Recognition for

Raul Ramos y Sanchez

D0771651

❖ Best Novel Award Winner
International Latino Book Awards

❖ Violet Crown Awards Fiction Finalist
Writers League of Texas

❖ Books Into Movies Award Winner
presented by Edward James Olmos

❖ USA Today Summer Reads Author

❖ LATINA Magazine "10 Hottest
Summer Reads" Author

❖ Named #1 among "2011 Top Ten
Latino Authors" by LatinoStories.com

❖ Listed among "Best Hispanic Writers
of the 21st century" by ChaCha.com

❖ Featured Author Ohioana Book Festival

Other novels by Raul Ramos y Sanchez

America Libre

House Divided

Pancho Land

Copyright © 2016 by Raul Ramos y Sanchez

Fiction—Coming of Age FIC043000; Fiction—General FIC000000; Fiction—Hispanic or Latino FIC056000

Beck and Branch Publishers | Printed in the United States of America | ISBN 978-0-9972644-1-8

A NOVEL

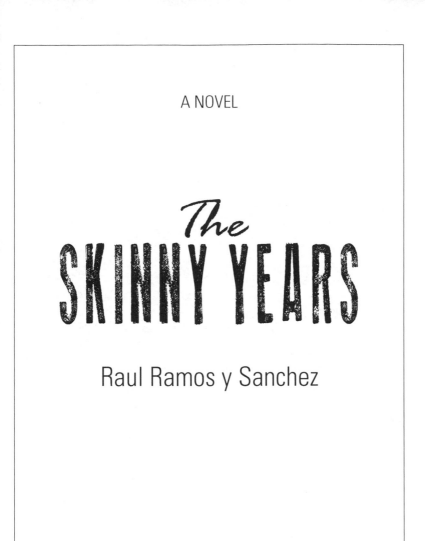

The SKINNY YEARS

Raul Ramos y Sanchez

Beck and Branch Publishers

Foreword

Write what you know. That's an adage shared by most writers and one I've followed in this novel. Not surprisingly, that's led some readers to ask, "Is this story about you?"

The short answer is no. But like most things in life, the full answer is more complicated. The characters in *The Skinny Years* are composites of my neighbors, family, friends, and enemies growing up in Miami during the 1960s. A few of my personal experiences are woven into the story as well. The result is a mashup of the real and the imagined, from the past and from the present, concocted into a narrative that's hopefully interesting. In other words, it's fiction.

This piece of fiction would not have been possible without the support and inspiration of many others.

I owe a special debt to the Yaniz family: Jorge, Edita, Minita, Fat, Chiqui, Barbara and Rob. Their house in Miami was my second home growing up. We share a bond that goes beyond blood. Others from my past who helped inspire this work include Everett Schooler, Billie Simons, Michael Meyer, Tony Mendez, Retha Sally Boone and my classmates at Jackson High.

To the readers of my novels, thank you for letting my words cohabit with your brain. You are the reason for the countless hours that go into this work. I also want to thank Sally van Haitsma for her help in shaping this novel and John L. Woods for his editing.

Growing up in Miami was not easy. But coming of age in that kaleidoscope of color, culture and creed has been an enduring gift. This novel is my attempt to share it.

—The author

What does *m'hijo* mean?
(It's pronounced ME-ho)

A GLOSSARY OF CUBAN EXPRESSIONS

At the end of this book, you'll find a glossary of Cuban expressions. I expect readers unfamiliar with Cuban idioms—including other Spanish speakers—may be grateful to know about this wordlist right away. Most of these expressions have no English equivalent and, frankly, the story would not be the same without them.

An Unexpected Gift

Forty-eight years. That's how long it had been since Victor last stood here. He looked around the walled courtyard, no more than ten paces wide, trying to see it through his eyes as an eight-year-old.

In his memory, the courtyard alongside his home was a vast landscape shaded by white-trunked royal palms and hibiscus bushes higher than his head, fat with pink flowers. In the courtyard's center, four stone paths met at a raised bed of orchids.

Before Victor now was a barren, weed-choked patio next to a decaying mansion. The house's once-white walls were crumbling and grimy with the patina of neglect that covered most of twenty-first century Havana.

Glancing around to make sure he was alone, Victor

dropped to one knee and pulled a zip-lock bag from his cargo shorts. As he shook the gray powder in the baggy onto the ground, a gust of wind carried a small cloud back toward him.

He laughed softly, wiping the dust from his face. "I hope that's not a sign you're complaining, *Mamá*," he whispered. "I know a sandwich bag may not be the way you imagined coming home. But it was the only way to keep my promise." A tear trailed down his cheek, leaving a dark spot in the ashes. "Rest easy, *viejita*."

Standing up, Victor looked around again. Did the chubby eight-year-old who played here forty-eight years ago ever imagine the time would pass so quickly? Victor closed his eyes.

A surge of dormant memories washed over him like a breaking dam.

They were an unexpected gift.

DECEMBER 31

A Portrait of Domestic Bliss

Victor headed toward the kitchen, hoping the cook would sneak him a plate of crackers and guava paste before dinner. Passing the living room, he heard voices and peered around the doorway, staying out of sight.

His mother and father, dressed for a formal event, were posing for a photo on the first step of the living room's curving marble staircase.

"Wait!" Juan Delgado called out to the photographer.

"What's the matter now, Juan?" Alicia asked her husband, rolling her eyes. "Your tuxedo looks fine."

Juan grimaced like someone sniffing week-old *bacalao*. "Alicia, I cannot believe you'd wear that garish trinket to the Presidential Palace," he said, glaring at the large brooch on her evening gown.

"I got it at *El Encanto* when I bought the dress," Alicia said, stroking the pink satin fabric. "The sales girl thought they looked divine together."

Juan leaned close to his wife, speaking softly in her ear. "Someone at *El Encanto* would never suggest this atrocity. I'm certain this is *her* doing," he said, nodding toward his mother-in-law hovering behind the photographer.

Alicia flushed as she glanced at her mother. "We never take her anywhere, Juan," she whispered. "I let her choose the brooch so she'd feel a part of this evening."

"Alicia, how could you?" he hissed in her ear. "You know that old *guajira* has the taste of a Colón Quarter whore."

"I heard that," his mother-in-law called out, locking him in a stare. "Mortgaging your *cojones* to pay for a fancy life doesn't make you better than anybody else, Juan Delgado."

Juan looked rattled for a moment, then recovered. "Considering where you come from," he said sneering, "you should be grateful your daughter married someone who can introduce her to the cream of Cuban society."

"Ha! I may be an old *guajira*, but if Batista and his low-life cronies have become the cream of Cuban society, then it won't be long before that scoundrel Castro is taking his morning shit in the Presidential Palace," the old woman yelled before shuffling out of the room.

"Your mother has a lot of class, Alicia," Juan said dryly. "Unfortunately, it's all low."

Watching the squabble from the doorway, Victor cringed. They were at it again.

His father and grandmother tried to hide their bad blood, acting more-or-less friendly when the children were around. The ploy fooled five-year-old Marta, but their fights were no secret to Victor.

He'd hoped tonight's New Year's Eve celebration would lift the mood of the adults in his family and bring a truce to the bickering. His parents loved fancy parties.

Victor heard footsteps behind him. His sister Marta had left her room. "What's all the yelling about?" she asked, looking into the living room.

"It's nothing," he said, steering Marta away. "Let's go play outside. Why don't you show me how high you can swing?"

A short while later, after Alicia had replaced her brooch,

the photographer was able to finish his work. The image he captured showed a moneyed couple in their mid-thirties smiling brightly in their lavish home—a portrait of domestic bliss.

❖ ❖ ❖

After taking Marta to their private playground and watching her swing for a while, Victor left his sister and headed back to the kitchen, hoping to cadge those crackers and guava paste.

Passing through the courtyard he spotted their nanny, Imelda, sitting on a marble bench. New Year's Eve was a day off for Imelda, so he was surprised to see her.

Thrilled, Victor ran to his nanny. "I've been practicing a song for you!" he said eagerly.

"I'm sorry, Victor," she said gently. "I don't have much time. I'm meeting someone in a few minutes."

"This won't take long, I promise."

Imelda smiled. "All right. Let's hear your song."

Victor climbed onto the low stone wall around the orchid bed and faced his one-person audience. Closing his eyes, Victor began to sing, inflecting his squeaky eight-year-old voice like the famous Desi Arnaz.

Reaching the first chorus of the bolero, Victor threw out his palms and leaned back, pouring his soul into the song. "*If you can't make your mind up, we'll never get started. And I don't want to wind up being parted, broken hearted.*"

Glancing at Imelda, Victor was thrilled to see her smiling.

Now humming the tune, Victor turned away from his nanny to conduct an imaginary orchestra, swaying his pudgy frame along with the music. After a few bars, he faced Imelda again and finished the song playing an invisible trumpet. *Ta-da, ta-da, TA-DAAAAAAA!* He held the last note, his pretend-horn pointing at the sky, then whirled his arms in a wide circle and gave a deep, theatrical bow.

"Bravo, Victor! Bravo!" Imelda said with a smile, clapping her hands.

Victor hopped down from the wall and nodded. "*Muchas gracias, señorita,*" he said with the grandiose humility of a seasoned celebrity.

"That was wonderful, just wonderful!" his nanny said in a shiny voice. After a moment, she smoothed out her skirt and touched the boy's chin. "You know, Victor," she said, her tone mellowing, "your teacher keeps telling me you never answer questions in class anymore and that you're always off by yourself at recess. Why can't you be more like this in school, *mi amor?*"

Victor's shoulders slumped as his soaring mood came crashing down to earth. Why did she have to bring up school?

Looking at his nanny, Victor once again felt the tug of those soulful dark-brown eyes and *café-con-leche* skin. His attraction to her was powerful but hazy, like the tantalizing smell of coffee—that mysterious and forbidden adult elixir.

How could he tell Imelda that the last thing he wanted at school was attention?

He was already the butt of everyone's jokes, a fat kid who was pitilessly teased because his last name, Delgado, meant "slender" in Spanish. If Imelda knew about this ridicule, his chances to win her would be gone for sure. There had to be some way to explain his dilemma to the woman who held his heart.

"I don't know," he finally mumbled with a shrug.

"Look, Victor. I want you to promise me you'll try to mix more with the other children in school when classes start again. Will you do that?"

Victor shuffled his feet. "*Está bien,*" he said feebly, staring at his shoes.

"Your mother told me the family is going to Varadero tomorrow."

"Are you going with us?" Victor asked excitedly,

picturing his nanny in a bathing suit, romping in the ice-blue water.

Imelda shook her head. "No, but I want you to remember something. The last time you were at the beach, you and Marta got so burned you came home pinker than a ham slice. So I want you both to play in the shade when you're not swimming. Will you do that?" Unlike Imelda, the Delgados' skin was fair.

Victor sighed. "I will. Don't worry."

"Good!" Imelda said, then delicately turned her wrist, looking at her watch. "I've got to go now."

"Can't you stay a little longer?" Victor said, his lower lip rising into a pout.

"I'm sorry. My *novio* is taking me to the Tropicana tonight and he's picking me up here."

"Is your *novio* rich?" he asked, hoping his family's wealth might give him an advantage over this unknown rival.

"That's not an appropriate question for a young gentleman to ask his nanny, Victor."

"I'm sorry."

"*Está bien*. You need to learn these things," she answered smiling. "Have a happy new year, *mi amor!*" she said, then pinched his chubby cheek and walked away.

Victor sighed as he watched Imelda crossing the courtyard, her voluptuous figure swaying through the ferns and hibiscus lining the walkway.

Someday, he told himself. *Someday*.

JANUARY 1

The Exile-In-Chief

Under the glow of a waning moon, Fulgencio waited patiently while the bitch squatted in the grass by the tarmac. Once the poodle had finished her business, Fulgencio called her to his side and boarded the plane waiting for him, its engines running.

The C-47 roared into the indigo sky carrying President Fulgencio Batista y Zaldivar, his immediate family, a few close supporters, two French poodles, and all of the cash from the Cuban treasury he could get his hands on.

Less than two hours earlier, Batista had hosted an extravagant New Year's Eve party in Havana's Presidential Palace. Now he was fleeing Cuba for the Dominican Republic, spooked by reports that Fidel Castro's rebels had captured Santa Clara, a provincial capital 175 miles from Havana.

Like all shocking news—or particularly juicy gossip—word of Batista's departure spread across the island with the speed of an atomic reaction. In the wake of Batista's pre-dawn flight, Cuba was transformed.

The island's army of 38,000 soldiers and reservists was

no longer strong enough to keep Castro and his ragged rebels at bay. The government troops laid down their arms.

Suddenly there were not enough policemen to keep the peace in Havana. Gleeful mobs attacked the symbols of Batista's power, smashing casinos, destroying parking meters, and ransacking the homes of several prominent presidential cronies. Government officials and collaborators spotted on the streets were denounced and sometimes beaten. The once-feared *Policia Nacional* made no attempt to control the chaos.

To no one's surprise, most of Batista's supporters made plans to leave the country—including Victor's father, Juan Delgado Morales.

A professor of law at the University of Havana, Juan's widely published anti-communist essays often glorified Batista as a valiant defender of democracy. Although Juan had been at the Presidential Palace that night and spoken to Batista in the reception line, he was not among the lucky few with any warning of the strongman's sudden departure. Too proud to admit he'd been wrong about Batista, Juan convinced himself Fulgencio's flight was a shrewd strategic retreat until democracy could be restored.

Nine days after Batista fled the country, Castro would enter Havana to a hero's welcome leading a convoy of captured government trucks and tanks. Perched atop the vehicles, Fidel and his bearded comrades drove through the cheering crowds, smiling and waving like scruffy prom queens on parade floats.

Two days before Fidel rolled into Havana, Juan had managed to secure seats for his entire household on one of the suddenly overbooked flights to Miami. The endeavor had taken persistence, connections—and a significant bite into Juan's cash accounts in bribes.

At Havana's Rancho Boyeros airport, Victor trailed in awe behind his father as Juan ceremoniously led his family up the steep ramp of a Cubana Airlines DC-3. Victor was proud of his father. He was saving everyone in their family from a fate worse than death under the rule of the communists—something which Juan made sure they all appreciated.

Climbing the ramp behind Victor was his mother and sister. Bringing up the rear and walking stiffly was Victor's wizened *abuela*—his grandmother. Her stilted gait as she navigated the stairs was not solely the result of age. She wore virtually every dress she owned beneath a heavy coat to conserve space in her crammed suitcases. "Besides," she'd confided to Victor earlier as they were packing, "it's cold in America. I've seen the snow in movies."

"But, *Abuela*, we're going to Miami."

"Don't be insolent, Victor. Miami is in America, no?"

At the top of the ramp, Juan stopped and turned to the long line of passengers waiting restlessly to board the plane behind him. "This is a dark day in the history of our great island," he announced, his bald pate glinting in the tropical sun. "Take heart, fellow patriots. Justice and liberty will prevail!" he said before ducking quickly into the cabin.

Victor glanced over his shoulder at the people on the observation deck, hoping that Imelda had come to see him off. Heartbroken that she was not there, he entered the crowded plane.

As the family took their seats, Victor saw his mother begin to cry. With a flamboyant sweep, Juan put his arm protectively around his wife. "Don't cry, *mi amor*. I assure you, we'll be back home in a few months—perhaps a year at the most. This malevolent scoundrel cannot last."

Already missing his nanny, Victor was comforted by Juan's words. He could not remember a time when his father had been wrong.

MARCH

The Yellow Bungalow

"*Dios santisimo!*" Alicia yelled after turning on the kitchen light. A squadron of shiny roaches foraging on the chipped linoleum began a frenzied dash for the baseboards.

Following his mother and startled by the scream, Victor dropped the bag of groceries he was carrying. Horrified, he watched a week's supply of food tumble to the floor, creating an explosion of eggs, milk, orange juice, bread, rice, beans, coffee, oatmeal, and chipped ham.

"You disgraceful ingrate!" his father screamed, slamming his hand on the kitchen table. "We just spent the last of our cash on these groceries!"

Victor cringed and bowed his head, hot tears trailing down his cheeks. His father had scolded him before, but never in a rage like this.

The shouting drew *Abuela* and Marta into the kitchen. The look of shock in their eyes sobered Juan. He exhaled slowly, rubbing his lips. An agonizing silence fell over the family standing in the small room. Their swift collapse into poverty was finally sinking in.

Six days ago, the Delgados had been casually searching

for a house in Miami Beach while renting a suite at one of the area's most luxurious hotels, the Fontainebleau. They'd even retained a private tutor for Victor to keep up his studies. Then the stunning news had arrived.

The Castro government had confiscated the family's vast land holdings, cutting off the source of their income. When the Fontainebleau presented Juan with the latest bill, most of their remaining cash was wiped out.

After a flurry of frantic searching, the family of five had moved into the only shelter they could afford: a cramped two-bedroom bungalow in Miami's Wynwood district. About a half-mile inland on the cheap side of the bay, Wynwood was a tightly-packed grid of small houses and apartments—a low-rent area where the cooks, cabbies, mechanics, and maids whose labor greased Miami's tourism machine rested their heads and raised their kids.

The contrast between their new house on Northwest 33rd Street and the home they'd left in Havana was staggering.

The Delgado household in Cuba had employed a maid, a cook, and a gardener to help manage their eight-bedroom, two-acre estate in Havana's posh Miramar district. They'd retained Imelda to watch the children six days a week and shuttle Victor to school.

The sprawling house also included a wing for the children's *abuela*, Alicia's widowed mother, who divided her time between stitching intricate doilies, tending a small personal garden, and feuding with her son-in-law.

The complex and grandiose home was a reflection of its owner.

Juan Delgado Morales had been born into wealth and assumed it as a birthright. Because most of his wealth was in land, Juan had always borrowed against the property to pay for his lavish life. Getting credit had never been a problem for a man of his station.

A descendant of one the island's most prominent families,

Juan could boast of having a former Cuban president in his blood line—and it was boast he made frequently. However, he always omitted one detail. His great-uncle had been a provisional president for a total of two days.

Juan's marriage to Alicia Betancourt Perez was seen by many as slumming. Not many men of Juan's station married a flower shop clerk he'd met buying a Mother's Day bouquet. But one look at the shapely, green-eyed honey-blonde left little doubt about Juan's motivation.

Along with her beauty, Alicia had inherited another asset that gave her a veneer of respectability in Cuba's elite social circles. Despite being raised in a working class household, Alicia's great-grandparents had once owned a large sugar estate outside Santiago de Cuba. Unfortunately for Alicia, that wealth was quickly squandered by the next Betancourt generation.

Now that legacy of loss was visiting Alicia's family again.

Victor stared at the food splattered across the floor. His family was poor now, he realized. Very poor. The faces of the adults around Victor betrayed the same grim revelation. The silence in the kitchen grew, enveloping the family in a painful stillness.

The hush was finally broken by the unlikeliest of sources.

"*Pápi*, why don't you go to work?" Marta asked.

Alicia knelt before the five-year-old, gently holding her shoulders. "Your father can't go to work, Marta. We're here as tourists. I know this is hard for you to understand, *m'hija*, but we're not allowed to work in America."

"So what are we going to do? Starve?" *Abuela* asked. "There are ways for a man to work under the table. It's been done before."

"Be reasonable, *Mamá*. Juan barely speaks English—and he's a professor of Cuban law," Alicia calmly explained. "Where could he find a job in this country?"

"He can push a broom, can't he? You don't need an American law degree to do that."

"*Mamá*, you know that's out of the question. A man of Juan's stature could never stoop to manual labor."

Abuela shook her head in disgust, then thrust her chin toward Juan. "I told you this one would turn out like his brother Panchito."

Victor watched his mother and father stiffen. He'd never met this mysterious uncle but was curious about someone whose mere name produced that much tension.

"Let's not dredge up old muck, *Mamá*," Alicia cautioned.

Juan, who had been surprisingly quiet, finally spoke. "This is not the time or place for this discussion," he said, gesturing toward the children.

"Well, somebody in this family has got to put food on the table," *Abuela* insisted.

After a long pause, Alicia finally spoke. "You're right, Mamá. But Juan isn't going to work," she said firmly. "I will."

"You?" *Abuela* said with a sour laugh. "*M'hija*, I love you dearly. But unless they have jobs in America for choosing centerpieces at charity balls, what in the world do you plan to do?"

"One of the maids at the Fontainebleau told me people work in hotels here without papers all the time—and they don't need to speak English."

Juan shook his head. "No, Alicia. You know the law. If you're caught working without a visa, *all of us* could be deported to Cuba. With my reputation as a defender of democracy..." Juan paused, dramatically lowering the pitch of his voice like a radio actor. "Well, I don't have to tell you what that would mean."

Victor's mouth was suddenly dry. He'd heard about *El Paredon*—the infamous wall where Castro's firing squads executed Batista supporters. He was sure his father would be shot if their family was sent back to Cuba. *Would they shoot an eight-year-old as well?* he wondered.

"I know it's dangerous, Juan. But it's a chance we have to

take," Alicia said. "How else can we live here?"

Juan thrust his finger in the air and puffed out his chest. "I will not permit my wife to work illegally, much less as a maid."

"So let me get this straight, Juan," *Abuela* said, inching closer to her son-in-law. "You're too proud to take a job. You're too proud to let your wife work. But you're not too proud to let your children go hungry?" she said, now nearly nose to nose.

"It's not as simple as that, you obstreperous old cow," Juan growled.

"Both of you, stop it!" Alicia shouted, stepping between them. "This is not the time to squabble!"

Victor's jaw went slack. He'd never seen his mother take charge like this before. Juan and *Abuela* were also stunned. After a moment, they lowered their eyes and backed away.

Alicia gently touched Juan's arm. "This job is temporary, Juan," she said soothingly. "Just as you said, Fidel won't last much longer. In a few months, we'll be back in our own home. Until then, we have to survive here... any way we can."

❖ ❖ ❖

Seated at the kitchen table beside his sister the following morning, Victor held out his plate and called out to his grandmother. "I want more eggs."

"We only had two eggs to scramble this morning because somebody dropped the carton on the floor, remember?" she answered, standing at the counter, brewing coffee.

"Then give me more toast."

"Victor, you're not going to order me around like you did the cook back in Cuba. Besides, it wouldn't hurt you any to skip the seconds. You want to look like your father when you grow up?"

Pouting, Victor rose from the table and was about to leave when his father entered the kitchen.

"*Buenos dias*, your excellency," *Abuela* said to her son-in-law with an exaggerated bow. "Are you here for your *café-con-leche* before you embark on another day of leisure?"

"Listen, old woman, I supported you for years. Don't forget that."

"Of course you supported us, Juan," she said sneering. "I've never forgotten how you worked like a cane field slave during *la zafra*—pretending to teach classes while you were really hoisting mojitos all day at the Yacht Club." Victor saw his father flinch as *Abuela* spoke. "Oh, you think I didn't know about that? Well, let me tell you something else, *chulo*. Maybe you'd like to explain to your children about that *mulata* in Marianao you visited every—"

"That will be enough!" Juan shouted before stomping out of the kitchen.

While Victor and Marta stared in confusion at their grandmother, the old woman turned back to her cooking. "That'll keep the flies out of the kitchen," she said under her breath.

❖ ❖ ❖

That night, Victor found it hard to fall asleep. He tossed fitfully on the hard cot in his new bedroom: the screened front porch of the yellow bungalow. The voices coming through the wall from his parents' bedroom were keeping him awake.

Hearing his mother and father late at night was nothing new. At the Fontainebleau, their repertoire usually included an assortment of moans and grunts concluded by his mother calling out to his father like a third-base coach urging a runner home.

But tonight, their voices sounded different. They were arguing.

"Tell her to control her tongue," he heard his father say, the anger in his voice unmistakable. "I will not tolerate her disrespect to me in front of the children."

His mother murmured something in reply, but he could not make it out. Then his father's voice rose again.

"I promise you this, Alicia, as God is my witness. If your mother continues behaving like this, I will leave you."

The sound Victor heard next was his mother's sobbing.

He closed his eyes and rolled over on the lumpy cot, trying to find a comfortable place. The image of his mother being led away in handcuffs by immigration officers vied with the vision of his father packing his bags to leave them.

Then he remembered Imelda. Would he ever look into those delicate brown eyes again?

Victor shook his head, trying to clear his mind. Staring into the darkness, he felt tears fill his eyes. After a very long time, he finally fell asleep.

❖ ❖ ❖

A dull pain in the big toe of his right foot woke Victor up. Looking toward the bottom of the cot, he saw *Abuela* squeezing his foot through the covers.

"Time to get up, *dormilón*," *Abuela* said, the morning sun etching the wrinkles on her face. "Go wash up and come to breakfast."

Entering the kitchen in his pajamas a short while later, Victor was startled by what he saw. His parents, grandmother and sister were seated around the metal table, silently eating breakfast.

Abuela rose and placed a bowl of oatmeal on the table. "Sit down and eat," she said drily.

An icy silence followed, broken only by the clinking of silverware. Just one thing could explain this, Victor realized. His mother must have told *Abuela* about his father's threat. This prickly peace was uncomfortable. How could a Cuban family possibly sit stiff and silent around a table? But the tense ceasefire still seemed better than having his father leave, Victor told himself.

Alicia put down her spoon and cleared her throat.

"Victor, you'll need to get dressed right away after breakfast. You'll be starting school today."

"No!" he said, rising to his feet. "Why can't I keep studying with Miss Dorothy?"

"Victor, we can barely afford food. How can you expect us to pay for a private tutor?"

"I won't do it! I don't want to go back to school!" he screamed before running out of the kitchen. Reaching his front porch bedroom, Victor threw himself on the cot and covered his head with his hands.

Until that moment, the thought of losing his tutor had not crossed his mind. For as long as he could remember there had always been a woman who had treated him like someone special. The plain-featured college student who'd come to the hotel had been kind, although no substitute for Imelda. But his tutor had at least been a welcome change from the torment of his classmates in Cuba. Now, those hellish days in school would be back again.

The sound of shuffling footsteps on the porch's worn tile floor told him *Abuela* was coming. The cot creaked as she sat down on its edge. "I guess things look pretty bleak right now, eh?"

Victor nodded without looking up.

"The worst times I can remember were back in 1929 when your grandfather and I were still living in Minas," *Abuela* told him. "That year, something happened in *Nueva York* and times got bad all over the world. The newspaper in our little town said some men in America had even thrown themselves off buildings after losing all their money. The next day, your grandfather's cousin Pépe came to visit with a story going around about some rich man who killed himself that way in Redencion, another little town not far away. Your grandfather looked at his cousin and said, 'Pépe, don't be a *comemierda*. All the buildings in Redencion are one story high. How many times do you suppose this man jumped off the building?'"

Despite himself, Victor laughed.

"Hard times come to everybody, Victor. Life is what you make of it, not what happens to you," *Abuela* said softly. "I know the children at your school were cruel to you and I saw you change. You used to be a happy child who loved being around people. That's your real nature, Victor. Don't let the *comemierdas* change you."

Victor sat up and hugged his grandmother.

"This new school can be different for you, Victor. It's a chance for you to start over again and be who you really are." Never one to get too mushy, *Abuela* patted him on the head and walked back into the house.

Victor rose from the cot and began dressing for school, hoping that *Abuela* would turn out to be right—somehow.

❖ ❖ ❖

The palms and jacarandas along 33rd Street were rustling in the afternoon breeze and Victor was humming a conga along with their rhythmic swooshing. *Kuru-ta-ta-ta. Kuru-ta-ta-ta,* he murmured, gyrating his hips as he walked. Victor realized some people inside the small homes and apartments along the street might be watching him and snickering as he danced down the sidewalk. He didn't care. His first day at school had gone better than he'd ever dreamed.

He'd been terrified that morning when his mother had forced-marched him the four blocks to Buena Vista Elementary. The tan, hard-edged building reminded Victor of a *cuartel*—the military outposts throughout Cuba where Batista's secret police had tortured captured rebels.

At the school's main office he slouched in a chair, mortified, as his mother pantomimed for the clerk her desire to enroll Victor at the school. (Victor would never see anything like it again until the first time he witnessed Kabuki theatre.) Mercifully, the clerk fetched the school's only Spanish-speaking counselor.

After a long session of paperwork, Victor hugged his

mother goodbye like a prisoner facing the gallows and followed the counselor along a hallway lined with classrooms smelling of crayons. This was the moment Victor had been dreading most.

Over two dozen young faces locked on Victor as he entered the classroom, his knees nearly buckling with each step. The counselor introduced him in English, which Victor did not understand. Then, to his astonishment, the students broke into a long round of applause.

Looking at their beaming smiles, Victor was intoxicated. He half-closed his eyes and leaned toward the sound, letting the applause soak in like sunshine. He had never imagined anything could feel this good—much less in a classroom. Seized by the moment, Victor clasped his hands together and shook them above his head like a boxer. The students giggled, clearly amused by the new kid.

After being paired with a Puerto Rican boy who would be his interpreter, Victor learned the counselor had introduced him as the son of a man battling communism and forced to leave his home in Cuba.

His good fortune at Buena Vista was not over, however.

During recess, a pretty blonde classmate approached him. Her name was Janice, Victor learned through his interpreter, and Janice's father thought Castro was a dirty commie and any Cubans who opposed him were heroes. Looking into Janice's pale blue eyes, Victor sighed blissfully, his brain a jelly of joy. *Step aside, Imelda. A new queen rules my heart*, he told himself.

Arriving at the yellow bungalow, Victor entered the front door eager to share the news of his first day in school. Passing through the empty living room, he found his grandmother folding laundry in her bedroom with Marta playing on the floor.

"*Abuela*, where are *mámi* and *Pápi?*" he asked excitedly.

"They went to sell your mother's jewelry so we'd have something to eat."

The news took the edge off Victor's glee. Despite his triumph at school, his family still faced serious problems. All the same, it might cheer *Abuela* to hear about his good fortune.

"The kids at school applauded me, *Abuela*," he said, face glowing with pride.

"That's good, Victor. I'm very glad to hear it," *Abuela* said smiling. "What did you do to win them over?"

"Well, I didn't actually *do* anything."

"They applauded you for nothing?"

"No, they applauded me because of *Pápi*."

"Your father?" *Abuela* said, suddenly looking like she'd tasted sour milk. "And what exactly has Juan done to deserve this applause?"

"*Pápi* is a hero. He's against Castro and communism."

"A hero?" The old woman looked at the ceiling and pressed her palms together. "*Señor*, give me the strength to stay silent."

"What do mean, *Abuela*?"

"Never mind."

"No, tell me."

Abuela shook her head. "I promised your mother not to say anything else about Juan."

"Why isn't *Pápi* a hero?" Victor demanded, his new popularity suddenly on shaky ground.

"Look, Victor," *Abuela* said, lowering her voice. "Your father is not a bad man—as spoiled, rich *bitongos* go. But he's hardly anybody's hero."

"That's not true. You're always talking bad about *Pápi* and making trouble."

"I'm not making trouble. I'm just trying to keep Juan from making a fool of my daughter—and apparently, my grandson now as well."

"No, *Abuela*. You're just jealous because *Pápi* is a hero who's fighting against communism and you're not."

Abuela let out a sharp, dry laugh. "Anyone who thinks

Juan Delgado's articles sucking up to Batista are 'fighting against communism' doesn't know a donkey turd from a chocolate cupcake."

"*Pápi* is right," Victor said, his eyes narrowing. "You *are* an obstre... obsret... some kind of an old cow."

Abuela's face reddened and her cheeks began to tremble like a volcano about to erupt. Then she exhaled slowly, rubbing her face. "Victor, I'm very sorry—but what I've said is true. Unfortunately, you'll have to learn that for yourself," she said calmly. "Now go outside and play. I've got work to do."

The next morning, with the first rays of the sun glowing low in the sky, the squawk of the screen door woke Victor up.

He rolled over in bed and saw someone leaving the house.

It was his mother in the dove gray uniform of a maid at the Fontainebleau hotel.

APRIL

The Anthill

The anthill rose like a miniature volcano from the scraggly grass around the yellow bungalow. Squatting above it, Victor dropped another pebble into the mouth of the mound. The ants immediately swarmed around the small stone, furiously digging a new opening to their nest. Watching the tiny creatures, Victor realized they had no idea a giant being loomed above them, creating disasters just to see how they'd react.

He'd discovered the anthill a few days earlier near the window of the bungalow's back bedroom, the one shared by his sister and *Abuela*. Since then, it had become his favorite spot in the yard.

Victor wondered why he'd never played with ants in Cuba. Then he realized their family's gardener had probably cleared all the anthills from their lawn.

As he placed a twig across the trail of the ants leaving the nest, Victor heard his mother's voice coming through the window. She sounded close to tears.

"I don't know what to do, *Mamá*," Alicia said. "The boss told me I'd be fired if I didn't finish the rooms faster. I'm trying, *Mamá*. I'm trying."

Then Victor heard *Abuela's* raspy voice. "*Cálmate, m'hija*," she said. "You learned how to ride a horse and make those fancy flower arrangements. You can learn how to make a bed faster. *Vamos*, let's practice on Marta's bed."

Victor stood and peeked into the window. The two women were stooped over the mattress, absorbed in the task and not aware he was watching.

The change in his mother's looks was still a shock to Victor. Alicia's long golden hair was gone, replaced by a closely-cut bob showing dark roots. But it was her eyes that had changed the most. Stressed and fatigued, her green pupils were nearly lost in folds of flesh above dark circles—a downfall made worse for Alicia by having to choose between buying makeup or food for her children.

Suddenly, his mother grabbed her back. "Ow! There it goes again," Alicia said grimacing.

"What did I tell you? Didn't I say you'd regret that foolish horseback riding? But would you listen to your mother? Oh, no. You had to be the equestrian queen."

"That fall was over ten years ago, *Mamá*. Can't you let it go?"

"Well, it seems like your back hasn't forgotten it."

Alicia's eyes flashed angrily. "You're trying my patience, old woman. The reason my back hurts is from bending over all those beds for the last two months," she said. "Look at my feet. They're like a pair of *chorizos* from standing all day. Are you going to blame that on my riding lessons too?"

"*M'hija*—"

"Just forget it, *Mamá*," Alicia said, furiously yanking the sheet off the bed. "You're bickering has upset Juan—and now you're beginning to annoy me too."

Abuela lowered her head and sighed. "I'm sorry if I upset you," she said before leaving the room.

Alicia followed her mother, her voice fading away into the house. "Wait, *Mamá*. Wait. I'm sorry. I've pulled double shifts these last few days and I'm..."

As Alicia's voice drifted away, Victor sat down in shock. Now his mother and *Abuela* were fighting, the first time he'd seen that happen. What else would go wrong in this upside-down new place?

Although his father didn't have a job, Juan seemed busy. He usually slept till lunchtime and left the house at night, returning through Victor's front porch room in the early hours of the morning.

At least his mother's job now gave them enough to eat and a place to live. But every day she worked, the chances grew that she'd be caught and deported.

There were only two bright spots in Victor's world: seeing Janice every day at school and his "son of a hero" status—but even that was losing its luster. More children of Cuban exiles were enrolling at Buena Vista every day. His exotic identity was no longer all that special. Worse yet, as he'd begun to master English, Victor had discovered not everyone shared Janice's father's admiration of Cuban exiles. Last week, he'd overhead a cafeteria lady grumble to a co-worker about "all these goddamn Cubans coming to Miami."

Victor looked down at the ants, working feverishly to undo the obstacles he'd set for them and was struck by a thought: Did God ever play the same way with people?

MAY

The Capri

The lights in the house were turned off but Victor could still make out shapes inside the screened porch by the glow of the streetlamp. He was in bed, fully dressed under the covers, pretending to be asleep.

Before long, the moment Victor had been waiting for arrived. His father emerged from the living room and slipped carefully through the screen door, trying to mask its squeak.

For several weeks, Victor had seen his father leaving the house late at night. Victor suspected his father was meeting with other anti-communists in an effort to take back their homeland from Castro. Tonight, Victor would follow him to find out for sure—and prove *Abuela* wrong.

After waiting a few moments, Victor slid out of the cot and tip-toed out the door. Reaching the sidewalk, he saw his father a half-block ahead walking along the row of streetlights toward 3rd Avenue.

When Juan turned left on 3rd, Victor realized he had a problem. The next corner his father would reach was a peculiar five-way intersection and Victor would lose his father's trail unless he was close enough to see which way Juan went.

Fortunately for Victor, adults stuck to the sidewalks. Nine-year-olds did not. Although only in the neighborhood for three months, Victor already had a mental map of the all the yards around his house.

By crossing through Mrs. Post's yard next door (who kept a pet boa constrictor in her garage) and detouring around the thorn bushes behind the Victory apartments, he could cut through the empty lot next to the Guerra's house (home of two pretty teenage daughters) and emerge at the five-way corner ahead of his father.

Victor's plan quickly met with a setback, however.

Dashing through Mrs. Post's backyard, he ran full-speed into one of the barely-visible support wires anchoring her clothesline. The thin metal cable caught him just above the ankle. "Unnfff," Victor groaned, going down like a soggy sack of rice.

Now limping badly, he continued the shortcut, finally taking cover in a hibiscus bush near the critical corner. His father arrived moments later and took a sharp right onto 34th Street. Without the shortcut, Victor would have lost him.

Trailing his father from the shadows, Victor saw Juan turn into the alley behind the row of businesses along 2nd Avenue. He broke into a run again to keep his father in sight—alarmed by where his father was heading.

The alley was familiar territory. Victor had walked past it many times on his way to Wynwood Park, always fascinated by its shady reputation. At school he'd learned the unmarked third door in the alley was ironically nicknamed "The Capri" after one of the largest casinos in Havana. According to the rumors, unlike the glamor of the real Capri in Cuba, this Capri was the site of a regular poker game among the neighborhood's deadbeats.

His heart fluttering, Victor reached the corner of the

alley. His father was approaching the third door. "Please don't go in, *Pápi*," he whispered to himself. "Please don't go in."

Victor's head dropped in dismay as his father opened the door and stepped inside.

For a time Victor stood there, hoping his father had entered the place by mistake and would come out again. After nearly a half-hour, that illusion evaporated and Victor started home.

Abuela had been right. His father was not an anti-communist hero. He was a low-life who gambled to amuse himself while his wife worked to support their family.

And, most shameful of all, Victor still did not want his father to leave them.

❖ ❖ ❖

"Are you sick, Victor?" *Abuela* asked the next morning after placing a bowl of corn flakes and milk before her grandson. "You usually finish your *confleis* before I walk away from the table."

Victor sat at the metal kitchen table, eyelids heavy, head cradled in his hands. "I'm not hungry."

"I'll eat his *confleis*," Marta called out from the other side of the table. Their new circumstances had quickly taught the five-year-old to eat whatever you could, whenever you could get it.

"You've had your share, Marta," *Abuela* answered. "Go watch *la tele*." Last week, the family had gone into debt for a three-in-one console TV, radio and record player that dominated the living room like a coffin in a funeral home viewing room.

Once Marta was out of the kitchen, *Abuela* sat down next to her grandson. "I heard the screen door open a couple of more times than usual last night"

Victor looked away from his grandmother. "I didn't hear anything."

"You must have been sleepwalking then. That's a very serious condition, you know. The cure is twenty-one shots in the bellybutton."

"I thought that was for rabies?"

"Yes, rabies—and for sleepwalking too."

Not amused, Victor lowered his head. "You were right, *Abuela. Pápi* is a bum."

"That's not what I said, Victor. Your father thinks Fidel is going to fall soon and he can go back to his spoiled life again. Juan is still the same man he was in Cuba. Nothing more, nothing less."

Victor closed his eyes for a moment, then spoke softly. "I hate it here, *Abuela*. I want things to be like they were before."

"I'm not going to kiss your forehead and tell you everything is all right, Victor. That would be a lie. But nothing is going to change by feeling sorry for yourself," *Abuela* said, rising to her feet. "Now finish your *confleis* and get ready for school."

JULY

Slender Mercies

Victor walked to the plate, looked at the pitcher, and fought back a shudder. The thirteen-year-old on the mound, who stood a head taller, was sizing him up with a cold glare.

It was Victor's first Little League at-bat, and to the short and chunky nine-year-old, it seemed the pitcher facing him was a giant who was already shaving—or at the very least had pubic hair.

Victor was not an intimidating sight.

Holding the team's smallest bat on his shoulder, his tubby frame was magnified by a yellow team jersey stretched tight across his middle, revealing a pink baby-fat belly. His sandy hair protruded at weird angles from an oversized batting helmet perched precariously on his head.

Unlike most Cuban boys, Victor had never played baseball before. His mother had not allowed him to associate with the coarse types who played the game in Cuba. Now, wanting desperately to fit it, Victor was facing what seemed to be a full-grown man about to hurl a rock-hard projectile in his direction.

"At bat, Victor Delgado!" the park superintendent called out, reading from the lineup sheet as Victor nervously approached the plate. The announcement brought a chorus of snickers from the small group of parents, siblings and gadflies on the weathered pine bleachers behind home plate at Wynwood Park.

Victor's parents were not among those in the stands. Alicia was still at work at the Fontainebleau; his father at home, getting ready for another night of poker.

While stepping into the batter's box, Victor heard a voice with a thick Spanish accent call out behind him.

"Heet one out of dee park, Skinny!"

The man's remark turned the snickers of the crowd into howls of laughter.

Victor, who had effortlessly soaked up English over the last seven months, understood the all-too-familiar mocking of his last name. Taking his stance in the batter's box, Victor's eyes began welling with tears. Before he could clear his vision, Victor heard the sharp pop of a hardball on leather.

"Stee-rike!" called the umpire.

Victor noticed the catcher and pitcher exchange a knowing grin as the boy behind the plate casually tossed the ball back to the mound. Victor gritted his teeth, determined not to be caught off-guard again.

It was a good thing.

The next pitch appeared to hover in place, not moving at all but simply growing larger. Then, more by instinct than logic, Victor realized the sphere was heading right for his head. He closed his eyes and lunged away.

When Victor opened his eyes, he was lying on his back, a cloud of dust from the dry clay infield billowing around him. The laughter from the crowd rose again.

"Ball one!" the umpire called out, stifling a smile.

Victor got up, ignoring the tears streaking his cheeks and prepared to face the next pitch. At that moment, he wanted nothing more than to stop the laughter. His small, portly frame shook with a white-hot wrath begging for release.

The opportunity came in a poorly-thrown curve that floated invitingly toward the plate.

Victor tomahawked the high pitch and the ball came off his bat sharply downward like a topspin tennis serve. Five feet from the mound, the ball hit a pebble on the hardpan infield and caromed upward wickedly, striking the pitcher squarely in the crotch. The boy collapsed into a fetal position, clutching his groin and gasping for breath, sure that his chances for fatherhood had passed.

Victor began trundling toward first base like someone harnessed to a sled.

With the pitcher down, the second baseman sprinted to the mound and picked up the ball. Now only a few steps from the base, Victor looked over his shoulder and saw the second baseman about to throw to first. With a last burst of energy, Victor dove head first for the bag.

"Safe!" the umpire yelled as Victor ended his dusty slide. Stirred by Victor's tenacity, the crowd rose to its feet and gave him the loudest cheer of the day.

Standing on first base, holding back a smile, Victor nonchalantly tipped his hat toward the bleachers like a major leaguer. The gesture delighted the crowd.

"Skin-ny! ... Skin-ny! ... Skin-ny! ..." the people in the bleachers chanted.

From that day on, outside of his home, Victor would rarely be called anything else.

SEPTEMBER

Grits with Un Huevo Frito

Dracula sat in the gathering dusk.

A scrawny ten-year-old without incisors, Dracula was perched on the top row of the deserted bleachers at Wynwood Park, sniffing glue from a brown paper bag. On the pine bench next to him, his cousin Felix waited impatiently for his turn.

Each day as darkness fell, the weather-beaten bleachers behind home plate at Wynwood became a hangout for an assortment of neighborhood miscreants. Glue-sniffers, reefer smokers, and the occasional wino, all shared the spot with the same studied indifference as wildebeests and impalas around a water hole.

After passing Felix a bag soggy with Testor's cement, Dracula's bloodshot eyes wandered toward someone nearing the bleachers. Waddling at a trot along the left field line was the tea-pot shape of Victor Delgado, a football tucked under his arm.

Skinny was hurrying home

Since the end of school that afternoon, Skinny had been absorbed in the new passion of his life: playing football. More suited to his physique than baseball, the sport gave

Skinny a chance to shine. Better still, immersed in the game's unvarnished aggression, Skinny had at last found an escape from the fears of his mother's being deported or his father's threats to leave them.

For the last three hours, Skinny and five other boys from his fourth grade class had been playing tackle on a grassy strip next to the park's rarely-used tennis courts. Skinny was the game's dominant player, repeatedly carrying his badly-scuffed ball for large gains with the other boys clinging to his bulky frame like remoras on a shark.

Only the approach of darkness had finally put an end to their game. Now, Skinny was hustling home, hoping to avoid a tongue lashing from *Abuela* for staying out so late. The sight of Dracula and Felix in the bleachers added an extra chill to the sweat already cooling on his body.

"Hey, Skinny! You want a sniff?" Dracula yelled, holding out the crinkled brown bag.

Even in the twilight, Skinny could see the toothless grin that had earned Dracula his nickname. Skinny also noticed that Felix looked pissed at Dracula's generosity.

"No thanks, Drac," Skinny said with a wave of his hand. He'd never sniffed glue and was not interested in a habit that seemed to only attract losers.

"It'll make you strong like a bull, man," Dracula said laughing while flexing a puny bicep.

"I gotta get home. Thanks anyway," Skinny replied, walking quickly by the bleachers

Skinny did not want to linger. In spite of his sinister nickname, Dracula was a harmless clown. But Felix was another matter. He and Skinny had a history.

Having flunked fourth grade the year before, Felix towered over the younger kids and was the alpha bully in Skinny's class. A week earlier, the big Puerto Rican kid had cut in front of Skinny in the school lunch line. With Janice watching from a few places in line behind him, Skinny screwed up the courage to object. Shocked by this audacity,

Felix shoved him to the floor and planted a hard right above Skinny's ear before a teacher broke up their scuffle.

"*Oye, maricón!* Come back here!" Felix yelled. "Drac said he wants you to take a sniff." Clearly, Felix had not forgotten their confrontation either.

Skinny stopped and faced Felix who was now charging down the bleachers, eyes narrowing like an angry dog. "There's no teacher around to save you this time, you little fuck," Felix said, drawing closer.

Before Skinny could decide whether to fight or run, a lanky kid with a mop of wavy red hair appeared next to him. Skinny had seen him around the park but didn't know his name.

The kid put his hand on Skinny's shoulder and said, "*Oye*, Felix. Have you got a problem with *mi amigo?*"

Felix stopped as if he'd hit a glass wall. "No, Loco...I mean...If he's your friend, man. Then he's okay," he said, turning up his palms and backing off.

The redhead calmly led Skinny away.

"I saw you playing baseball the day that *comemierda* in the bleachers called you skinny. He thought he was being *comico*," the redhead said after they were out of earshot. "You really showed him up, though," he added with a nod of approval.

"My name's Victor. But everybody calls me Skinny now. I don't mind."

"My name's Enrique. Everybody calls me *El Loco*," he said, extending his palm.

Skinny shifted his football to the other side and shook his hand.

From the accent of Loco's few words in Spanish, Skinny knew the redhead was Cuban. Like most of the kids at Wynwood Park—Latin American and Anglo—Skinny had already mastered the patois that would one day be called Spanglish.

"*Gracias* for sticking up for me with Felix," Skinny said

as they reached the edge of the park.

"*No fue nada.* Felix is a chickenshit who tries to pick on anybody smaller."

What Loco did not mention was that the scar above Felix's left eye was a reminder of the first and only time Felix had tried to bully the redhead just over a year earlier. Loco had responded with a rain of blows with the remnant of a broom handle. When it was over, Felix needed six stitches and Enrique Garcia had earned the nickname "El Loco." No one around Wynwood Park had messed with the redhead since then.

"Do you go to Buena Vista?" Skinny asked, wondering why he'd never seen Loco at school.

"No, I go to Corpus Christi."

Skinny knew about the parochial school in the neighborhood. "*Mi mamá* wanted to send me there. But we didn't have the money."

Loco snorted in disgust. "You're lucky. I hate it. Some of the nuns are worse than the *Policia Nacional*," he said as the boys reached the edge of the park.

Wynwood Park was the center of the universe for Skinny and his neighborhood cohorts, a square block of green space where everything that mattered took place.

Originally designed as a haven for young and old, Wynwood Park had a toddler area with swings and slides, shuffle board and tennis courts for adults, and a limestone-walled lodge for community activities. But like a swarm of locusts descending on a wheat field, the post-war baby boom had transformed the park.

The shuffle board courts were covered with crudely-painted hopscotch squares and the fenced-in tennis courts were now used only for stick ball games and home run derbies. When school was out, the lodge became a thermonuclear reaction of screaming children that released checkers, crayons, Ping-Pong paddles, Parcheesi pieces and other particles in random directions.

The only places at Wynwood still used as originally intended were the baseball diamond in the center of the park along with a pair of cracked asphalt basketball courts.

Leaving the park, the boys made their way south on Second Avenue past the cluster of stores facing the playground. Walking side-by-side, the pair traversed the squares of yellow light spilling from the storefronts onto a sidewalk lined with parked cars. They passed the doorway to Leo's Drugstore with its tart medicine smell and the entrance to Armando's Market exuding the salty-sweet aroma of fish and ripe bananas.

Eager to impress his new friend, Skinny tossed his football in the air. "Unitas has Berry open in the end zone." Skinny said as he ran under the ball, imitating the booming voice of a TV announcer. "It's a touchdown!" he yelled, after catching his own throw. "The fans are going wild!" he said then exhaled hoarsely, mimicking the roar of a crowd as he struck a triumphant pose.

Skinny continued his performance as they made their way down the sidewalk, throwing the ball to himself while delivering a play-by-play account with each catch.

"*Oye*, Skinny. You're the quarterback, the receiver and the announcer," Loco said. "When you start selling beer in the stands, get me a Schlitz, will ya?"

Skinny laughed but stopped throwing the ball when they neared a gleaming turquoise and white Studebaker parked in front of Ramon's Barbershop. The immaculate two-door sedan belonged to a neighborhood figure known only by one name: Chucho. Skinny gave the vehicle a wide berth. Messing with Chucho's car was not a good idea.

Like everyone in the neighborhood, Skinny knew Chucho worked in Ramon's Barbershop—but had nothing to do with cutting hair. If a police cruiser was in the area, Chucho would pick up a broom and pretend to sweep. Otherwise, the barbershop was the office where Chucho conducted his real business: *La Bolita*—the mob's illegal lottery.

All during the day a procession of men and women would visit the barbershop. Some would hand Chucho a piece of paper. Others would simply call out a number and an amount. All the transactions were done on credit—but God help you if you tried to stiff Chucho. Word was, if Chucho sent his *esbirros* to collect, the first late payment would be your front teeth. Another late payment and you'd be food for the fish in Biscayne Bay.

At the entrance to the barbershop, Loco raised his palm. "*Espérame aquí* for a minute, okay?" he said before going inside. Watching his new friend through the plate glass window, Skinny's eyes widened as he saw Loco walk toward the back of the barber shop. He was heading straight for Chucho.

Chucho was holding court in his usual spot, the blue Naugahyde guest chair farthest from the door. Sporting a crisply ironed *guayabera*, mohair slacks, two-toned wingtips and a thick gold ID bracelet, Chucho appeared regal and serene.

With a nod of respect, Loco handed Chucho a scrap of paper from his pocket. The bookie briefly examined the document and then smiled at Loco, exposing a gleaming gold tooth below a meticulous pencil mustache. Satisfied with Loco's work, Chucho playfully slapped the boy on the shoulder and handed Loco something from his pocket.

When Loco returned to the sidewalk, Skinny was bouncing with excitement. "How long have you been working for Chucho? How much does he pay you? Does your family know?"

"*Oye*, Skinny. There are some things it's better not to ask about, *entiendes?*" Loco said softly. "Let's go to Leo's and get a cherry Coke. I'm buying."

"Aw, man! I can't. I'm already late and I have to get home and eat."

Loco smiled and patted Skinny's arm. "*Está bien*. I'll see

you around," he said, walking back toward the park.

"*Esperate*, Loco. Aren't you going home?"

"No, but you better go," he said over his shoulder.

"If you don't have to go home, why don't you come over to my house and eat? It's not far. I live next door to Mrs. Post."

"The lady with the snake?"

"Yeah. *Mi abuela* is fixing grits. She puts *un huevo frito* on top—when we have eggs."

Loco stopped. "*Muchas gracias*, but no. I should go."

"Aw, c'mon. We've got plenty," Skinny lied. Since *Abuela* had discovered American grits, the cheap and filling staple had become the mainstay of almost every meal. Still, *Abuela* carefully doled out the portions and they never had any leftovers.

Loco hesitated, then walked toward Skinny. "*Está bien.* Thanks, man."

❖ ❖ ❖

The rusty spring on the screen door groaned as Skinny and Loco entered the yellow bungalow. Walking into the front porch, Skinny gestured toward the sagging cot in the corner. "That's where I sleep," he explained to Loco.

The bang of the screen door closing brought *Abuela's* voice from inside the house. "Ingrate! Rascal! Reprobate!" she yelled, her voice growing louder as she walked through the house, nearing the front porch.

"Is that your *mamá?*" Loco whispered, eyebrows rising in alarm.

"No, my mother's working a double shift again. That's *mi abuela*," Skinny said, matter-of-factly. "She always gets like this when I come home late."

Loco headed for the door. "I better go."

"*No es nada*," Skinny said, grabbing his arm. "She'll stop in a minute."

Abuela entered the front porch in a full-gale rant. "What kind of country is this where a child of nine stays out until all hours of the night? Are you listening to me? Or am I just wasting air here?"

Casually ignoring the tirade, Skinny introduced his friend. "*Abuela*, we have company for dinner. This is *El Lo...* I mean, Enrique."

"What's this? We don't have enough mouths to feed in this house already? Now our little prince of the street is bringing home every stray cat in Miami," *Abuela* said before walking back into the living room. "This kind of thing never happened in Cuba, Victor," she called out, her voice fading as she made her way back to the kitchen. "Even your worthless *Tio* Panchito respected the sanctity of the home at dinnertime."

Loco retreated toward the door, but Skinny held him back. "It's okay. *No es nada.* You'll see."

As if on cue, *Abuela* called out from the kitchen. "Go wash your hands then come and eat—both of you!"

By the time the boys had cleaned up and entered the kitchen, *Abuela* had two bowls of steaming yellow grits on the table waiting for them. (Many years later, in the middle of night, Victor would wake up and realize the portion of grits *Abuela* served his friend that day had been her own.)

"Your sister ate the last of the eggs," *Abuela* explained. "If you had come home at a decent hour, you wouldn't have gone without *un huevo frito* for your grits."

The boys silently wolfed down their food as *Abuela* continued to grouse.

"*Dios santisimo.* Look at the time, Victor. It's almost seven o'clock. Now you won't be able to take your bath until nine."

Skinny wiped his mouth with the back of his hand. "But *Abuela*, people here take a bath after they eat all the time—and nobody gets an *embolia.*"

"I don't care what these *comemierdas* here do. My great-aunt knew a woman from Matanzas who took a shower after eating. That woman collapsed of an *embolia* and died—right on the spot."

"What if I only wash my hands after I eat? Will I just pass out or something?"

"Don't try to be funny, Victor, This country is making you stupid. *Embolias* are real. Anyone with a brain in their head knows that."

Skinny shrugged. *Abuela* was wrong. But he had enough of a brain in his head not to argue anymore. He'd learned that the hard way with his grandmother.

After finishing their meal, the boys passed through the living room where Marta sat in a trance watching *Father Knows Best*. Something brown and furry scuttled across the floor, catching Loco's eye.

"Whoa! What was that?" the redhead asked.

"Speedy Gonzalez," Marta answered without looking away from the television.

"That's what my sister named the mouse," Skinny explained with a strained smile. "He's been living here longer than we have."

Loco shook his head. "That wasn't a mouse, man. That was a—"

"Hey, let's go to my room," Skinny interrupted, hustling his friend out of the living room. Once they were on the porch, Skinny leaned close to Loco and whispered, "It's better if Marta thinks he's a mouse, like in the cartoons. That way, he's not so scary."

"Sure, man. I understand," Loco said nodding. He then reached into his pocket and produced two wrinkled dollar bills. "Here, Skinny," he said, holding out the money. "Give this to your *abuela*."

The sight of the money made Skinny's hands tingle. Two dollars would keep his family in grits and eggs for a week. But thrilled as he was by Loco's offer, it was a time-honored tradition among Cuban males to refuse any compensation for a favor—for a while, at least.

As custom required, Skinny recoiled as if the bills were on fire. "No-no-no-no-NO!" he said, stepping away.

Loco knew the ritual as well. "Tell her it's to buy some eggs, okay?" he insisted, trying to press the money into Skinny's hand.

"No!" Skinny answered, vigorously shaking his head. "*No es posible.*"

"*Vamos*, Skinny. Take it. Are you trying to offend me?" Loco said, capturing the perfect shade of indignation that would seal the deal.

The sound of footsteps approaching the house interrupted the ceremony. Through the porch screens, Skinny saw his father's short round figure silhouetted by the amber streetlights of 33rd Street.

A wave of shame washed over Skinny. Why did his low-life father have to show up tonight, the first time a friend had come over to the house?

Juan opened the screen door with a flourish and Skinny was surprised to see his father smiling broadly, eyes gleaming behind his thick tortoise-shell glasses. With a courtly nod of his bald head, Juan acknowledged Loco's presence. "Ah, I see you have a guest, *m'hijo.*"

"Yes, *Pápi*. This is Enrique."

"And does Enrique have a family name?"

Skinny shifted uneasily, realizing he did not know his new friend's last name.

"Garcia," the redhead offered.

"You are Cuban, correct?" Juan inquired.

"*Si, señor*," Loco replied, showing the respect expected of a minor.

Juan nodded elegantly, content for the moment with this information. "Well, Victor. Would you and Enrique like to hear some good news?"

"Sure, *Pápi*," Skinny answered. *Did he find a job?* he wondered. His father seemed eager to reveal something—

and the old man loved an audience.

Sitting down on Skinny's bed, Juan pulled a pack of Camels from the pocket of his Ban-Lon pullover, and studiously lit a cigarette. "Boys, I have just returned from a meeting that not only struck a major blow against the evils of communism but has proved quite lucrative as well." Juan paused and made a stately sweep with his hand. "Sit and attend."

The boys made themselves comfortable on the floor beside the cot as Juan continued.

"Although I am not at liberty to divulge its whereabouts, there is in this neighborhood a safe house for the Central Intelligence Agency of the United States. At this location, I revealed to those brave defenders of liberty, secrets heretofore unknown about the evil tyrant who now rules the fair island of Cuba."

Juan paused for a deep drag on his Camel. "You see, boys. I knew Fidel when we were both law students. Back then, Castro was one of the many young revolutionaries of every political stripe opposing the government.

"In fact, I met Fidel through my good friend Ernest Hemingway—God rest his soul. Hemingway and I were like this, by the way," Juan said, holding out two fingers crossed over each other. "Anyway, Papa and I were sitting in *El Floridita* having a few daiquiris when he told me about this young firebrand, Castro. After I met Fidel, I discovered he was a powerful presence, a person of consequence. But while many others lauded and admired Castro, I immediately sensed his evil cunning."

As his father stopped for another drag, Skinny glanced over at Loco and was thrilled to see the redhead mesmerized by his father's tale.

"While I cannot reveal the details on Fidel I provided to the CIA, suffice it to say the information will be used to topple the bearded despot. And as recognition for my valuable contribution to the cause of liberty," Juan said, reaching into his pants pocket and producing a neatly folded wad of bills. "I was awarded the sum of forty-three dollars."

The sight of the money made Skinny's pride surge—and his mouth water. Not only was his father turning out to be the hero he'd always hoped, they'd have more than grits and eggs to eat for a change.

Juan winked and placed a finger before his lips. "Not a word to your *mamá* or *abuela*, eh?" he said, quickly pocketing the bills. "We want this to be a surprise."

"Of course, *Pápi*," Skinny answered.

Juan rose to his feet. "Now, if you young gentlemen will excuse me, I must freshen up before my evening appointments," he said before retreating to the master bedroom.

"I should go, *tambien*," Loco said after Juan left the porch.

"Why don't you stay a little longer?"

"It's getting late," Loco said, making his way toward the door.

"Where do you live, Loco?"

The redhead hesitated. "It's not far," he said before stepping outside.

"You gonna be at the park tomorrow?" Skinny called out as Loco disappeared into the darkness.

"Sure, man," Loco yelled back. "I'll see you around."

Alone on the porch, Skinny settled into his cot and lay back smiling. He'd finally made a friend—and thanks to his father, they'd soon be eating more than grits.

This had been his best day ever since leaving Cuba.

❖ ❖ ❖

For the next several days, Skinny kept his father's secret. *When will he break the news?* he wondered. The suspense was agonizing.

Each night as Skinny fell asleep, his imagination would

play a cavalcade of delights the forty-three dollars would buy...palomilla steak grilled with onions...crispy tostones... arroz con pollo...grilled flounder...grated coconut with cream cheese...

After more than a week without a change in their diet of grits and eggs, Skinny came to a bitter realization.

His father did not intend to share the money.

OCTOBER

Abuela Routs the Demons

Joey Cook did not like cats. In fact, Joey hardly liked any living things at all.

A spindly ten-year-old with buck teeth, a crooked neck and ears like two open doors on a VW Beetle, Joey was at the bottom of the ruthless pecking order in his all-boys class at Corpus Christi Elementary. Being punched, pinched, kicked, and shoved were as much a part of Joey's school day as the prison-like electric bell that announced the start and end of classes. Not surprisingly, Joey had become the merciless torturer of any creature smaller and weaker.

Most recently, this had been an unfortunate litter of kittens whose mother had made a den under a porch near Joey's house. The remains of the cats were found by several neighbors in a series of grisly tableaus.

Among those neighbors was Skinny's grandmother. She'd seen ritualistic killings like this before in Cuba and to *Abuela* it meant only one thing: *brujeria* was afoot.

Brujeria—literally, witchcraft—was the derogatory name given by many in Cuba's upper classes to *La Regla de Lucumi*, a unique religion that had evolved on the island. A fusion of Catholic saints with African deities that began among Cuba's slaves, Lucumi had spread to every class and color. Nonetheless, many non-believers like *Abuela* considered it a satanic cult with dark powers.

Now, in *Abuela's* eyes, *brujeria* had surfaced in Miami—and fearing for the safety of her family, she sprung to their defense.

To ward off the evil eye, *Abuela* threaded black and orange beads onto safety pins and insisted the children wear them at all times. More afraid of ridicule than the evil eye, Skinny hid the beads in his pocket once he was out of his grandmother's sight.

As an added precaution, *Abuela* wheedled a small vial of holy water from the parish priest and began dabbing the sign of the cross on each child's forehead every morning. "May the saints protect you," she'd intone. "And don't take any coins from strangers. That's how the *brujos* pass on a hex."

Abuela even had a theory about the origins of the witchcraft. "I think Castro sent his *brujos* to get revenge on the exiles in Miami," she explained to her grandson.

Like his grandmother, Skinny was also preoccupied with demons and goblins—but of a totally different kind. Tomorrow was Halloween and Skinny was nearing a state of rapture.

Even after Loco explained Halloween, Skinny could hardly believe it. Strangers in America would actually give you free candy. All you had to do was knock on their door wearing a disguise and utter one magic word…"trickertreet."

However, there was still one obstacle between Skinny and sugar snack nirvana. He needed a costume. Fortunately, Loco had that problem worked out. The redhead had instructed Skinny to meet him in front of Leo's drugstore before dark on Halloween.

Arriving at Leo's, Skinny found Loco sitting on the sidewalk, a half-full grocery bag on the curb beside him.

"Did you remember to bring a bag?" Loco asked, rising to his feet.

"*Aqui esta!*" Skinny said excitedly, holding out a small paper sandwich bag.

Loco shook his head. "I can tell you've never done this before," he said then pulled out a folded grocery bag from the one he'd brought. "Here, take this one."

Skinny unfolded the large bag, eyes wide in amazement. "We'll get this much candy?"

"*Por seguro*," Loco assured him.

Thrilled, Skinny broke into an impromptu song. "*Dulces, mamá, dulces*," Skinny sang, shoulders churning in a rumba. "*A comer dulces, cha-cha-cha!*"

"*Oye*, you want to get our costumes ready and go grab some candy or be Xavier Cugat?"

Skinny laughed and stopped dancing. "What are we going to be?"

"Pirates," the redhead answered as he pulled a tin of black shoe polish from his grocery bag. In a couple of minutes, Loco had dabbed a greasy beard and mustache on Skinny and used the drugstore window as a mirror to do the same for himself.

"What now?" Skinny asked, slightly embarrassed.

"Roll up your pants a few times and put this on your head," Loco said, handing Skinny a red scarf from his bag.

Skinny grimaced, holding the scarf out at arm's length with two fingers like it might carry leprosy. "Eww! What's this?"

"It belongs to *mi mamá*. What's the problem?"

"I'm not putting on a lady's scarf. People will think I'm a *maricón*."

"*Oye*, Skinny. You want candy or not?"

"*Por seguro*."

"Well then cut the *macho* act and put on the scarf. This isn't Cuba. Nobody here is going to think you're a *maricón* for wearing a scarf on Halloween." (Skinny would eventually discover this statement was not entirely true, especially during Halloween in Coconut Grove.)

Reluctantly, Skinny tied the scarf over his head like a pirate in the movies, rolled up his pants and looked at his reflection in the large window. "Hey, I'm Errol Flynn!" he shouted. Inspired by his transformation, Skinny struck a series of swashbuckling poses while admiring his reflection in the glass, oblivious to the grinning customers watching from inside the drugstore.

After finishing his own costume, Loco tapped his distracted friend on the shoulder. "C'mon, Captain Blood. Let's go get some candy," he said, leading Skinny toward the row of houses across from the park. "By the way," he added, "what's your *Abuela* giving out?"

Skinny froze, suddenly pale. Until that moment, it had not occurred to him that his family would be expected to give out candy as well.

"*Ay, cojones!* I need to get home!" he said, breaking into a run. "I never told *Abuela* about Halloween!"

"I'll go with you," Loco said, taking off behind him.

❖   ❖   ❖

An eerie wailing from the front door startled *Abuela* as she cracked another egg into the cast-iron skillet. The voices were shrill and insistent, uttering a bizarre incantation. In her sixty-seven years, she'd heard nothing like it.

"Triko-tree! Triko-tree!"

After the signs of *brujería* in the neighborhood, *Abuela* was wary. Evil sorcery was lurking, she was sure of that. She inched to the kitchen door and peered toward the front of the house, straining to focus her failing eyes. What she saw nearly stopped her heart.

Lucifer was at the door.

The Prince of Darkness was accompanied by Death himself, his skull's face staring in a wicked grin. Judging by their short stature, it was clear both had assumed the form of gnomes. Worse still, as they continued their eerie incantation, each demon was thrusting an orange gourd toward her with an evil smiling face.

"Triko-tree! Triko-tree!" they shrieked again.

Oblivious to the danger lurking at the door, Marta sat in the living room transfixed by the television.

Abuela fought a sudden weakness in the knees and the urge to urinate. She braced herself against the kitchen door, her mind racing. She had to compose herself. Her grandchild was in danger.

Then, with piercing clarity, an inspiration came to her.

Rushing to the kitchen sink, she filled a saucepan with water from the tap, then ran into the living room where she grabbed the plastic crucifix hanging on the wall.

"Be gone from this house! Leave us in peace!" she screamed in Spanish as she charged toward the front porch brandishing the crucifix and the saucepan. "This is holy water! This is holy water!"

❖ ❖ ❖

"Trick or treat! Trick or treat!" Michael and Tommy Brewer called into the yellow bungalow's screen door.

The porch light was on and the boys could see the gray glow of a television set flickering on the walls of the living room. An overhead light was visible in the kitchen at the back of the house.

"Trick or treat! Trick or treat!" they screamed again, holding out their pumpkins expectantly.

After several seconds, Michael and Tommy finally saw a figure moving toward them in the house. At last, someone was coming to the door.

What they saw next left them petrified.

From the gloom of the living room, an old woman charged toward them screaming something they couldn't understand, waving a crucifix and holding a saucepan. Her gray eyes glared wildly, exposing the white around her pupils. Paralyzed with fear, the boys stood rooted to the ground, their expressions of terror hidden behind their masks.

The deranged old woman opened the screen door and thrust the crucifix toward them, still shouting angrily. Thinking she might want him to take the crucifix, Tommy extended his basket tentatively toward the cross.

It was the wrong thing to do.

The old woman emptied the saucepan of water in his face.

Drenched and terrified, Tommy turned and bolted with Michael trailing less than a step behind.

❖ ❖ ❖

Skinny was panting for breath as he and Loco arrived at the corner of 33rd Street. Looking down the block, Skinny saw a column of kids in costume, all streaming past the yellow bungalow on the sidewalk.

"Look, Skinny. Nobody's going to your house," Loco pointed out.

"You're right," Skinny answered, staring in amazement. The trick-or-treaters were stopping at every other door on the street except his. "I better go see what's wrong."

As the boys started down the concrete walkway toward the front porch, a girl's voice called out behind them.

"Hey! Don't go there, you guys! They say that old lady's crazy."

Skinny's head sagged. "Oh, great," he said dejectedly. "Now, the whole neighborhood will think anyone who lives here is a nut job."

"*Oye*, don't sweat it," Loco said, patting Skinny's shoulder. "Looks like your *Abuela* figured out how to get through Halloween without anything to give out," he said, then held up his empty grocery bag. "So how about we go get some candy?"

A smile slowly formed on Skinny's face. Maybe being crazy wasn't so bad.

DECEMBER

The Last Journey of the Three Kings

Skinny opened the Christmas songbook he'd brought home from school and pointed to the smiling fat man on the first page. "This is Santa Claus, *Abuela*. That's who I was telling you about," he said to his grandmother.

Sitting beside *Abuela* on the living room's frayed couch, Skinny was taking great pains to show her how *Navidad* was celebrated in America. The last thing Skinny wanted was a repeat of their first Thanksgiving.

Gathered around the table, their mouths watering, the family had watched anxiously as Juan began to carve the turkey. As the family's guide to Thanksgiving, Skinny had explained this was always done by the man of the house. *Abuela* had basted the bird for hours and it was now golden brown and smelled like heaven—until Juan plunged the knife deeper. Suddenly, the acrid odor of burned plastic filled the air.

No one had told *Abuela* that American turkeys came stuffed with a plastic bag holding the neck, heart, liver, and gizzard.

That disastrous meal was now driving Skinny to make

sure his family got Christmas right.

"In America, the Three Kings don't bring children their *Navidad* presents—the presents come from Santa Claus," he said slowly to *Abuela*, hoping it would sink in. "And children get their gifts on December twenty-fifth, not on the sixth of January like in Cuba."

"That's ridiculous," *Abuela* said scowling. "Everyone knows the Three Kings brought the gifts for the baby Jesus in the manger, not someone who looks like Karl Marx after four shots of rum," *Abuela* said, pointing to Santa. "Look at him. He's got a beard like Castro and he's wearing a red suit—that's the color of the communists! My God, Victor. What are they teaching you in this country?"

Marta, who had been serving high tea to her dolls in the corner, perked up at the talk of presents. "Are the Three Kings coming soon?" she asked, remembering the bounty of toys during *Navidad* in Cuba.

"No, Marta," *Abuela* answered. "In this country children get their gifts from a fat degenerate."

Disgusted, Skinny slammed the book shut and stomped out of the living room, certain he'd be the only kid in the neighborhood without any gifts on Christmas morning.

"Where are you going?" *Abuela* called out as he swung open the screen door.

"To the park," Skinny said over his shoulder.

The old woman charged onto the porch in a surprising burst of speed. "Change your clothes first! Your mother just bought you those pants!"

"I'll be fine," he said as the screen door banged shut.

"Go ahead. Keep haunting the streets like a shameless urchin, Victor. You're going to wind up just like your worthless *Tio* Panchito."

Skinny shrugged. Maybe if he knew what his shady uncle had done, the threat he'd heard so often would make sense. The only time he'd asked *Pápi* about his brother, the old man had said that children can ask questions when chickens pee. His mom and *Abuela* had been equally mum on the subject.

After making his way to the park, Skinny saw Loco in a two-on-two basketball game on the fractured asphalt court. "I got next!" Skinny yelled, reaching the gate in the court's chain link fence.

When the new game started, Skinny found himself playing against Loco whose team had won. Fortunately, Loco was not guarding him. The redhead would always take the best player on the other team—which was definitely not Skinny.

The game was tied at eight apiece when Skinny caught a pass near the foul line. The lane was open and Skinny began a lumbering drive to the hoop. It ended two steps later as he stumbled over a crack in the pavement.

"Shit!" Skinny yelled, landing hard on his right knee. Grabbing his leg, Skinny saw a hole the size of quarter in his new dress pants. Inside was a raw patch of skin that looked like a strawberry.

Skinny tried hard to hold it back, but he began to cry.

Loco walked over knelt beside him. "Are you hurt?"

"No, it's the pants. They're new," Skinny said, sobbing softly. "*Mi mamá...* she worked a double shift all week to buy our clothes for Christmas."

Loco's idea of a cure was a now-familiar offer. "Let's go to Leo's and get a cherry Coke. I'm buying," the redhead said, helping Skinny to his feet.

"Thanks, man," Skinny said, hobbling for a few steps before getting back to his normal waddle. As they were about to cross 2nd Avenue, Skinny stopped. "Loco, how does your family celebrate *Navidad?*"

"Why do you want to know?"

"It's *mi abuela*. She thinks things should be like they were in Cuba. You know, putting hay under your bed for the Three Kings' camels, eating *lechon* on *Nochebuena*, all that kind of shit."

Loco paused, rubbing a thumb over his lips. "I don't have any brothers or sisters and *mi mamá* has to work. So we don't really celebrate Christmas."

"Where does she work? Most places are closed on Christmas."

"She works in Miami Beach."

"Is she a maid or something?"

"Look, I don't want to talk about it, okay?"

"*Está bien*, Loco," Skinny answered. "It's just that... well, you've been to my house and met *mi familia*, but I don't know anything about your family. I mean, we're friends, right?"

Loco exhaled slowly and nodded. "Yeah, Skinny. We're friends," he said and sat down on the curb. Loco stared at the pavement for a moment, then spoke just above a whisper. "*Mi mamá* works at Trader Ted's. She's a dancer there."

Skinny swallowed hard, trying to hide his surprise as he sat down beside Loco. Like anyone in Miami old enough to read, Skinny knew about Trader Ted's Lounge. Billboards for the place were everywhere, all showing scantily-clad women with beckoning smiles saying *Come and see us*. Word on the street was the dancers there were hookers.

Although embarrassed for his friend, Skinny was also strangely happy. Revealing the truth about his mother meant Loco trusted him. Now, Skinny realized, he owed his friend a secret in return. After a pause, he said, "A mother who works at Trader Ted's is still better than a father who doesn't work at all."

"I don't understand, Skinny. Your dad works. He showed us the money."

"No, man. He got that money from the CIA just one time—and he never shared it with our family. *Mi papá* doesn't do anything. He just lays around the house in his underwear all day and then goes out at night to play poker. He says there's no reason for him to find a job 'cause Fidel's

going to fall any day. So *mi mamá* is the only one who works."
Skinny was too scared to say anything about the danger of
his mother being deported—even to his best friend.

"Well, at least your father is still around," Loco said, still
staring at the ground.

"What do you mean? Did your father die or something?"

"No, he's not dead. He's still in Cuba."

"He can't get out?"

"He doesn't want to."

"*Que dices?* Are you kidding?"

"My father left us to go fight in the mountains with Fidel.
That's why *mi mamá* divorced him and came to Miami. She
was afraid Batista might do something to us because of my
dad. Now that Castro's in charge, my father is some kind
of big shot."

"When was the last time you saw him?"

"I was pretty little when they got divorced—around five,
I think. But we got a letter from him this year, after Fidel
took over. He asked *Mami* to bring me back to Cuba."

"Are you going to do it?"

"My father's a communist, Skinny," Loco said, shame in
his voice. "I don't want to go back."

Skinny grew silent, remembering his life in Cuba...his
bedroom full of toys and games...the sumptuous meals
prepared by their cook...swimming whenever he wanted in
their private pool...the constant attention from Imelda.

"If my father was still a big shot in Cuba, I'd go back,
Loco. *Por seguro*, I'd go back."

DECEMBER

Ike's Christmas Gift

With a courtly flourish, Juan raised a tumbler of rum into the air. "*Salud* and *Feliz Navidad* to President Eisenhower," he said beaming, "the world's most valiant defender of freedom!"

"*Salud!*" Alicia and *Abuela* echoed, lifting their glasses. Even Marta and Skinny joined in the toast, raising reused jelly jars full of Kool-Aid.

Skinny looked into the happy faces around the wobbly kitchen table, sharing in their delight. This was their second *Navidad* in America—and they had good reason to celebrate.

For the first time since they'd moved into the yellow bungalow, their table held a heaping platter of *lechon*, the exquisitely-seasoned roast pork traditionally served during *Navidad* in Cuba. Skinny knew his mother had saved a month's worth of tips to pay for the pricey pork, a sacrifice that made his first mouthful of the succulent meat even more delicious.

"This house finally smells like Cuba," *Abuela* said as they began to eat.

But even as the family tucked into their *lechon*, they had

an even greater reason to celebrate this Christmas Eve. The president of the United States had given them a gift as well.

Any Cuban fleeing the Castro regime could now work legally in the U.S. thanks to a presidential directive issued less than a week before. Eisenhower's new law also promised economic relief for the swelling tide of exiles arriving in Miami and gave them a new identity: Cuban Refugees.

Although Skinny did not understand it all, one thing was clear. His mother no longer had to work under the table.

It was like being adrift in a lifeboat and finally seeing a rescue ship on the horizon. The gnawing fear he'd lived with for over a year was gone. His entire family no longer risked being deported to Cuba and suffer God-knew-what horrible fate.

Their good fortune had become like a new toy for Skinny. He loved to revisit the thought and let it roll around in his mind, enjoying the glowing feel of it. They were finally safe.

Abuela, who had downed several tots of rum during the meal, rose unsteadily and offered another toast. "Here's good riddance to *huevos fritos* and grits for a while—that is, unless God sends down a lightning bolt and fries the bearded one's *huevos*," she slurred, setting off a gale of laughter.

Juan refilled his glass and raised it again. "I offer a toast to the legions of freedom that are once again on the march," he said. "Even as I speak, the CIA is recruiting an army of noble Cuban patriots who will soon return to our island and reclaim it from the throes of tyranny."

Skinny looked away and rolled his eyes. His father was still hanging on to the dream that they'd be back in Cuba any day now. *This means he still won't get a job—even if it's legal,* he decided.

Juan's voice rose as he lifted his glass higher. "Thanks to the steadfast support of that illustrious statesman, President Eisenhower, I trust that we will very soon be toasting the fall of the treacherous tyrant who holds our homeland hostage. Next year, in Havana!"

"And thank you, President Eisenhower, for keeping Alicia out of *Cielito Lindo!*" *Aburls* slurred before downing another shot of rum. The others laughed. *Cielito Lindo* was the name Miami's Cubans had given to the notorious jail cells in the pyramid atop the 28-story Dade County Courthouse.

Skinny joined in the laughter. Their mood was too cheerful to resist.

Then his mother stood.

Skinny could barely remember his mother as she'd been in Cuba. Only an ember remained of the sparkle and glamor Alicia had once radiated. Even so, something about his mother's expression made Skinny uneasy. She was smiling, but her tired eyes seemed focused somewhere far away.

"I have some news...to share with the family...," Alicia began hesitantly. "We're all together this *Navidad* and grateful for the blessings of *El Señor*. So this is probably the best time to tell you..." she said, her smile growing tighter. "By this summer, Victor and Marta will have another little brother or sister."

Abuela's boozy eyes widened suddenly. "*Dios santisimo*, Alicia! Not now!" she said, covering her mouth in shock.

"Mamá, *por favor!*" Alicia answered, glancing quickly toward Marta.

Like the flip of a switch, Abuela broke into a broad smile. "I meant, not now because I haven't had a chance to knit any booties yet," she said looking at Marta, her words now pouring out like syrup. "This is wonderful news...just wonderful. We're going to have a baby in the house."

Marta giggled gleefully. "Will I get to hold the baby, *Mami?*"

"Of course, *m'hija*. You're going to be a big sister."

"I can't wait, *Mami*," Marta said, her eyes alive with delight. "This is our best *Navidad* ever!"

Skinny knew better.

Although only ten, he understood what his mother's pregnancy really meant. She brought in the family's only paycheck. How long would she be out of work to deliver the baby? They'd be penniless the entire time—that much was sure. Besides that, there would now be another mouth to feed. Even with the new government help, their future now looked much the same as their past: miserable.

After the meal, with Marta put to bed and the adults still sluggish from the rum, Skinny quietly slipped out of the house. Arriving at the corner of the block, he found Loco sitting on the curb, waiting for him as they'd agreed.

"You should have come to eat with us, man," Skinny said. "We had *lechon* and everything."

"*Gracias*, Skinny. But it's okay."

"When does your *mamá* get home tonight?" Skinny asked, sitting down beside the redhead.

"Late."

"Will you open your presents with her tomorrow morning?"

"Naw, she sleeps in. And besides, I already know what I'm getting."

"She told you?"

"She took me to the Five-and-Ten on 7th Avenue, gave me ten bucks, and let me pick the stuff myself. She says I'll be sure to get the toys I want that way," Loco explained. "Funny thing is, I could buy more toys than that for myself. But it makes her feel better, so I just play along."

"Well, at least you're getting toys," Skinny said sighing. "All I'm getting is clothes."

"How do you know?"

"Same as you. *Mi mamá* took me to the store last week to make sure the clothes would fit. Only we didn't go to Richards or Burdines. No, she takes me to this little place downtown on 2nd Street owned by a Jewish guy," Skinny said, shaking his head. "First, she makes me try on all these clothes, then she starts to haggle with the guy. She picks up a shirt and asks the guy how much. When he tells her, she drops it like its red hot. Then she does the same thing with a pair of pants, and then socks, and then shoes. Finally, she puts all the stuff in a pile and asks how much. By this time, the guy is saying 'Lady, have a heart. I've got children, too.' She told me on the bus ride home that when he started begging, she knew we finally had a good deal."

Loco whistled softly. "Your *mamá* is *candela* when it comes to haggling."

"Maybe, but I don't really know why she takes me along. Everything she buys is too big."

"She might be expecting you to grow into them."

"Well, all I know is, I'm gonna look like a *pendejo* when school starts again."

"Yeah," Loco said smiling, "and you're worried about what Janice will think, right?"

The mention of her name made Skinny's heart race. For over a year he'd watched Janice from a distance, never daring to speak to her although he'd easily mastered English. But she was never far from his thoughts. He'd finally let Loco in on his secret a while back. Ever since, he'd been terrified his friend would taunt him for being such a pussy. Cuban males of every age were expected to be fearless skirt chasers. "I never shoulda told you anything about her, man," he said nervously. "Please don't tell anybody, okay?"

"Skinny, friends don't talk about stuff like this to anybody else, okay?"

Picking up a bottle cap from the gutter, Skinny studied it, then tossed it across the street. "*Mi mamá* is having a baby," he said flatly.

Loco's face brightened. "Good for you, man" he said. "You want a brother or a sister?"

"I don't want any at all."

"Why not?"

"We barely have enough money to go around as it is."

"Having family is better than having money, Skinny."

"That's easy for you to say. You and your *mamá* have money," Skinny griped. "You have everything you want."

Loco exhaled slowly. "You really think so, don't you?"

The look in Loco's eyes made Skinny feel very small. He'd never thought much about his friend's life at home. "Does it feel bad being by yourself all the time, Loco?"

Loco stared at Skinny for a moment—then laughed. "*Oye*, it's getting late," he said, rising to his feet. "I'll see you around, man. I want to get home and watch *Bonanza*," he said before walking away.

APRIL

Saturday Morning News

The twin engine Cessna roared across the TV screen, signaling the start of *Sky King*.

Skinny got up from the floor and hiked up his pajamas. "Tell *Abuela* I'm at the park when she gets up," he said to his sister. The Saturday morning cartoons were over. WTVJ would now start the boring stuff—shows with real people that only Marta would sit through.

With the sound of the TV show drifting out to the porch, Skinny changed into a tattered t-shirt and khaki gym shorts—his usual weekend clothes. He then put on his battered black high-tops and dashed out of the house.

Within a block of the park, Skinny could already hear the mosquito-pitched din of children playing, a siren song that sped up his pace. When he got to Wynwood, Skinny found most of the kids his age gathered around the swings in the sand-covered toddler playground—a part of the park his peers normally avoided. Breaking into a run, he reached the crowd and discovered the reason behind the excitement.

Loco and Peanut O'Connor were competing in long jumps from the swings.

Swinging side-by-side with the élan of trapeze artists, each boy was taking turns propelling his weather-beaten wooden swing into a high arc and then launching himself, arms flailing, to a landing in the playground's soft sand.

So far Peanut had the longest jump. The wiry tow-head stood proudly on a spot that looked to Skinny like an impossible distance to beat. But Loco seemed determined as he began to swing.

"Do it for Cuba, Loco!" Skinny yelled, his voice lost among the other shouts around him.

Then, like a school of fish acting with a single mind, the children turned their attention to a woman entering the playground. She walked stiffly toward the merry-go-round, a folded newspaper pressed against her chest, tears streaming from her eyes. The competition was forgotten and the yelling died, leaving an eerie stillness.

"Nancy," the woman called out hoarsely.

Skinny's classmate Nancy Santos had been laughing alongside another girl on the merry-go-round—until she saw her mother. In that instant, Skinny saw the light of childhood leave her eyes.

Nancy ran to her mother, hugging her tightly.

"What happened?" Skinny whispered to a girl in their class.

"I'm not sure. Nancy said her father's been gone for a while," she said softly.

Nancy's mother slowly led her away, the crying child clinging to her side.

Silently, the pack of children followed them, some of out of concern, others simply curious. As the procession passed the lodge, the park superintendent stepped in front of the children and slowly lifted his hands. "I think they need to be alone now. You kids go back to the playground," he said gently.

"Why are they crying?" a girl near the front asked.

The super looked at the ground for a moment, then

said, "Mrs. Santos lost her husband at the Bay of Pigs. It was in the paper this morning."

As the group turned back toward the playground, Skinny felt a sense of relief—followed by a wave of guilt.

His father might be *un habitante*. But at least he was still alive.

AUGUST

Either Blowfish or Spam

"What the hell is that?" Skinny asked as Loco hoisted the thrashing fish onto the sea wall. It looked like something out of a cartoon—a bloated, spiky thing the size of a softball with bulging eyes and a sphincter-like mouth clamped around Loco's hook.

"It's a blowfish," Loco answered. "They puff up like that so the other fish can't swallow them."

"Can you eat it?"

"Nobody I know eats blowfish."

Skinny's face tightened. The blowfish was the first thing either of them had coaxed out of Biscayne Bay in nearly two hours of fishing. "Well, we need to catch something, Loco," he said anxiously. "You heard *Abuela*. *Mi mamá* needs fish—for the baby and everything."

As Skinny had expected, the birth of his new brother Rafael had been an ordeal for the entire family. After four days of labor, the doctors at the hospital had gotten tired of waiting and talked Alicia into a caesarian delivery. Three days after coming home, with Alicia still too weak work, the news they'd been dreading arrived from the Fontainebleau.

Alicia had lost her job.

Since that day two weeks ago, the family had survived on the meager handouts of the Cuban Refugee Center—a diet *Abuela* warned would not be enough to sustain Alicia as she nursed the baby and regained her strength. And, while Skinny was anxious to help his mother, there was another reason he was desperate to bring home some fish— he wanted some himself.

Most of their meals were now either the government's chalky powdered eggs or its suet-laden spam, items so vile that only belly-mauling hunger pangs could drive Skinny to eat them. In desperation, he'd once brought home packets of mustard and ketchup from Burger King, spread it on bread and pretended he was eating a Whopper.

So when Loco offered to loan Skinny a pole and take him to the best fishing spot they could reach on foot, Skinny jumped at the chance.

Only a ten minute walk from Wynwood Park, Loco's fishing spot was at the base of the Julia Tuttle Causeway, a man-made peninsula jutting a quarter-mile into Biscayne Bay. From there, you could cast your line into one of the deepest channels in the bay, a place where the best catches waited.

But so far, Loco's choice spot had produced zilch—and Skinny was getting frantic.

"*Cálmate*, Skinny. We've still got a lot of time to catch something worth eating," Loco said as he carefully pinned the blowfish under his shoe and gently removed the hook from its mouth.

"Stupid fucking fish!" Skinny yelled as he kicked the unhooked blowfish back into the gray-green water.

Loco stared at his street-bruised Keds for a moment. "*Oye*, Skinny. You ever fish before?" he said, looking up.

"Uh, yeah...sure...but not for a really long time," Skinny lied. During their flush days in Cuba his mother had considered fishing unseemly.

"Then you probably remember that sometimes the fish just don't bite. Look, if we don't catch anything, I can loan you some money and we can buy your *mamá* a snapper at Armando's," Loco said. He then poked Skinny's ribs and smiled. "We'll tell *Abuela* you caught it."

"No, Loco. I can't borrow any more money from you. I can't pay back what I owe you already."

"Don't be a *pendejo*, Skinny. How about if I ask your father? He'll let me loan you some money."

Skinny scowled. "*Mi papá*," he said and theatrically spit in disgust. The effect, however, was less dramatic than he'd hoped. The bay breeze blew the loogie back onto his chest. "*Mierda*," he said disgustedly, wiping at the wet spot on his t-shirt. "You know, Loco. Your father may be a communist. But mine is something worse. *Mi papá es un habitante*."

"Your father is not a bum, man. He may not work but he's smart—and nobody can talk like he does."

"Yeah, talk...That's all he does."

Loco baited his hook again and cast the line into the bay. "C'mon, Skinny. You can't catch anything if you don't put a line in the water," he said before sitting down on the sea wall.

Reluctantly, Skinny retrieved his rod, tossed his line into the channel, and plopped down beside his friend.

For a long while the boys sat wordlessly, listening to the bay's gentle waves lap against the sea wall and the cars that passed like heavy sighs on the causeway above them.

Then Skinny's pole began to quiver.

"Look, Loco," Skinny whispered.

"Yeah, I know. You're getting a nibble."

The end of Skinny's pole lurched suddenly downward.

"What do I do?" Skinny yelled.

"Yank on the rod to set the hook, like this," Loco said, demonstrating with his own pole.

Skinny pulled back on the rod and felt a powerful surge of resistance. The tip of his pole bowed sharply toward the water as the line began to unspool from his reel in a screeching whine.

"Let him take the line," Loco said calmly. "If you don't, he's going to break it. See how far your pole is bending? He's big."

Skinny's heart thundered as the fish tugged harder on the pole. "You better take over, Loco. I don't know how to do this!"

"You're doing okay. Stay with it."

For several minutes, the fish kept up the fight. But Skinny could feel the desperate being on the end of his line growing weaker. The sensation was sad yet exhilarating. He was taking a life so that someone in his family could eat. Suddenly, Skinny felt bad about kicking the blowfish.

Finally, under Loco's subtle guidance, Skinny reeled in his first fish.

"It's a sea trout," Loco said as the fish broke the surface. "Your *mamá* is going to eat good tonight!"

❖ ❖ ❖

The last glow of daylight was bleeding from the sky as Skinny and Loco neared the yellow bungalow, fishing poles on their shoulders, strutting like victorious soldiers. They were bringing home enough fish to feed everybody—and Skinny was especially proud. Of the five fish dangling from the loop of line in his hand, the fat Sea Trout he'd landed first was the prize catch of the day.

Swaggering down the concrete walkway to the porch, the boys stopped suddenly, startled by angry shouts from inside the house.

Abuela's raspy voice drifted through the open door. "... if you had a job, our family wouldn't be in this mess, Juan. But, no. It's too much to ask the prince of the high and mighty Delgados to do an honest day's work. The sweat might muss what's left of his hair."

"How many times do I need to tell you?" Juan's answered

loudly. "It's pointless for me to pursue employment here when The Tyrant's fall is imminent."

"You've been using that excuse since the day we landed in Miami," *Abuela* yelled back. "That's a load of *mierda* and you know it."

"Alicia, tell your mother to be silent!" Juan shouted. "It's senseless trying to discuss politically complex issues with an ignorant *guajira*. Someone who is incapable—"

"Listen, Juan," *Abuela* cut him off. "For two years I've held my tongue as you laid around here smoking cigarettes, playing cards and scratching your fat *culo* while my daughter cleaned toilets to support this family. Now that she's lost her job giving birth to your child, you're still using the same lame excuse about Castro. Well, I've got news for you, Juan. If the men who had the *cojones* to land at the Bay of Pigs didn't topple Castro, who will? Are you planning to volunteer?"

"Alicia, I warned you!" Juan shouted back. Then the yelling stopped.

Skinny and Loco stood motionless, waiting to see what would happen next. They did not have to wait long.

Framed by the light spilling from the living room door, the boys saw Juan Delgado stomp onto the screened porch and open the door. "I'm leaving you forever! Do you hear me? Forever!" he yelled back toward the house. "Don't try and stop me!" he said at the door. After pausing for a moment, he walked outside, letting the screen door slam behind him.

If Juan recognized his son and Loco standing in the walkway, he showed no sign of it. He simply walked past the boys as if they were invisible.

Skinny watched his father's squat figure disappear down the street, unable to speak.

"What's going on, Skinny?" Loco asked.

"*Mi papá* is not coming back," he said, his voice shaky.

"Are you shitting me?"

Skinny shook his head. "When we first moved here, *Pápi* said he'd divorce my mother if *Abuela* ever yelled at him again," he whispered, eyes welling with tears. "Now, he's leaving us."

"But Skinny, you always talk about your father like he's a piece of shit."

"Yeah, I know," Skinny said, letting his pole and the fish fall to the ground. He then covered his face and cried.

❖ ❖ ❖

"Pssssssst, Skinny!" Loco called out softly from the screen door. "Skinny, wake up!"

Skinny opened his eyes and rolled over in his cot, squinting into the morning sun. Through the rusty porch screens, he saw Loco outside the door, holding two white take-out bags. "Come in," he mumbled without getting out of bed.

"I brought some breakfast for you and *la familia*," Loco said, holding out the bags as he stepped inside the porch. "Donuts from the Mayflower."

"Gracias," Skinny replied dully, rubbing his eyes.

Loco put the donuts on the window ledge by the door and walked over to Skinny's bed. "*Vamos, chico*. Get up," he said, playfully tugging on Skinny's toes through the covers.

"I don't feel like it."

"Look, I know your father left last night. But things are going to be okay. Your *mamá* has been supporting the family all by herself anyway. She'll find another job."

As Loco spoke, *Abuela* walked out onto the porch. "What's this?" she asked pointing at the bags on the window ledge.

Loco opened one of the bags and showed her the donuts. "They're for your family, *señora*."

"May God bless you, *niño!*" *Abuela* said excitedly. She then turned and yelled toward the kitchen. "Look, Alicia! This thoughtful boy brought *donas* for our family!"

From the other side of the wall, Loco heard a muffled protest. "*Silencio, cojones!* I'm trying to sleep!" Loco's jaw dropped as he recognized Juan Delgado's voice.

"It's eight in the morning, Juan! Time for decent people to wake up!" *Abuela* shouted back. "If you didn't live like a godless vampire, someone talking in the morning wouldn't bother you!" she yelled, then carried the donuts into the house, leaving the boys alone on the porch.

Smiling broadly, Loco walked to the edge of the cot. "Your father didn't leave you, Skinny," he said, cheerfully. "He came back."

"Yeah," Skinny said, staring vacantly at the ceiling.

"So what's the matter?"

"I don't know which is worse, Loco." Skinny said softly. "Having a father who leaves you—or having a father who doesn't have the *cojones* to stay away."

SEPTEMBER

Un Pinpollo

Skinny craned his neck. He stood on tiptoes. He jumped. It was no use.

No matter how Skinny tried, he was too short to inspect his new school clothes in the only mirror in the house: the medicine cabinet door above the bathroom sink.

Then an inspiration struck him.

He hopped onto the toilet lid, opened the cabinet door and turned the mirror toward him. From this perch he could finally see his outfit.

Skinny liked what he saw.

The trendy gray continental slacks and striped Oxford button-down minimized a paunch that had grown less noticeable over the last year. Before long, Skinny was absorbed in his reflection, imagining the impression he'd make at school in his new clothes.

He folded his arms and jutted his chin. *Que macho, caballeros!* he told himself.

Then he tilted his head and winked. *Come here often, sweetheart?*

He was striking a rakish stance, hands on his hips, when a voice from the hallway startled him.

"*Dios santisimo!* Look at this handsome *pinpollo* in his new clothes," *Abuela* said smiling.

Skinny jumped down from the toilet, his face suddenly scarlet. "I was...well...uh..."

"Don't be embarrassed, Victor. Be proud," *Abuela* said. "Your *mamá* worked hard to buy those clothes. *Gracias a Dios*, she found a job in time for you to go to school dressed decently."

Skinny had to agree. After nearly three months without work, Alicia had used most of her first paycheck to buy him two pairs of slacks and three new shirts along with a pair of black penny loafers—a sacrifice for which Skinny was painfully grateful.

But despite his mother's new job, their family was still only a paycheck away from powdered eggs and spam. Alicia's new job as a maid at the stodgy Everglades Hotel downtown paid less than the extravagant Fontainebleau in Miami Beach—and they now had one more mouth to feed. All the same, the new threads were making Skinny hopeful about better times ahead.

"I like the clothes *Mamá* bought me this time," Skinny told his grandmother. "I finally talked her into buying them at Richards. She said it reminded her of *El Encanto*."

"All this interest in how you look—somebody might think you've got your nose full of a girl, Victor."

Skinny blushed. As usual, *Abuela* was on to him. Over the last few months his thoughts about Janice were no longer just a warm-and-cuddly longing—especially at night. More than once, he'd woken up sweating yet strangely thrilled after a dream with hazy images of female bodies. These dreams were usually accompanied by a distressing dampness in his underwear. But not even the threat of torture by Batista's *Policia Nacional* could have made him tell any of this to his grandmother.

"I've got to get ready for school," he said, hoping to evade the subject.

"Don't play innocent with me, Victor. I'm the one who

washes your sheets and underwear, remember?" she said grinning slyly. "Have you got your eye on a girl at school?"

"No."

"Is she Cubana or *Americana?*" *Abuela* asked, ignoring his denial.

"I told you, *Abuela.* I don't have a girlfriend."

"Listen, Victor. You're at the age where you're getting interested in girls and I want to set you straight from the very beginning."

"*Abuela,* I don't want to hear this," he said, walking past her toward his bedroom.

Abuela followed him to the porch. "First of all, you need to find a good Cuban girl. Forget about these *Americanas.* They're all spoiled and crazy, and to tell you the truth, they're indecent. They go out with boys without a chaperone."

"You think only Cuban girls are decent?"

"Listen, Victor," *Abuela* said, shaking her head with disdain. "I heard from the butcher at Armando's about this *Americana* he knows. He said if every man who slept with her honked the horn when he drove by her house, nobody in the neighborhood would get any sleep."

"Fine, *Abuela.* I won't go out with American girls," Skinny said, eager to see her go away.

"Promise me you won't backslide, eh?"

"I won't," Skinny said.

Apparently satisfied that she'd schooled her grandson, *Abuela* finally left him alone.

With his grandmother gone, Skinny's thoughts turned to Janice. Now that he had nice new clothes, this would be the year he'd finally talk to her.

When school starts this year, I'm not going to be the same old Skinny, he promised himself.

MAY

You Can't Breathe Underwater

Mrs. Mitchell pushed the cat eye glasses higher on her nose and glanced at the wall clock. "We have two minutes left, people," she announced to the class then raised a Social Studies textbook, sending the loose skin under her arm into a flutter. "For tonight's homework, you will read chapter four. You'll have a quiz tomorrow."

Skinny sat hunched protectively over his copy of the book as she spoke. Not that he was attached to it. Just the opposite, actually. He was terrified someone would notice that virtually every male pictured in the book had been given a crudely-drawn penis and balls. This salacious handiwork was a legacy of one of the book's many previous owners. But every time he opened the book in class Skinny feared that Mrs. Mitchell, or worse yet, a female classmate would think he was responsible.

When the bell rang, Skinny closed the book and exhaled in relief. The end of Mrs. Mitchell's class always meant mixed feelings. This was his last class of the day and he was finally free to hit the park. But Social Studies was also the only class he shared with Janice now that they were both in Junior High.

He stole a final glance in Janice's direction. As usual, she was chatting cheerfully with her friends, oblivious to his existence. *Someday*, he told himself as the bell ending class rang. *Someday*.

Resigned to his shyness, Skinny bent down to retrieve his other books from the storage space under his seat. When he sat up, he was startled to find Janice Bockman standing near his desk.

"Hi," she said smiling.

Skinny looked around to see who she was talking to. When he realized they were last two people in class, his jaw began to tremble. "Y-y-you sure you got the right kid?" he stammered.

Janice giggled. "Don't be silly, Skinny."

My God. She knows my name! A rush of euphoria coursed through his body like an electric shock. As he jumped to his feet, Skinny bumped the edge of his desk, sending his books tumbling toward the floor. In that instant, Skinny saw a nightmare about to unfold.

His Social Studies book was on the top of the pile. If it fell open, Janice would see the torpedo-like penises scrawled on its pages. There was only one thing to do.

Like a soldier throwing himself on a live grenade, Skinny hurled his body onto the books. "Uuuufff!" he blurted, losing his breath as he slammed into the floor.

"Are you okay?" Janice asked, frowning with concern.

"Yeah...Sure...No problem!" Skinny called out, flopping on the floor like a beached fish, fumbling desperately to close the cover on the books under his body. Once the books were secure, he stood up, dusting himself off.

Still trying to smile, Janice held out a folded piece of notebook paper. "I have something for you."

Skinny tried to keep his hands from shaking as he unfolded the sheet. Written in a swirly school-girl cursive, it read:

POOL PARTY!!!
You're invited to our new pool!
Bockman House. Saturday at 10am. Bring your own towel.

Skinny stared at the paper, stunned. "Are you inviting everybody in class?"

"No. Dad said I could only invite two people from school."

"And you picked me?"

Janice tilted her head and smiled the way you would at someone in the hospital. "My dad said to invite the kids who would appreciate it most. Will you come?"

"Yeah! Sure! I'll be there!" Skinny answered, nodding like a woodpecker.

"That's great," Janice said, then walked to the door and waved. "See you Saturday!"

Skinny watched her walk out of the classroom with fireworks bursting in his chest.

❖ ❖ ❖

Standing on the sidewalk in front of the Bockman's house, Skinny stared nervously at the only two-story home for blocks. The house was small compared to his home in Cuba, Skinny reminded himself. But among the small, boxy cottages in Wynwood, it seemed like a palace.

The closer he'd gotten to the Bockman's house this morning, the more Skinny's nerve had faded. Wearing a bathing suit borrowed from a neighbor and carrying a castoff Everglades hotel towel did not help his confidence. In fact, Skinny's doubts had started only moments after Janice's invitation.

What had Janice meant by "the kids who would appreciate it most"? The question had tortured him for the last two days. Still, the thought of seeing Janice again—in a bathing suit, no less—helped him kick that qualm down the road each time it surfaced.

Swallowing hard, Skinny walked to the door and rang the bell.

A stout, middle-aged woman in a flowered sun dress opened the door. "You must be Skinny," she said smiling. "Come on in."

Skinny followed Mrs. Bockman through a large living room where a slender man with copper-colored hair sat working on a fly fishing lure and smoking a pipe. He rose and extended his palm.

"Glad you could make it, son," Mr. Bockman said shaking Skinny's hand. "Hope you enjoy the pool."

"Thanks for inviting me, sir," Skinny answered.

Mr. Bockman's eyebrows rose. "Wow. Janice wasn't kidding when she said your English has improved. I'd swear you were born speaking it."

Skinny beamed at the compliment—and the fact Janice had mentioned him to her parents.

After meeting Janice's dad, they continued through the house to the kitchen. There, Mrs. Bockman led him through open double doors to their newly-built pool. Seated at a patio table on the concrete deck, Skinny saw Janice in a modest one-piece bathing suit and a fully-dressed Norman Lee.

"Janice," Mrs. Bockman called out, "your other guest is here."

Janice smiled and waved him over. "Hi, Skinny. You know Norman, right?"

"Hi, Norman," Skinny said with a small wave.

Norman Lee was new to the neighborhood, a lanky good-natured kid from Georgia with a honey-thick drawl. The thing about Norman was this: He had a bright pink harelip scar under his nose. It was something Skinny tried hard to ignore—but it always made his throat catch with pity each time he saw the kid.

Looking at Norman, Skinny came to a realization that made his stomach flop.

Janice's reason for inviting him now made a miserable kind of sense. *This isn't a pool party. It's a pity party.* The "kids who would appreciate it most" meant the deformed, the fat and the poor. He knew the Bockmans meant well. But it made him feel small enough to crawl under the belly of ant.

"Well, now that you're all here, it's time to open the pool," Mrs. Bockman announced in a sunny voice. "Norman, why don't you go get changed? The bathroom's just inside on the right. I'll be in the kitchen if any of you need me."

Norman rose excitedly and disappeared into the house.

Meanwhile, Janice pulled on her bathing cap, walked to the edge of the small pool and gracefully dove into the deep end.

"Get in, Skinny!" Janice called out after surfacing in the shallow side.

Skinny joylessly took off his shirt and shoes, lowered himself into the water and swam over to her.

"Hey, you swim pretty good," Janice said.

"I've been swimming since I was little," Skinny said dully. "We used to have our own—" Skinny stopped and turned around as he heard the clomping of footsteps on the deck. Coming toward the pool at a full gallop was Norman Lee in his white jockey briefs.

"Yeeeehaaaw!" Norman yelled as he launched himself feet-first into the deep end. *KERSPLOOOSH!* The splash sent small waves sloshing over the edge of the pool.

Janice looked at Skinny, covering her mouth as she laughed. "Oh, my God! Norman's in his underwear!"

Skinny smiled back, the sound of her laughter brightening his mood. But then Skinny noticed something wrong. Norman was thrashing wildly in the water. "Hey, I don't think he knows how to swim," he said to Janice.

Janice's smile changed to a look of horror. "Mom! Mom! Come here!" she yelled.

Without thinking, Skinny swam toward Norman. Diving

under the water, Skinny saw the gangly Georgian, limbs flailing in panic, trying desperately to reach the surface. As he swam closer, Skinny could hear Norman's gurgling cries of terror. For a moment, Skinny watched helplessly, not knowing what to do. Then an inspiration came to him.

Diving until he was directly below Norman, Skinny stood on the bottom of the pool and pushed the drowning kid toward the surface. Looking up, Skinny could see that Norman's head was finally out of the water. The question now was: How long could he keep this up before coming up for air?

The answer came with a heavy splash. Looking above him, Skinny saw a pair of chunky legs in white cotton panties billowing inside a flowered skirt. Mrs. Bockman had jumped into the pool, fully dressed. In a matter of seconds, she pulled Norman to safety.

Skinny surfaced and found Norman gasping for breath, clinging to the side of the pool. Mrs. Bockman was beside him, her hair wet and plastered to her neck and shoulders.

For a long moment, everyone stared at Norman, expecting an explanation.

"Y'know somethin'," Norman sputtered in his Georgia twang. "You cain't breathe underwater."

A short while later, with everyone safely on the pool deck, Janice's dad put his hand on Skinny's shoulder. "Nice going, son. Mrs. Bockman told me what you did."

Glancing at Janice, Skinny saw her smile, eyes glittering with approval.

The fireworks in Skinny chest began again. He didn't dare hope Janice was ready to fall into his arms like a hero in the movies. But there was a whiff of something more than friendship in the chlorine-scented poolside air.

SEPTEMBER

Duck and cover

Squeak...Squeak...Squeak...

Skinny rolled his eyes as he heard the dreaded sound draw nearer. The screech of ungreased wheels from the hallway meant only one thing: His Social Studies class was about to suffer through another mind-numbing educational film.

Sure enough, a few seconds later Mrs. Mitchell wheeled the battleship gray 16-millimeter movie projector into the classroom.

What would follow next was all too familiar. They'd close the windows and lower the blinds, turning the classroom into a furnace. Air-conditioning in most South Florida schools was still decades away. Then Mrs. Mitchell would fumble with the machine for a while, oblivious to the sudden outbreak of spitball fire—with Skinny as a favorite target.

With these painful preambles complete, Mrs. Mitchell addressed the class. "We have a special film today," she said. "I want you to pay close attention because this is a subject that could be a matter of life and death."

Yeah, sure, Skinny thought. *Like the life and death importance of irrigation.*

As usual, the film started somewhere past the opening credits. Mrs. Mitchell usually took up several feet of film to get the projector threaded. The announcer's voice began as a low-pitched growl, then rose to a normal tone as the ancient projector got up to speed: "Beeeeeeeeeeee-suuuuuuuuuuuurrrrrrrrre-to-remember what you'll learn today."

Skinny sighed and rolled his eyes, instantly bored. By the end of the film, however, Skinny and his classmates would be nearing a state of terror.

With the Cold War threatening to become a nuclear cataclysm, the Office of Civil Defense had embarked on a campaign to teach school children how to survive a nuclear attack. In vivid detail, the film showed students the horrors they could expect. The explosion would start with a skin-searing flash brighter than the sun followed by a hellish blast wave that toppled buildings and shredded bodies. Worst of all, the attack could come at any time—sometimes without warning. The wail of the air raid siren might be your only chance to "duck and cover" and survive.

When the film was over, Mrs. Mitchell said, "All right class, we're now going to practice this defense drill here in our classroom. When I say 'duck and cover,' I want each of you to get under your desk and cover up just like the children in the film. Are you ready?"

Skinny glanced at Janice and the other anxious faces around him. He had no doubt every kid in the class was taking this seriously.

"Duck and cover!" Mrs. Mitchell called out.

The classroom became a blur of children scrambling for the floor. Because of his bulk, Skinny was among the last in the class to get on his knees, place his forehead on the floor and cover the back of his neck.

It might have been the compression of his abdomen or

maybe the two pimento loaf sandwiches at lunch, but the crouch made Skinny break wind like a Sousaphone.

Blaauurrttt!

For an instant there was silence.

Then the kid next to Skinny began to giggle. Like the breaking of a dam, every child in the classroom burst into laughter.

"Quiet, everyone!" Mrs. Mitchell called out. "That's enough! Get back in your seats."

The laughter died down but Skinny avoided making eye contact with anyone, afraid he'd start to laugh again.

"Apparently, you've failed to understand the seriousness of this drill," the gaunt, gray-haired teacher said. "So for the next fifteen minutes, you will sit silently. You may not read. You may not write. I want you to think about what you've just seen."

Ignoring the teacher's directions, Skinny focused on Janice instead. Seated three desks ahead, he studied how the strands of her golden hair converged into a flowing ponytail. His eyes traveled down her shoulders and waist to the slim ankles above her bobby socks and saddle oxfords. If this was Mrs. Mitchell's idea of punishment, he was ready to fart in class every day.

But before long, the images from the film bubbled up—and along with them came the chill of fear, despite the heat from the closed windows.

An atomic bomb would wipe out everything and everyone he knew. After watching this film, the chances it could happen were suddenly very real. Skinny had heard his father talk about Fidel's new alliance with the Russians. Would Castro find a way to punish his family for leaving Cuba even here in America? That thought added another brick to his growing wall of fears.

Yet there was something different about this new danger. For once, this was not just a threat to him and his family. Looking around the room, Skinny could see that

Janice and the other kids in his class were afraid too. And for reasons he could not understand, Skinny found this vaguely comforting.

OCTOBER

A Cold War Wound

Loco and Skinny nervously approached the Bockman's house and rang the doorbell.

"Hello, Enrique," Mrs. Bockman said after opening the door.

"Hi, Mrs. Bockman. We're collecting for the telethon. You know, for the kids with 'cerbal palsy," Loco said, holding out a reused peanut butter jar with a crudely cut slit in its lid. The few coins in the jar jingled meagerly as he spoke.

"Why, that's very nice of you," she said smiling.

Standing behind Loco and holding his own jar, Skinny had his mind on other matters. He was craning his neck, trying to peer into the house past Mrs. Bockman's wide torso. It was still early on a Saturday morning and Skinny was hoping to catch a glimpse of Janice or her sister Laura lounging in their panties.

Skinny's curiosity did not escape Mrs. Bockman. As the mother of two nubile young girls, she was aware of the effects her daughters had on adolescent males. She was also familiar with Enrique and Skinny from chaperoning school sock hops and knew these two were smitten but harmless.

"Are you collecting too, Skinny?" Mrs. Bockman asked.

Skinny pulled back his head like a frightened turtle. "We're taking turns, Mrs. Bockman," he said, eyes darting guiltily. "Enrique does one house and I do the next one."

"Yes, I think I see what you're doing," she said, holding back a grin. "You boys wait here while I go get some change."

Once Mrs. Bockman was away from the door, Loco swatted Skinny's arm. "*Comemierda!*" Loco whispered hoarsely. "Did you think she wouldn't notice you trying to sneak a peek at some *papaya?*"

Skinny cringed. "I'm sorry, man."

"Stick to business, will you?"

That business was Miami's Cerebral Palsy Telethon of 1962.

Since its start at seven the previous evening, the telethon had been broadcasting continuously. The boys were genuinely moved by the sight of their less fortunate peers—but the pair was also driven by an irresistible bonus...

All the children who collected money for the telethon in their neighborhoods were invited to appear on the air.

To participate, the children were instructed to bring their donations by one o'clock to the Olympia Theatre, the site of the telethon broadcast. Thrilled at the prospect of being on television, the boys hastily prepared their collection jars and began badgering the neighbors.

When Mrs. Bockman returned to the door, the boys leaned forward eagerly. "Here you are," she said, dropping a nickel and a dozen pennies into Loco's jelly jar.

"Thanks, Mrs. Bockman," Loco said with a grin and hurried away.

"Tell Janice to look for us on TV, okay?" Skinny added over his shoulder.

Looking back toward the Bockman house from the sidewalk, Skinny could not hold back his excitement. "You think Janice will dance with me after she sees me on television?" At a sock hop the week before, he'd nearly asked her to dance but had lost his nerve walking across the gym floor.

"I wouldn't get my hopes up, Skinny. Janice has a lot of *gallos* chasing her," Loco said. "Besides, I'd say it's five-to-two the Russians will drop the bomb before you grow the *cojones* to ask her to dance."

"That's not funny, Loco."

"Lighten up, *chico*. In any case, nobody is going to see you on television if we don't fill up these jars," Loco said, pulling Skinny down the sidewalk.

Like most kids in their neighborhood, Skinny and Loco were cultural bees, cross-pollinating Wynwood's households. The neighbors the boys were hitting up for donations were a mix of Anglo and Latin American names: Schooler, Myers, Perez, Kellog, Sanchez, Roberts, Jimenez, Anderson. Although varied, every household had something in common. Whether from Hartford or Havana, Ponce or Peoria, most had moved to Miami from somewhere else.

In the city's racial landscape, Wynwood was a slice of turkey between two pieces of rye—a layer of Anglos and Latin Americans sandwiched between the African-American neighborhoods of Overtown in the south and Liberty City to the north. The labels "Hispanic" and "Latino" were inventions more than a decade away. Racial segregation was a black or white proposition.

Skinny and Loco, of course, were oblivious to these abstract notions. Like bees in search of nectar, they were intent on raising money.

After scouring the homes along 33rd Street, the boys reached the corner and turned north on Third Avenue. The first house was a pastel green duplex with a driveway on either side.

"I know the kid who lives here," Loco said, pointing to the left side of the duplex. "He goes to Corpus Christi."

"Yeah, I've seen him at the park. *Se llama* Joey Cook, right?"

"Yeah."

"He seems kinda weird, though."

Loco shrugged. "Y *que*? If his parents want to give us some money, we'll take it. *Vamos*, Skinny. We gotta be downtown by one o'clock."

As they neared the door of the duplex, a dog in the yard next door began barking. Before they could knock, the door opened slowly and Joey poked his head out.

"What are you guys doing?" Joey asked, his thin neck swiveling as he glanced around suspiciously.

"We're collecting for the telethon," Skinny explained.

Joey mulled this over for a moment. Then his face lit up. "Hey, you guys want to raise a lot of money real fast?"

"Sure!" Skinny said excitedly.

Loco was more cautious. "What do you have in mind?"

"Come in. I'll show you," Joey said, waving them inside.

Skinny scrunched his nose in disgust as they stepped inside. The place smelled like acetone, maple syrup and piss. But that wasn't the worst of it.

The tiny living room crammed with cheap furniture looked ransacked— every drawer and cabinet had been flung open, the rugs were overturned and the couch cushions askew. Empty bottles of Jim Beam littered the floor.

"What happened?" Loco asked.

"Never mind. Come here," Joey said before leading the boys to a door at the end of short hallway. "Look at this," he said, opening the door.

In a small, dimly-lit bathroom an unconscious man sat naked on the toilet, mouth agape, head lolling.

Skinny's eyes widened. "Is he okay?" he whispered.

"You don't have to whisper," Joey said with a matter-of-fact air. "My father won't wake up when he's like this."

"What happened to him?" Loco asked.

"HE'S JUST A FILTHY FUCKING DRUNK WHO PASSED OUT TAKING A SHIT!" Joey screamed suddenly, the tendons of his thin neck flaring with rage.

Skinny and Loco stepped back, stunned.

"See," Joey said, his manner icy-calm again. "I told you he wouldn't wake up."

Loco had seen enough. "C'mon, Skinny. We gotta go."

"Wait! Wait a minute," Joey pleaded. "Don't you guys want to raise money for the telethon? My father always hides his wallet before he gets drunk," he said, looking behind a gilt-framed portrait of the pope. "If you guys help me find it, I'll split the money with you."

"Thanks, Joey. But we'll keep collecting the way we started," Loco said, heading for the door.

Joey hung his head for a moment, then looked up, his eyes alive with hope again. "Hey, can I hang out with you guys and help you collect?" he asked, grabbing Skinny's arm.

Loco grabbed Skinny's other arm and pulled him away. "I'm sorry, Joey," he said. "There's already two of us. We're not going to raise much money if we have to split it three ways. We'll see you around," he said before leading Skinny outside.

As they hurried up the driveway, Skinny looked back and saw Joey staring at them from the doorway, an empty expression on his face. He understood the feeling.

"You sure we can't bring Joey with us?" Skinny said, staring at the pavement as they walked.

"I think we should stay away from Joey. He's messed up, man."

"What you really mean is he's just like me, right down to having a deadbeat for a father."

Loco stopped and looked Skinny in the eye. "You're nothing like Joey Cook, okay?" he said then put his arm around Skinny's shoulder and smiled. "*Oye*, you want to be on television or not?"

"Sure."

"Well then, you better smile, *chico*," Loco said, tugging on Skinny's chubby cheek.

Skinny laughed as the two continued down Third Avenue.

Almost three hours later, their jars were nearly filled. After counting their haul at the bus bench on Second Avenue, Skinny had collected $5.79 and Loco $6.47.

"Okay, here's the deal," Loco said, holding up his jelly jar. "We can each take out forty cents for bus fare there and back."

"You sure about that?"

"Hey, they gotta let us do that if we're going to take this money downtown."

"How about lunch, then?" Skinny asked. "We've been doing this all morning and I'm getting pretty hungry."

"You're always hungry, *chico*," he said patting Skinny's belly. "Don't worry. I'll buy us some lunch at Walgreens after we're on TV."

"Loco, if you have money for lunch, why didn't we just put it in these jars? We could have saved a lot of time!"

Loco shook his head. "That wouldn't be right, man," he said. "Besides, we haven't got time to argue. Here comes the bus."

❖ ❖ ❖

When the boys arrived at the Olympia Theatre, the ornate marquee read: CEREBRAL PALSY TELETHON – PLEASE GIVE.

Skinny had been to matinees at the Olympia before but today the theater's entrance had a conspicuous new addition. Next to the ticket booth was a large metal bowl filled with coins. A paunchy guard with a sour expression stood nearby.

Looking at the shiny bowl, the game plan seemed clear. Skinny leaned close to Loco and whispered, "It looks like we put our money in that bowl over there and then the guard lets us go inside to be on television."

Loco nodded. "I think you're right."

Agreed on how to proceed, each boy walked up, opened his jar and poured the coins into the shiny bowl.

"Five dollars and thirty-nine cents," Skinny announced proudly to the guard after emptying his jar.

"Six dollars and seven cents," Loco said, nodding toward the guard.

The fat guard ignored them, staring straight ahead.

Skinny's heart was thumping as he and Loco strutted side-by-side into the Olympia's fancy lobby, a place that always reminded Skinny of a vampire movie. Even the gleaming candy case and the smell of popcorn could not distract him. The moment they'd worked for all day was finally here. "This is it, man!" he whispered to Loco. "We're going to be on television!"

The double doors into the theatre were just ahead. As if they'd rehearsed their entrance, each boy grabbed a polished brass handle and they opened both doors at once.

"What the hell?" Skinny said, staring inside in shock.

He'd expected a brightly-lit theatre packed with a cheering crowd, all gazing adoringly at a handful of children waving like heroes from the stage. Instead, the theatre was dark and empty except for a handful of people in the first few rows.

The only thing breaking the gloom was a small, bright cone of light on the left side of the stage. There, under the watchful eye of a mammoth TV camera, a procession of children shuffled past a large metal bowl like the one out front, pouring their coins in as they went. A few smiled and waved at the camera. The rest trudged along like they were in the cafeteria line at school.

On the other side of the stage Skinny recognized the Telethon's backdrop. On television, it had looked huge and glamorous, a place of bright lights and excitement. In reality, it was only about a dozen feet of painted wood and light bulbs in front of a bare brick wall. The set was dark and empty—the movie star host was probably taking a break.

"Shit, Skinny. We dropped our money in the wrong place," Loco said, then pointed to the line of children along the left wall waiting for their turn before the camera. "That's where we were supposed to go to."

Skinny slapped his forehead, realizing their mistake. "Coño! That bowl outside was for people walking by."

Loco's shoulders sagged. "All that work...for nothing."

Skinny stared at the stage, watching the children file past the camera. This was not what he'd expected, but it was still a chance for Janice to see him on television. The thought gave him courage.

"We can still be on television, Loco. I've got an idea."

"Forget it, man. Let's go home," Loco said, walking away.

Skinny grabbed his arm. "We can do this," he said then pointed toward the entrance. "I'll get the guard's attention and you can take our jars back and fill them up from the bowl out front."

"That's stealing, Skinny."

"No, it's not. We collected that money, right? We just put it in the wrong place."

Loco shook his head. "I don't know, Skinny. That sounds risky."

"Oye, Loco. Do you want to be on television?"

"Yeah," Loco answered warily.

Skinny pinched Loco's cheek. "Then you better smile, chico."

They both laughed and then Loco said, "Let's do it."

As Skinny watched Loco walking toward the silver bowl outside, he had a troubling thought. Was this how his Tio Panchito started his shameful ways? Skinny pushed the thought aside. It was too late now. Loco was depending on him.

Skinny walked outside and approached the guard. "Excuse me, sir. Can you tell me where the boys' bathroom is?"

"Inside the lobby, on the left," the guard answered in an icy voice.

From the corner of his eye, Skinny saw Loco approaching

the metal bowl behind the guard. "Where is that again?" Skinny asked.

The guard took a few steps toward the lobby and pointed. "Right there. Can't you read?"

With the guard away, Loco lowered his jar into the bowl and began carefully scooping up coins.

"It's kind of dark in there." Skinny said, tugging on the guard's sleeve. "Could you walk in with me and wait?"

"Listen, sonny. I don't have time to wet nurse a bunch of—" As the guard spoke, Loco's nearly-full jar slipped out of his hand, sending a fountain of coins crashing to the floor. The guard spun toward the sound. "Hey, what do think you're doing there?" he yelled.

For an instant Loco froze, a look of guilt in his eyes. Then he bolted for the street.

"Come here, you!" the guard shouted and began chasing Loco. After a few steps, the flabby rent-a-cop realized he'd never catch him. He then turned toward Skinny. "That punk a friend of yours?" he asked suspiciously.

The look on Skinny's face betrayed him.

"*You* I can catch, tubby," the guard said with a cruel grin.

"Look, sir. It's not what you think. We just put our money in the wrong place," Skinny jabbered as the guard drew closer. "It wasn't really stealing."

"You can explain that at the police station," the guard said reaching for Skinny's shoulder.

Instinctively, Skinny ducked, leaving the guard grabbing at air.

Skinny knew there was no way anyone would believe him now. His only choice was to run. With the guard blocking his way to the street, Skinny bolted into the darkened theatre.

Trundling down the center aisle, Skinny could hear the heavy footfalls of the guard behind him. He was gaining ground.

"Stop him! Stop him!" the guard yelled. "He's a thief!"

Skinny felt his heart rising into his throat as every face in the theatre turned his way.

With guard almost on him, Skinny made a hard left down a row of seats. Glancing over his shoulder, he saw the guard stumble and fall heavily in the center aisle while trying to match his detour. Looking ahead, he saw the line of children waiting along the wall to go on stage.

Staring in wide-eyed terror, the children backed away as Skinny neared them, clearing his path to the stage. Skinny felt a rush of power. He was a desperado, someone to be feared. Spurred on by their awe, Skinny charged up the steps to the stage.

Just outside the range of the camera, he stopped, uncertain what to do next.

The guard was still down, holding his ankle in pain. The cameraman and the children around the silver bowl on stage were staring at him, too stunned to react. Then he spotted his salvation.

On the wall behind the curtains, was a doorway. Above it, like an oasis in the desert, a sign with glowing red letters said: EXIT. His panic fading, Skinny headed for the door. As he crossed the stage, a thought popped into his head that brought him to stop.

He still had a chance to be on television.

The cameraman was startled when the face of a sweaty, overweight kid suddenly appeared in his lens, completely filling the frame. "I collected five dollars and thirty-nine cents—but I dropped the money in the bowl outside by mistake," Skinny said breathlessly into the camera. "Oh, yeah…Hi, Janice," he added, flicking a small wave with his fingertips. He then stepped back, took a deep bow, and lumbered away.

As an adult, Victor would call this the first television appearance he ever arranged.

❖ ❖ ❖

"Did you see me? Did you see me on TV?" Skinny yelled, bursting into the living room of the yellow bungalow.

"*Silencio, imbécil!*" his father snapped, then gestured toward the television. "Can't you see the president is speaking?"

Skinny's excitement died like a fat steer entering a slaughterhouse. He looked around the room, crushed and confused.

His entire family was huddled around the TV, staring anxiously at the sober-faced president. Most shocking of all, his father and *Abuela* were sitting side-by-side on the couch. *This must to be something serious*, Skinny realized, his throat getting dry.

"What is Kennedy saying now, Marta?" Juan asked his daughter, leaning closer to the black & white screen.

"Something about a quarantine for Cuba," Marta translated. "Are people in Cuba sick, *Pápi*?"

"This is much worse than a disease, *m'hija*," Juan answered, his eyes glazed.

The look on his father's face scared Skinny, a fear that grew like an icy stone in his belly.

"What's happening, *Pápi*?" Skinny finally asked.

"There's going to be a war," Juan answered, his voice cadaver cold. "They've uncovered Russian missiles in Cuba."

Skinny swallowed hard, imagining the smoking trail of a rocket from Cuba crossing over the ocean, zeroing in on Miami.

❖ ❖ ❖

Peeking anxiously around the corner of the building, Skinny finally saw Janice leave through the side door of the school. Retreating out of sight for a few steps, he began walking nonchalantly in her direction. Running into her at the corner on his way home from school would now seem like an accident—which was hardly the case.

He'd been desperate to talk to Janice since his telethon adventure on Saturday. But for once, Skinny's obsession with Janice had been matched by another fixation: his terror of the bomb. Eventually, it was that very fear that gave him the nerve to plan this encounter. He might die without a chance to declare his love to Janice—or at the very least make out with her.

Skinny waved casually to Janice as their paths crossed. "Another boring day in Mrs. Mitchell's class, huh?" he said, falling into stride beside her.

"My sister had her for Social Studies three years ago. Laura says if Phyllis Diller opened a fashion academy, Mrs. Mitchell would be her star pupil," Janice said laughing.

Skinny laughed along—with no idea of what she meant.

"Hey, did you watch the telethon on Saturday?" Skinny asked, unable to restrain himself.

"No. I went to the movies with Laura."

"Oh," he said, his heart sinking.

After a few steps, Janice said, "Isn't it awful about the missiles in Cuba? We watched the president on Saturday. Dad said there's going to be a war."

"My father did too," Skinny answered, encouraged by this common ground.

"You're a Cuban, Skinny. What do you think is gonna happen?" she asked, looking at him as if he'd really know.

"Hmmm," Skinny said, rubbing his chin, relishing the chance to impress her. "Well, I think Castro is a fire... a fire something," he said, trying to recall his father's words. "And he's—"

A deep rumbling in the distance made Skinny stop.

"Look!" Janice said pointing skyward, eyes widening in alarm.

Heading toward them from the north was a long line of planes stretching back to the horizon.

"Don't worry, they're ours," Skinny reassured her. He recognized their shapes from his collection of model planes in Cuba. "They're cargo planes, probably heading for Homestead. My father said that's where they're staging the invasion of Cuba."

The planes were above them now, their engines blotting out any chance of conversation with their deafening roar. Scared but trying to hide it, Skinny glanced at Janice.

Trembling as she stared at the planes, Janice slipped her hand into his palm.

For minutes, the long line of planes passed overhead. Wavering between fear and rapture, Skinny was frightened by the roar of the engines but thrilled by the softness of Janice's palm. As the planes disappeared into the southern horizon, Janice let go of his hand.

Skinny sighed, relieved the terrifying noise was over but missing Janice's touch.

"Do you think the Russians will drop the bomb?" Janice said, still shaken.

"Naw, they wouldn't dare," Skinny blustered.

Janice's blue eyes rose to meet his. "I'm scared, Skinny," she said softly.

"Don't worry, Janice. I'm Cuban and I know about these things. It'll be okay," he said forcing himself to smile. "Come on. I'll walk you home."

"Thanks, Skinny," she said, smiling back. "You're a good friend."

Skinny's heart nearly stopped.

A friend? Oh, God. Not that. A bullet in the chest could not have wounded him more. She'd called him a *friend.* His chances with Janice had just dropped to zero.

For so long he'd dreamed of a moment like this, walking beside Janice, talking to her, being a part of her world. And now, although he was close enough to touch her, he felt a million miles away.

❖ ❖ ❖

...WOO...WOO...WOO...WOO...

Skinny rolled over in bed, stirred by a distant wail.

...WOO...WOO...WOO...WOO...

The pulsating sound was strangely familiar. But still foggy with sleep, he could not figure out where he'd heard it.

...WOO...WOO...WOO...WOO...

Skinny sat up and shook his head, trying to clear his thoughts. Then he finally remembered. He'd heard it in the movie in Mrs. Mitchell's class.

It was the Civil Defense signal to take cover immediately. The bomb could fall at any moment.

"Duck and cover! Duck and cover!" Skinny yelled in English as he leapt from his cot on the porch and rushed into the house.

"Duck and cover!" he screamed again in panic, pounding on the door of his mother and father's bedroom. Finding it locked, Skinny ran into the room where *Abuela* and his siblings slept, threw open the door and turned on the light.

Blinking like a mole in the sunlight, his grandmother sat up in her metal folding bed. Marta and Rafael were still sleeping.

"Duck and cover, *Abuela!* Duck and cover!" he yelled in English.

"I can't understand you, Victor," the old woman said. "Speak Spanish."

"Get under the bed!" he answered in English, then caught himself and repeated it in Spanish. "*Abajo de la cama!*"

"Victor, did you take a bath after dinner?" she asked, suspecting an *embolia*.

His siblings were awake now, staring and bewildered.

Only seconds remained before the bomb fell. He would have to show his grandmother and siblings what to do.

"Watch me! Do this!" he said in Spanish and then dove under his grandmother's bed.

Unfortunately, he did not get very far.

The underside of the folding bed was lined with angled iron braces. As he lunged headfirst under the bed, Skinny rammed his skull into one of the metal supports.

The pain was like a Zen epiphany.

Lying on the floor, finally fully awake, Skinny realized with excruciating clarity what had happened.

The wailing he'd heard outside was a police car siren.

Ten minutes later, Skinny sat in the kitchen with *Abuela* tending his wound. She'd staunched the bleeding and was using a tray of ice cubes wrapped in a towel to reduce the ugly bump on his head. "Are you sure you didn't take a bath after dinner?" *Abuela* asked again.

By morning, the swelling was gone. But the crescent shaped scar would remain for the rest of his life.

The history books say that a few days later Kennedy and Khrushchev haggled out a deal over the missiles in Cuba, ending the near-panic that had gripped South Florida and the nation. But Victor's memories of that time did not include such grand bargains.

As an adult, whenever he was asked about the odd scar on his nearly hairless head, Victor would smile and say it was his wound from the Cold War.

APRIL

An Unseen Line

Janice brought the straw in the stubby Coke bottle to her mouth and delicately pursed her lips before taking a sip. Sitting across the table from her, Skinny watched in delicious agony, imagining Janice was about to kiss him.

This is almost like a date, just the two of us sharing a table, he told himself.

Skinny looked around, hoping someone from school might notice. The chances of being seen together were good on a Sunday afternoon at the luncheonette in Shell's City.

One of Dade County's first supermarkets, Shell's City drew shoppers from every corner of Miami. And with the in-store luncheonette next to the checkout lines, everyone seated at the tables was under the eyes of a steady parade of customers pushing shopping carts.

Janice glanced at the clock and finished the last of her Coke. "You better drink up, Skinny," she said, tapping his half-full bottle. "Mom should be done with her shopping soon."

The fact he was there to help Mrs. Bockman carry groceries and not really on a date with Janice didn't bother

Skinny. Over the last few months he'd helped the Bockmans clean the pool, trim the hedges, sweep away leaves and other odd chores around the house just to be near Janice. The Bockmans had welcomed his help—especially Mr. Bockman who seemed glad for some male company in a house full of females.

Skinny looked across the table into Janice's sky-blue eyes. He would have lugged a thousand bags of groceries just to be near her. Although Skinny could not put it into words, his attraction to Janice went beyond her beauty. Janice was part of a world Skinny longed for—a world where holidays were familiar traditions, not humiliating ordeals—a world of harmony and picnics and lemonade—a world where you were not on the outside looking in.

For the last few months he'd endured the torment of hanging out with Janice as a "friend." Every time they'd been together, he'd thought of telling her how he felt. Now, sitting close to her, breathing in her scent, the moment finally seemed right.

"Janice, there's something I have to tell you," he said softly.

"What's that?"

Before Skinny could answer, a woman in rollers at the next table spoke up. "Just what do *they* think they're doing here?" she said loudly, her voice dripping with contempt.

Looking over his shoulder, Skinny saw a family of four, in what looked to be their Sunday-best, sit down at a table. They had the same *café-con-leche* skin as Imelda.

"You don't intend to serve them, do you?" the woman in rollers asked the waitress.

"I don't rightly know what I'm supposed to do ma'am," the waitress whispered.

"Well, I'll have you know that if you serve the likes of them, I'll never set foot in this store again," the woman said, making no attempt to lower her voice. "And I'm sure there are plenty of others who'll do the same."

"All right, ma'am. Please don't get upset. I'll ask my boss," the waitress said before disappearing into the kitchen.

A tense silence fell over the diner.

Watching the family, Skinny felt an ache in his chest. As an overweight kid, he was no stranger to scorn—but nothing ever as cruel as this.

When the waitress came out of the kitchen, her boss's instructions quickly became clear. She completely ignored the family, acting as if they were invisible.

For a painfully long time the family sat quietly, waiting to be served. Finally, following the father's lead, they slowly rose and left.

"Wasn't that awful?" Janice whispered. "I felt so bad for them."

Skinny nodded, too stunned to speak.

"Was there something you wanted to tell me?"

"Uh... I forget," Skinny said, the magic of the moment gone.

No one had given him a second look when he sat down with Janice at the luncheonette. All the same, Skinny sensed he was somehow different. The thought was not comforting.

Looking at the faces around him, Skinny came to a queasy awakening. The world had dividing lines you couldn't see— until you crossed them.

JULY

The Roller Kings

Billy Ray Talbot loosened the drag on his ancient Penn reel and carefully lowered his line into the water over five stories below. He'd been fishing from the humpback bridge on the Julia Tuttle Causeway since they'd finished the roadway across the bay a couple of years before. The fishing wasn't bad. But the thing Billy Ray liked most about the spot was having it all to himself—on most days anyways. Not many fishermen would walk over a mile to stand on a shadeless sidewalk while cars zoomed by a few feet away. And that was just fine with Billy Ray.

The view was aces, too. On calm days like this when the bay was glassy, the skyscrapers of downtown Miami reflected in the water looked like they were floating in the air, blue sky above and blue sky below. It was peaceful here—once you learned how to tune out the traffic. The pint of Old Grand Dad always in his tackle box helped on that account.

Billy Ray's bastion of peace, however, was about to be invaded.

A sound like a half-dozen garbage cans being dragged

along the pavement rose beyond the crest of the bridge about fifty yards from Billy Ray.

Turning toward the noise, he saw a kid in a blue ball cap and white t-shirt arrive at the peak of the bridge on one of those new skateboard things. A moment later, another kid dressed the same appeared—and then another, and another, until there were six of them, all bearing down on Billy Ray and picking up speed as they came down the slope.

"Watch out for the fisherman!" Loco yelled at the five boys behind him.

Bringing up the rear of the line, Skinny did not hear Loco. He was looking down, alarmed by a skateboard that was beginning to wobble dangerously. This was not the place to take a spill. On Skinny's right was a fifty-foot drop into the bay. On his left was a speeding stream of traffic.

When Skinny finally looked up, he was only a few feet from the fisherman. "Look out!" he yelled, managing to steer his unruly skateboard away from the man.

Billy Ray pressed himself against the railing, barely escaping a collision. "You crazy goddam sons-a-bitches!" he screamed as the last kid rolled past.

"Sorry!" Skinny called out over his shoulder as he continued down the slope.

There was no stopping now, Skinny knew. The slope of the bridge would carry them another half mile at least. They could not afford to waste that kind of energy if they were going to make it all the way to South Beach.

Almost two miles later, the six skateboarders reached the end of the causeway where it met Alton Road. It was now nearing noon under a merciless July sun.

"Let's rest for a while," Loco said, pointing toward a shady spot under a clump of sea grape trees.

Relieved, the group collapsed onto the grass, panting and sweat-soaked.

"This blows, man. How long before we get to South Beach?" Hector Rivera asked lying on his back.

"We keep going straight until we hit Collins Avenue, then we turn right," Skinny replied.

Fanning himself with his ball cap, Peanut O'Connor asked, "So how far is Collins Avenue?"

"Just a little farther," Skinny said, not sounding very sure.

Peanut nodded toward the causeway they'd just crossed. "My uncle says the Julia Tuttle's the longest bridge in the world 'cause it connects Havana to Tel Aviv."

"Peanut, your uncle sounds pretty smart ... for a Georgia cracker," Hector said smirking. "I heard that he was your uncle—and your daddy too."

Peanut jumped to his feet, fists clenched. "Take that back, asshole."

Loco stepped between them. "Save your energy, Peanut. South Beach is still a ways to go."

"I still don't understand why we're doing this," Hector whined.

Skinny rolled his eyes. "I already told you," he said. "Because we can't let the Knights show us up."

The Knights on Wheels had started the whole skateboard craze at Wynwood Park. Mostly Anglo kids with store-bought boards, they wore matching polo shirts with an embroidered crusader's helmet on the pocket. Eager to be part of the cool new group, Skinny had asked to join the Knights. But they'd rejected him and his homemade skateboard.

Wounded by the snub, Skinny came up with a plan for revenge. He recruited Loco to be president of a new skateboard club, the Roller Kings. With the Knights turning down more kids than they accepted, new members were not hard to find.

For their club uniforms, Skinny asked each member for a white t-shirt. The club's artist Bobby Reyes then drew a large red crown on the shirts with a laundry marker. The cheap blue ball caps Wynwood gave out free to its Little

Leaguers topped off their uniforms.

The newly-minted Roller Kings had been feeling pretty good about themselves—until last week.

Just before the start of a Little League tournament, the Knights had wowed the crowd in the bleachers at Wynwood by doing a series of coordinated tricks on the sidewalks circling the park. Skinny was sure it was meant to put his club in its place. Determined to top their rivals, Skinny had come up with a daring idea: a skateboard trip all the way to South Beach.

Hector propped himself up on his elbow. "It would have been a lot easier to cruise around the park like the Knights did."

"No!" Skinny snapped. "We need to do something different, something people will talk about." What Skinny left unsaid was that their skateboard skills and equipment were no match for the Knights.

Loco picked up his board and rose to his feet. "We better get going, guys. We've got a ways to go."

Before getting up, Skinny quickly inspected his rebellious board. Like all the other boys in the Roller Kings, his skateboard was simply two halves of an old steel roller skate nailed to a salvaged piece of lumber. Looking for a problem he did not want to find, Skinny decided he was ready to roll.

Nearly an hour later, after crossing two small bridges and weaving their way through sidewalks crowded with tourists, they boys finally reached Collins Avenue and huddled in the shade of a tall hotel.

"Goddammit, Skinny," Hector said, his face flushed and sweating. "That was a long fucking way. How much farther do we have to go?"

Skinny looked at the street sign and gulped. They were on 41st Street. Skinny knew South Beach was on 1st Street, still forty blocks away.

Before Skinny could answer, Loco spoke up. "*Oye,*

Hector. You want people to say you were the guy who chickened out on this trip?"

Hector lowered his eyes. "I'm not chickening out, okay?"

Loco smiled. "All right then, let's get going. We can stop at the Walgreens over there and I'll buy everybody an iced tea and a bagel," he said, pointing to the drugstore a block away.

Entering the air-conditioned drugstore was like stepping into heaven. After the waitress brought his iced tea, Skinny poured nearly an inch of sugar into the tall glass and stirred it, turning the tea milky. Chomping into his egg bagel, Skinny glanced down at his skateboard and noticed the steel on the bottom of his wheels getting shiny and thin.

He pushed that worry aside and kept eating. There was nothing he could do about it now.

Once the Roller Kings hit the pavement again, Skinny quickly noticed how much Miami Beach changed as you traveled south. This was nothing like the Miracle Mile north of 41st Street with its extravagant high-rise hotels like the Eden Roc and Fontainebleau. The small hotels around here looked old and worn, just like their guests—mostly retirees staring vacantly from cramped verandas, looking like they were just waiting around to die.

As the boys approached Wolfie's Restaurant on 21st Street, still two miles from South Beach, the inevitable happened. The bottom of Skinny's skate finally wore away. Without warning, the front wheels of his skateboard locked up, spraying ball bearings onto the pavement and sending Skinny stumbling into a row of bushes next to the sidewalk.

"Shit," Skinny said, untangling himself from the gardenias.

As the other boys gathered round, Hector picked up Skinny's skateboard. "The wheels on this piece of shit are shot, Skinny. We'll have to go on without you."

"No," Loco said. "We all go together or nobody goes."

Hector grimaced in disgust. "Then that means we're all

walking back to Wynwood—and we won't get back until dark."

Skinny closed his eyes, sorry he'd ever dreamed up this trip. He'd dragged all of them for miles in the heat trying to prove they were better than the Knights. Now his plan had failed.

After a long silence Loco said, "I'll call my mom. She can come pick us up."

Skinny looked at Loco, not believing what he'd heard. He'd never been to Loco's house, much less seen his mother—and Skinny knew why. The redhead was ashamed of where she worked. Now, to get them out of this jam, Loco was going to let all of them meet his mother.

Loco had come to his rescue once again. Skinny had never been more grateful—or more curious.

❖ ❖ ❖

"There she is," Loco said as a mint green Valiant swerved onto Collins Avenue.

The car pulled up to the curb near the boys and a busty redhead behind the wheel called out to Loco. "I have not too much time, Enrique. So please to hurry," she said with a thick Spanish accent.

Not a very sexy car, but a very sexy woman, were Skinny's first thoughts about Loco's mother.

When Loco opened the front passenger door, the other boys began jostling to get in first and sit next to his mother.

"Get in, Skinny," Loco said, resolving the contest.

Skinny slid into the bench seat next to her. "Hi," he said nervously..

"Hello," she replied with a smile that was friendly but also said *don't get any ideas*. Skinny imagined she'd had a lot chances to practice that smile.

After the other boys had crammed themselves into the car, Loco's mom stomped on the gas and pulled away, tires squealing.

"You're going to get a ticket driving like that," Loco warned her.

"Ay, don't *desesperate* me, Enrique."

Skinny could not picture many traffic cops giving Loco's mom a ticket. She probably knew that too.

Skinny found her driving exhilarating—in more ways than one. During the trip back home, her swerving forced him against her several times, making his thigh tingle when they touched. By the time they arrived at Wynwood, Skinny was both aroused and guilt-ridden. *This is your best friend's mother*, he reminded himself.

After the boys were out of the car, she called out through the window in her broken English. "You have to have very be careful, Enrique!" she said, then peeled rubber as she pulled away.

Once the car was out of sight, Hector took off his Roller Kings t-shirt and tossed it at Skinny. "I'm out," he said and walked away.

Loco's face hardened, a look of kick-ass in his eyes. He started after Hector but Skinny held him back.

"Let him go, Loco. We don't need *pendejos* like him around."

"Skinny's right. Hector is a *comemierda*," Peanut added in his Georgia-inflected Spanglish. "We tried. There's nothing wrong with that," he said before heading home. "I'll see you guys around."

The other boys nodded and walked away as well, leaving Skinny and Loco alone.

"Loco, I know you didn't really want to call your mom. You're a good friend, man."

"We didn't have any other choice. Besides, I knew she'd have some time before work."

As they spoke, the two found themselves walking toward the empty bleachers.

"You heard anything more from your father?"

"I don't want to talk about him."

"Why not?" Skinny asked sitting down on the first row of the pine benches.

"Because I don't."

"Did something happen to him?"

Loco laughed softly. "You've been taking lessons from *Abuela,* haven't you?" he said, sitting down beside Skinny. "Man, you just don't quit with the questions."

"Hey, I'm just interested in how my best friend is doing. Is that wrong?"

Loco shook his head. "No, I guess not."

"So tell me about your father."

"Well, I had this dream and... I think my father's dead, Skinny," Loco said, his voice just above a whisper. "In my dream he was floating on a piece of rock in this sea of lava, screaming for mercy. Then the floating rock turned over and he disappeared."

Skinny was quiet for a moment. "Do you believe in that heaven and hell stuff?"

"I hear about it from the priests and nuns at Corpus Christi every day. But I'm not sure."

"I'm not either. But why would your dad go to hell?"

"He's a communist, Skinny."

"Loco, even if all that stuff about hell is true, I don't think being a communist is enough to send you there. *Mi papá* hates communists and he deserves to be in hell a whole lot more."

AUGUST

The Storm Season

"Shhhhh!" Skinny hissed at his siblings when WTVJ interrupted the afternoon movie with another special bulletin.

"Hurricane Cleo is now approaching the Florida Keys," the grim-faced weatherman said, pointing to a map showing a menacing spiral icon just below the southern tip of Florida. "The Weather Service predicts the edge of the storm will reach greater Miami shortly after dark and advises all residents in our viewing area to take immediate precautions. Stay tuned to WTVJ for more bulletins."

Marta looked up from the tower of empty oatmeal boxes she was helping three-year-old Rafael build. "You better go tell *Mámi* and *Pápi*."

"Naw," Skinny said, waving his hand in disdain. "It's the same old stuff."

His parents and *Abuela* were outside, struggling to lower the bungalow's corroded storm shutters. Because he understood English better than anyone else in the family, Skinny had drawn the cushy job of monitoring the television reports on the approaching hurricane.

For days, Miami's airwaves had been flooded with alarming reports on Cleo, the Category Two hurricane bearing down on the city. Skinny had seen the TV weather map with Cleo's dotted trail so many times, the image was now etched into his brain. But having never been through a hurricane, what Cleo would actually look like was still a mystery to him.

At first, he imagined Cleo as a much bigger version of the tornado from the *Wizard of Oz*, a colossal funnel cloud spiraling high into outer space. When *Abuela* explained that a hurricane was simply a vast circular storm and you couldn't actually see a funnel cloud, he was disappointed. After all the hype, he expected something a lot more dramatic.

Now, with the storm approaching, Skinny was feeling smug about his reaction: He wasn't afraid at all. Unknown to Skinny, the reason behind his bravado lay with another storm—one brewing inside him.

The storm had begun a few months before, around the time his voice had started changing. Nature was infusing his body with unprecedented levels of testosterone. The results were not unusual for a fourteen-year-old male.

Along with a budding plot of pubic hair, he'd developed a short-fuse temper and the unshakeable conviction that all adults had been placed on earth with a single purpose: to thwart his will and make his life miserable in every way possible.

But another side-effect of Skinny's hormonal storm had emerged—one that he found particularly mortifying. He was now plagued by unexpected erections.

They happened so frequently, he now had a mental code name for this uninvited visitor: Lorenzo—a secret he shared with no one, not even Loco.

The worst episode had come two months earlier.

As he stood for the Pledge of Allegiance on the last day of school, Nancy Jimenez had spotted Lorenzo's unmistakable presence in his pants. For the rest of the day, the girls from his homeroom had whispered and giggled whenever he was around.

Just last week, he'd spent a humiliating half-hour pressed against the side of the Bockman's pool, waiting for the bulge in his bathing suit to subside. If Janice had noticed Lorenzo, she'd been kind enough not to comment.

In spite of these shortcomings—or perhaps because of them—Skinny had come to a profound conclusion...

He was now A MAN.

And like any real man, he would no longer put up with shit—from anybody. On the heels of these lofty thoughts, Skinny's mother entered the living room.

"When do they say the hurricane will be here?" Alicia asked her son.

"Same as before. Right after dark." Skinny said, sprawled on his cot which had been brought into the living room from the front porch in anticipation of the hurricane.

"Victor, your father wants you to get him three packs of cigarettes from Armando's," Alicia said, holding out a dollar bill. "And bring back the change."

"What am I—his slave? Why can't *Pápi* go get his own cigarettes?"

"Be reasonable, *m'hijo*. Your father is busy with the storm shutters. The stores will be closing soon and he doesn't want to be without his Camels during the hurricane."

"If it's so important, why don't *you* go?"

Alicia exhaled slowly, trying to keep her composure. "I'm busy outside, too. It's only a couple of blocks, *m'hijo*. So please, be my sweet little boy and do this small thing for your family."

"Stop it! Stop treating me like a baby!"

"All right, Victor. I tried asking you nicely," Alicia said, eyes flashing. "Now I'm *telling* you. Stop behaving like a shameless ingrate and go to the store—right now!"

Skinny jumped to his feet. "No! I'm through being

ordered around by you and *Pápi* and *Abuela*. You can all go to hell!" he screamed then ran past his mother and out the door.

❖ ❖ ❖

The palms in Mrs. Post's front yard were fluttering like flags as Skinny reached the corner. *Nothing unusual*, he assured himself. He'd seen the wind whip the trees like this during the thunderstorms that came like clockwork on summer afternoons in Miami.

Looking east toward the bay, Skinny saw a bank of purple clouds gathering in the distance. To the west, a gauzy afternoon sun was fading quickly. With the freshening wind pressing his thin madras shirt against his chest, Skinny was struck by an idea.

What if he stayed out through the entire storm? After all, this whole hurricane thing was just more grown-up *mierda* like the duck and cover drills. He could take care of himself now. There wasn't anything to fear.

Yeah, this'll show them, he thought as he broke into a run again. *They'll see I'm too big to be bossed around anymore.*

His plan began to materialize as he reached Armando's Market—the place he'd resisted going for the cigarettes. He'd ride out the hurricane in the lodge at Wynwood. By then, his family would probably think he was dead. Wouldn't they be surprised when he showed up after the hurricane? They'd have to show him some respect then.

After running several blocks, Skinny began to get winded. He'd lost a good deal of his baby fat but was still far from slender. So he slowed to a walk.

After another block, Skinny noticed he was the only person on the street. No vehicles of any kind were moving. That worried him.

A needle-fine drizzle began to fall, stinging his face as he walked. Within sight of Wynwood, the wind got stronger. The trees began to thrash, their branches clawing the air menacingly.

By the time he reached the park, the baseball field was alive with eddies of leaves and paper scurrying like rats across the grass. Shielding his eyes from the debris, Skinny ran toward the lodge. At the door of the limestone structure, he made an alarming discovery: The lodge was locked.

He stood in front of the empty building, fears rising, uncertain what to do. The storm was blowing harder now. Sheets of rain raced across the open field in waves. With a menacing roar, the wind rose again. The trees went into seizures, shuddering in violent spasms.

An icy stream of fear began to flow through Skinny. He could not stay in the open. That, he knew for sure. Trying to hold back his panic, Skinny looked around him, desperately searching for cover. To his right was a dry corner of the L-shaped building sheltered from the wind. He ran to the spot and squatted against the wall, relieved to be out of the rain.

Under cover for the moment, he wondered what to do next. To go home would mean being humiliated. There was no way he'd do that. He'd have to stay here until the hurricane was over.

As the minutes passed, the spraying rain found its way into Skinny's little haven. Before long, his clothes were soaked and he began to shiver.

The sky darkened quickly into night and the wind rose again, spawning a howl like the wailing from a horror movie as it passed through the trees. *Ooooouuuuuu. Ooooouuuuuu.* Cold, frightened and feeling very much alone, Skinny's mind wandered into a fantasy.

He imagined his body being swept up into the funnel of the hurricane, flailing desperately as the ground below him disappeared. He tried hard to fight it, but Skinny began to cry.

Wiping the tears from his rain-soaked cheeks, he spotted a squat figure in a raincoat walking below the row of trees around the edge of the park. His bald head was shining under the streetlights.

Skinny stood and ran as fast as his feet would carry him toward his father.

"Do you have any idea how worried your mother is?" Juan shouted angrily as the boy reached him.

"I'm sorry," Skinny said, hugging his father.

"*Esta bien*," Juan said, his voice softening. "Let's get back to the house before this storm gets any worse," he said, opening his raincoat and pulling it over both of them.

❖ ❖ ❖

"I don't know whether to hug you or kill you!" Alicia screamed at Skinny as he entered the house, soaked and shivering.

Abuela nodded toward her grandson. "If that boy doesn't get into a hot bath right now, a cold is going to kill him for sure."

Alicia exhaled slowly. "You're right, *Mamá*," she said. "Take him into the bathroom. I'll get him some dry clothes."

After his bath, Skinny joined the family for a hurried meal and was relieved to find the talk around the table was about the hurricane. The growing roar of the wind and rain buffeting the yellow bungalow had captured everyone's attention.

"We're lucky to still have electricity," Juan said, scooping the last of the *congri* onto his plate from the cast iron pot on the table.

"Victor, go see when the television says the storm will end," Alicia said.

As Skinny rose from the table, the house went dark.

"You had to crow about the electricity, didn't you, Juan?" *Abuela* said. "Now you jinxed us."

"That's enough, *Mamá*," Alicia cautioned. "This isn't the time to start bickering."

Noticing a faint blue glow seeping through the shutters in the living room, Skinny walked to the window and looked through a gap in the shutters. "*Dios santisimo!*" he yelled, eyes wide with alarm. "Look at this!"

The rest of the family rushed to the windows.

One of the power lines that ran along the street was down. The severed cable was writhing on the wet pavement like an angry snake, spitting blue sparks at the cars parked along the curb.

Abuela made the sign of the cross. "Most holy God, protect us," she said, her voice trembling.

"Victor, call the electric company!" his father yelled. "This is dangerous!"

Running across the living room, Skinny picked up the phone. "Aaaayyy!" he screamed in terror and threw down the receiver.

"What happened?" his father asked.

"The phone shocked me! It's full of electricity!"

"*Mámi*, I'm scared!" Marta called out, starting to cry. Sensing the growing panic around him, Rafael began bawling as well. Skinny's breath grew short as a powerful urge to flee came over him.

"Calm down! All of you!" Alicia called out, picking up Rafael. "We're not in any danger. These things happen during a hurricane," she said steadily.

They all grew silent, Alicia's voice stemming the panic.

Breathing normally again, Skinny peeked outside. "The power line's gone dead," he announced.

"Someone must have called the electric company and they shut down the power," Juan said, sounding vindicated. "I told you that's what we need to do."

In a weary voice Alicia said, "*Mamá*, it's time to get out the candles."

"What candles?" *Abuela* asked.

"The emergency candles I asked you to buy yesterday. Don't you remember? I put the money on the kitchen counter before I left for work."

"Oh," *Abuela* said softly. "I thought that money was for my Lady Clairol. My roots have been showing a lot of gray lately, you know."

"*Mamá*, please don't tell me you forgot the candles."

Abuela shrugged. "Fine then. I won't tell you. But don't expect any candles to magically appear."

"You foolish old hag! How could you leave us in the dark?" Juan yelled. "Haven't you been through enough hurricanes to know we'll need candles?"

"I've been through many storms, Juan. But I've spent them with men who knew how to—"

"That's enough, *Mamá*," Alicia interrupted. "And Juan, stop insulting my mother. Arguing is not going to bring us any light. What's done is done. Let's make the best of it."

"I just remembered!" *Abuela* said, cackling with glee. "We still have a votive candle left over from when you were pregnant with Rafael."

"That's good, *Mamá*! Go get it!"

After stumbling through the darkness to her room, *Abuela* returned to the living room bringing light. The candle she held was in a narrow glass etched with the image of the Virgin Mary. "Thanks to Our Lady, we'll have enough light to see—and her protection from the storm."

Juan reached into his pocket and pulled out a crumpled pack of Camels. "I'm almost out of cigarettes," he said, glancing sourly at Skinny while he lit a smoke.

Alicia sat on the couch next to Marta, put an arm around her daughter and began slowly stroking her hair. "Maybe you can settle the children with a story, Juan," she asked, hoping the storytelling would calm her husband as well.

"An excellent idea, *mi amor*," Juan said proudly raising his chin. "I'll tell the children about the better half of their ancestral history—*my* family."

"Oh, good...a fairy tale," *Abuela* said in a sugary voice. "The children will love it."

Juan flicked an eye dagger at his mother-in-law, then dramatically cleared his throat. "Your great-grandfather, Alfonso Delgado Sanchez, was born in a small village in northern Spain. As fate would have it, when Alfonso was fifteen, an influenza epidemic took both his parents. The youngest of three orphaned children, Alfonso bade his brother and sister goodbye and walked to the port of Santander where he took a job on a merchant ship. After traveling the world's oceans, the ship made port in Havana. There, Alfonso learned workers were badly needed in the countryside. Taken by the beauty of the island, he moved to the town of Madruga and began cutting wood to earn a living. Before long, he'd earned a reputation as a man of trust. If Alfonso said there were two hundred logs in the pile, you didn't have to count them.

"He worked hard, saved his money and after several years bought a few acres of land eight miles from Madruga. He cleared the land and began growing fruit and vegetables. To raise cash, he'd haul his produce into Madruga and sell it in the town plaza on Saturdays."

"That's how he got rich—selling vegetables?" Skinny asked skeptically.

"Be patient, *m'hijo*. I'm coming to that," Juan said. "You see, in those days, Cuba was fighting for its independence from Spain. So the Spaniards brought in a ruthless new captain-general named Weyler to put down the rebellion. Weyler tried to starve out the rebels by moving people in the countryside into something he called reconcentration camps. Everyone, rich or poor, was moved into these camps and over the next year more than two-hundred-thousand people died. But, for your great-grandfather, it was the most fortunate period of his life—for it was then that he met and fell in love with Teresa Maldonado."

Marta's drooping eyelids flickered back to life at the talk of a romance.

"Without being thrown together in the camp, it's unlikely Alfonso and Teresa would have ever met, much less fallen in love. You see, they were from completely different worlds. She was the only child of the richest family in

Madruga, while Alfonso was a poor orphan with only a few acres of land. But fall in love, they did. And an unfortunate cat was instrumental in bringing them together."

Juan stopped and dragged deeply on his cigarette, stoking the intrigue of his tale. "The incident took place the night before *Nochebuena*. The people of Madruga had been in the camp for over six months and the food rations had been reduced to a single dry biscuit a day for adults. No one had eaten any meat for months. Near dawn, Alfonso noticed a cat had wandered inside the camp's fence. He was fat and yellow as corn. Apparently, there was no shortage of mice in the deserted village. Desperate for food, Alfonso lured the cat into a shed and dispatched it."

"Poor kitty!" Marta said. "That was horrible!"

"Remember, *m'hija*," Juan said gently. "Your great-grandfather was starving. He was doing whatever he could to stay alive."

Marta was sobered by the comment. She knew all too well how hunger felt.

"As he skinned and dressed the carcass, Alfonso was consumed by the thought of cooking and devouring it. Then he remembered Teresa and her family. They were hungry too. So he decided to share his prize with them. After all, tonight was *Nochebuena*, the time for a family feast."

Marta grimaced. "Eat a cat? Ugh! That's disgusting, *Pápi!*"

"Precisely, *m'hija*. Your great-grandfather knew the Maldonados would never bring themselves to eat a cat. They were a proud family, the ones through which we carry the blood of a Cuban president. So Alfonso told them it was a piglet. That way, they could eat the cat and save face."

"Did they eat it?" Marta asked, eyes widening.

"With gusto. In fact, the Maldonados never forgot Alfonso's generosity—or his tact. Your great-grandfather always insisted that the *Nochebuena* 'piglet' was the main reason Teresa's father consented when Alfonso asked for her hand in marriage two years later," Juan said proudly.

"Of course, by then the internment was over and Alfonso had doubled the size of his *finca* and opened a produce shop in town. Still, when he married Teresa his wealth increased many times. Thanks to the connections of the Maldonados, Alfonso and Teresa were able to send their boys to the University of Havana. Their oldest son, Tomas, became the family's first doctor. Your grandfather, Rafael, became the first Delgado lawyer.

"So you see, my children, you can say with pride that your Delgado ancestry is rooted in both honest toil and aristocratic breeding," Juan concluded grandly.

Skinny looked at Marta. His sister's eyes were closed, her small mouth gaping in rhythmic breaths. The tale had lulled Rafael as well. With his siblings asleep and his father in a talkative mood, Skinny decided to probe into a long-standing mystery. "So, *Pápi*, if we Delgados are so great, why did *Tío* Panchito turn out the way he did?"

Abuela leaned forward, eager to hear Juan's reply.

Juan scratched his chin and studied his son. "I suppose it's time you knew about your uncle," he said after a moment.

"Juan, you don't have to do this," Alicia offered.

Abuela snorted in derision. "Don't worry, *m'hija*. He doesn't have the nerve to tell the boy the truth about his brother."

Juan lowered his gaze. "I won't deny it. My younger brother brought great shame to our family and squandered every advantage given to him," he said, nervously flicking his cigarette over the ashtray. "Instead of following our family's tradition, Francisco spurned the university and became a wastrel."

"Francisco?" Skinny said. "I thought his name was Panchito?"

"I will explain that presently, *m'hijo*. Be patient. This is a delicate subject."

"Keep in mind, Victor," *Abuela* said, wagging her finger. "Whenever you hear someone say this is a delicate subject, you can be sure they're about to lie."

Alicia sighed heavily. "*Mamá*, would you please keep quiet and let Juan tell his story?"

Juan stubbed out his cigarette and lit another before continuing. "Our family first found out about Francisco's illicit ways when he was stopped for speeding in the Bentley convertible *Papá* gave him on his eighteenth birthday. When the officer began to write the ticket, my idiot brother offered the constable a bag of cocaine as a bribe. Can you imagine such audacity? *Papá* pulled a lot of strings to get Francisco off—but that only made things worse. My brother came to believe he could get away with anything.

"One night, two drunken women appeared at our house in the middle of the night and began chanting outside Francisco's window. '*Panchito, Panchito, dame un besito porque quiero un pesito.*' That's how we discovered his nefarious nickname—from two drunken whores screaming 'give me a kiss because I want a dollar.' For once I was glad my mother had passed away. I cannot fathom the shame this would have brought her."

Juan's eyes narrowed, "Panchito whored and gambled so much, you would have thought he was an American tourist."

Abuela cleared her throat loudly.

Juan paused and glared at his mother-in-law. "Panchito didn't gamble like a gentleman, playing cards in refined company. He loved the casinos. And the drugs...my God, the price of a yacht went up that fool's nose.

"These things alone would have been a cause for shame. But there was something worse, a disgrace our father would never forgive and took with him to his grave."

"What did he do?" Skinny asked.

"Panchito became a communist," Juan answered in a raspy whisper. "Can you imagine that? Here was this dandy who fought duels with pimps and kept the city's cocaine dealers in silk suits...and he fancied himself 'a man of the people.' It appalled our father."

Juan took another deep drag and shook his head. "I sometimes wonder if Castro would have succeeded without Panchito's help. When the rebellion started, Panchito was the one who gave Fidel the money to buy a boat in Mexico called the *Granma*. Castro used that boat to land his first cadre of rebels in the mountains of Oriente.

"While Fidel attacked government outposts in the countryside and recruited peasants for his army, Panchito was Castro's silent partner in Havana. He used our family's money to supply the rebels...weapons, ammunition, medicine, uniforms, whatever they needed, Panchito gave it to them. After a while, *Papá* noticed huge sums of money being drained from our accounts. All the clues pointed to Panchito. When our father confronted him, Panchito confessed without any qualms. The scoundrel knew *Papá* would never turn him in—even though he'd betrayed everything our family stood for. Our father died of a stroke a year after Castro landed in Oriente. But I will always be convinced it was my brother who killed him."

As Skinny watched Juan's eyes grow misty, he was touched by his father's sorrow. And yet...the thought he might have an important uncle in Cuba intrigued him. "Hmm. So where is *Tio* Panchito now?" he asked with a little too much nonchalance.

His father saw through him like a screen door. "So you think maybe your *Tio* Panchito can give you back the lavish life we had in Cuba, eh?" Juan said with a smirk.

"No, *Pápi*...I was just, well...sort of curious."

Juan's smile faded. "Panchito celebrated the day Batista left Cuba and the communists came to power. He'd worked for many years to help the rebels win. But a higher justice befell my brother," Juan said, his voice turning dry. "One of the pimps who had it in for Panchito publicly denounced him as a government collaborator. And who was going to doubt the pimp? Everyone knew the Delgados were Batista supporters. Since all of Panchito's work for the revolution was done in secret, no one came forward to clear him." Juan's voice dropped to a whisper. "Not long after we arrived in Miami, we learned your uncle was sent to jail. A few days later, he was killed by an inmate."

Juan took another long drag on his Camel. "Fidel didn't lift a finger to save him. Castro certainly didn't need Panchito anymore. Maybe Fidel didn't want a carouser like Panchito around to pollute his glorious revolution. Who knows? One thing is certain, though. In the end, Panchito no longer had our father to get him out of trouble."

Exhaling a long cloud of smoke, Juan sat back in his chair, staring at someplace far away.

After a moment, *Abuela* said, "You did a good thing telling the boy, Juan. He's finally old enough to understand," she said, then pointed a finger at Skinny. "And you better learn from it."

For a long time, no one spoke. The sound of the hurricane became a numbing drone. Eventually, Juan and *Abuela* nodded off in their chairs.

Then without warning, the noise died.

Skinny walked to the window, baffled by the strange silence. "Is the hurricane over?" he asked his mother softly, peeking outside through the gap in the shutters.

"No," Alicia answered. "We're in the eye of the storm."

Looking at the sky through the narrow opening, Skinny saw stars shimmering in an ink-black sky. "I'm going outside!" he whispered excitedly, heading for the door.

"No!" Alicia hissed. "It's too dangerous. This calm won't last long."

A surge of rage rose in Skinny's chest. Once again, his mother was denying him something. Then he remembered the terrifying moments he'd spent in the park. "When will the storm start again?" he asked, his anger fading.

"It's hard to say...maybe a half hour, maybe a few minutes. It depends on how close we are to the center."

As Skinny returned to the window, cascades of rain began pelting the house. Within seconds, the height of the storm returned, the wind once again lashing the trees—only this time, the gusts were blowing in the opposite direction. "You were right, *Mamá*," he whispered. "I didn't know a hurricane could be like this—really dangerous, I mean. I hope it's over soon."

"Storms always end, Victor. Good or bad, the weather never stays the same."

Abuela stirred in her chair. "Well, you better get used to bad weather, *m'hija*," she muttered sleepily to Alicia. "Because with this one starting to grow hair on his *huevos*, that's not the last storm we're going to see."

1964
SEPTEMBER

Wynwood, B.C.

The start of eighth grade at Robert E. Lee Jr. High was barely underway when Skinny encountered a new force of nature. Her name was Carol.

Carol was the Prometheus of Wynwood, bringing the dangerous and exhilarating flame of sexual passion to the boys in Skinny's circle. Shortly after arriving from Tuscaloosa to live with her grandmother in Miami, her fame quickly spread. The reason was simple: Any boy who met Carol in the dark stairwell to her grandmother's second floor apartment would be taken to a new territory beyond closed-lip kisses and holding hands.

In later years, Victor would regret his lone dalliance with Carol. In reality, she was a troubled fifteen-year-old, new to the neighborhood, trying desperately to be liked. But at the time, Skinny and his cohorts were too blinded by hormones to grasp this sad truth. As a result, Carol's stairwell saw more traffic than a liquor store on payday—a procession of adolescent males that changed the sexual landscape of Wynwood Park.

The world B.C. (Before Carol) had been much simpler.

Before Carol, Skinny's nebulous knowledge of sex had come mostly from the world of advertising. His imagination raced feverishly at the possibilities of the words "*CLOSE COVER BEFORE STRIKING*" on a matchbook from Trader Ted's Lounge featuring a scantily-clad woman. Another alluring mystery had come from a blurb on the condom dispensing machine at the gas station on 36th and 1st: "*Little women like Big Chief, saves him money, saves her grief.*"

Carol's arrival transformed relationships in Skinny's world as well.

Going steady with a girl usually meant listening to the radio together in her living room and maybe sneaking a peck on the lips before going home. Although Skinny was still stuck in "friend" limbo with Janice, their relationship wasn't much different—except for the kissing. That furtive brushing of the lips was the momentous line of demarcation between friend and boyfriend.

After Carol, however, the stakes of the game escalated—and Skinny's first take on this new sexual landscape was envy.

Bragging about how far you'd gotten with a girl became the new measure of status among the *gallos* at Wynwood. "*Cenaste?*" was the first question they asked each other after any romantic adventure—a crude pun on two Spanish words: *cena* and *senos*—dine and breasts.

How can I compete with that? Skinny wondered. His only brag-worthy feats had been with Carol— a deed as common among the *gallos* at Wynwood as a tourist with a sunburn in South Florida.

But Skinny's envy quickly faded as he came to a terrifying realization: Janice was now fair game for these second-base lotharios.

NOVEMBER

Couples only

"You put your left foot in, you put your left foot out. You put your left foot in and you shake it all about..."* sang the recorded voice from the scratchy loudspeakers at Skateland Roller Center.

Gathered in the center of the worn planked floor and dancing to the Hokey Pokey were a handful of teenage girls on skates. Noticing their drab clothes and lack of makeup, Loco shook his head. "Poor girls," he said to Skinny. "They're going to wind up as *solteronas*, for sure."

Along with dozens of other adolescents, Skinny and Loco were outside the rink waiting for the song to end, leaning against the railing that surrounded the floor. The *Hokey Pokey Song*, repeated every two hours at Skateland, invariably cleared the teens from the floor faster than a shout of *la migra!* in a sweat shop. Only families with small kids—and the hopelessly unhip—took part in the *Hokey Pokey*. This being a Saturday night, the families were gone. After all, no sane parent would bring small children to a place packed with hormone-addled adolescents careening about on skates.

"I should get to the bathroom and check my hair," Loco said, patting his auburn, pomade-stiffened pompadour.

Skinny scoffed. "Your hair looks fine, man."

"I don't want to wait 'till the last minute," Loco said, smoothing out his wispy sideburns. "You know how long the line gets."

Skinny knew the redhead was right. Very soon, both sexes would be crowding into the restrooms for some last-minute primping in anticipation of the fifteen-minutes that had brought most of them to Skateland...Couples Only.

The Couples Only session never varied. The lights would dim and a spotlight trained on a rotating mirrored globe would send a galaxy of shimmering reflections whirling gracefully across the floor. For fifteen minutes, the shabby rink became a dreamlike landscape. In contrast to this romantic setting was its participants.

Awkwardly holding hands, a procession of teenaged pairs would gracelessly skate in circles to the same three ballads: *Unchained Melody*, *Earth Angel*, and *Mr. Lonely*.

But despite its ungainly nature, over the last couple of months (an eternity in teenage time), Couples Only at Skateland had evolved into an event of epic proportions among Skinny's peers.

For the *grillos*, Couples Only was a public display of their appeal and popularity, especially when the boy who asked you to skate was someone cool. For the *gallos*, it meant you were probably going to make out later in the parking lot behind the rink—and maybe even get to second base.

"You put your whole self in, you put your whole self out..." the voice over the loudspeaker sang.

"C'mon, it's almost over," Loco said to Skinny rolling toward the opening in the railing around the rink. When the *Hokey Pokey Song* finally ended, a God-like recorded voice from the loudspeakers said: "All Skate." Like the bursting of a dam, Skinny and Loco, along with most of the other teens in the building, flooded back onto the rink.

The air was thick with pheromonal tension as the pack began a shark-like circling. This half-hour All Skate session before Couples Only was the time when the *grillos* checked out the *gallos* and the *gallos* planned their moves.

Weaving through the skaters, Skinny watched it all like a spectator at a ball game. He lacked the confidence to play this game—or the inclination. Janice was the only girl he cared about. But she'd never been to Skateland.

Then, as if fate had willed it, he spotted Janice near the skate rental window.

His stomach fluttering with excitement, Skinny kept circling the floor, watching Janice as she got her skates and sat down beside a couple of girlfriends from school. Smiling as usual, she began putting on her skates.

Janice's presence was not lost on Loco. He fell into stride alongside Skinny. "*Oye*, didn't I tell you she'd show up one of these nights?"

Skinny nodded. "Yeah, you were right."

"Skinny, this is your chance, man. You have to ask her out for Couples Only."

"What if she says no?"

"I'm not the only one here who's noticed Janice. Look around."

Sure enough, Skinny could see a number of *gallos* checking Janice out as they circled the floor. The fluttering in Skinny's stomach tightened into a knot.

"I'm gonna ask her to skate. You watch me," Skinny said, trying his best to sound confident.

"*Andale, hombre!*" Loco said, slapping him on the back. He then leaned close to Skinny and whispered, "I'm going to ask Susie Dexter to skate. Peanut says she'll let you feel her titties in the parking lot."

After Loco skated away, Skinny looked at the clock, knowing Skateland's schedule by heart. Twelve minutes remained until Couples Only at 9pm. *Should I go ask her to skate now?* he wondered. After playing that out in his mind,

Skinny decided to wait. He'd have to talk to Janice for at least ten minutes before Couples Only began, a prospect more terrifying than finding Mrs. Post's boa in his bed.

The minutes crawled by as he circled the floor, watching Janice while hiding inside the pack. Luckily, she was still sitting down, chatting with her friends. As the top of the hour drew closer, his palms began to sweat. When the clock reached one minute till nine, Skinny took a deep breath. *This is it*, he told himself then started in Janice's direction at full speed before he lost his nerve.

He was near the opening in the railing and still going flat out when the lights dimmed and the recorded voice-of-God sonorously intoned "Couples Only."

Unsettled by the sudden change of lighting, one of the Hokey Pokey girls staggered in front of Skinny. "Look out!" he yelled as she hit the floor, braided pigtails flying.

Skinny swerved hard, trying to avoid her. But their legs got tangled and he stumbled to his knees beside her.

"Ow!" she said, holding a badly scraped elbow and grimacing in pain.

"Are you okay?"

"It really hurts," she said, tears forming behind her heavy-framed glasses.

"You'll be all right," Skinny said, helping her up. "They've got band-aids in the office."

With his arm around the girl, Skinny looked up and saw Janice.

Their eyes met for a moment and he was puzzled by Janice's expression. Why was she looking at him like that, as if there was something she didn't understand? Then Hector Rivera appeared behind her. What Skinny saw next pierced him like a dagger.

Janice was heading into the rink—holding Hector's hand.

Part Dos

JULY

A Saucer Sighting

Skinny was drifting into that gauzy world on the border of sleep when the screech of the screen door drew him back to reality. Without rising from the cot, he scanned his front porch bedroom. Backlit by the streetlights shining through the screens, he watched his father enter the porch and step inside the house. Glancing at the clock on the milk crate by his cot, he saw it was just after midnight.

The old man is home early.

That meant only one thing: his father must have lost again—and nothing pissed off Juan Delgado more than a bad night of poker.

He should have been upset that his father still refused to work and help the family. But Skinny had given up on his father long ago. *Just lay low and get some sleep*, he told himself. *You've got a big day tomorrow.*

Skinny pulled the tattered sheet over his head, uncovering his feet in the process. The child-sized cot his parents had bought in 1959 was now too small for his sixteen-year-old frame.

Most of the growth had come in the last two years, completely transforming Skinny's body. Without gaining any weight, he'd grown five inches taller and now carried 140 pounds on a wiry five-foot nine-inch frame. Seven years after being dubbed Skinny, his nickname was no longer ironic.

With his head under the covers, Skinny's thoughts turned once again to Janice, a wound whose scab he could not resist picking.

Their friendship had evaporated after that night at Skateland and by the end of the school year, the Bockmans had moved away. Now, nearly two years later, he still had regrets about Janice and what he could have done differently.

He'd gone out with other *grillos* since then—his confidence had gone up as his waist size had gone down. But his longing for Janice when he was with other girls was a secret that made him feel sleazy.

Enough of that, he told himself. Tomorrow was the first day of his new summer job at the Siena Hotel and he needed to sleep. The first bus to Miami Beach came by 36th and 2nd at quarter after six.

The shrill scrape of coat hangers on a metal rod told him the old man was hanging up his clothes. When his father's footsteps headed toward the kitchen, Skinny sighed and gave up any thoughts of sleep. The refrigerator opened with a wheezy gasp. No doubt the old man was after some water before turning in.

Skinny did not expect what he heard next.

"What is this infamy?" his father screamed, his voice echoing through the darkened house. "What in the name of God is this family coming to?"

Jumping out of bed, Skinny ran to the kitchen. Moments later, he was joined by the rest of the family, bleary-eyed and confused. In the dim light of the open Frigidaire stood Juan Delgado Morales in a pair of crumpled boxer shorts and a sleeveless undershirt.

"Who, in the name of all the blessed saints, is responsible for this abomination?" Juan screamed, pointing to the center shelf of the refrigerator.

There, between a carton of eggs and a bowl of peeled potatoes, was a turd on a chipped saucer. The bolus was smooth and brownish-green with split at one end, reminding Skinny of the gaping mouth of a moray eel.

For a long time, nobody spoke.

"I have a doctor's appointment tomorrow. He asked me to bring a specimen," *Abuela* finally said. Since her mild stroke the year before, *Abuela's* behavior had become increasingly strange.

Juan glared at his mother-in-law, his breath hissing fiercely through his nose. "Well, you have finally succeeded. You've managed to bring this household down to the level of your family—a bunch of uncouth *guajiros* who wipe their *culos* and baste *lechón* with the same banana leaf. Are you happy now?"

Abuela shrugged. "I might not have been ready to do my business in the morning."

"*Abuela* needed to keep her poo-poo fresh, *Pápi*," Rafael explained.

"Do you see, Alicia? Now she has our children thinking this is normal behavior!" Juan screamed. "This is it. I cannot have the decency of my home violated in this way. I'm leaving you, Alicia—and don't try to stop me!"

Juan then stormed into the bedroom and began noisily getting dressed. "Shouldn't you go talk to him?" Skinny asked his mother.

Alicia yawned and rubbed her neck. "Don't worry about your father, *m'hijo*," she answered wearily. "Go back to bed. You have a long day tomorrow."

❖ ❖ ❖

The teenager in the pink bikini stole a glance at Skinny as she stretched out on the chaise lounge, rubbing suntan lotion on her legs.

Skinny lowered his eyes and kept working, painfully aware of the chasm in class his porter's uniform created between them. He was grateful the girl and her parents were the only guests on the huge pool deck at the Siena. The fewer people who saw him in the gaudy, gold and turquoise tunic the better.

Thankfully, his first chore of the day was almost done. Over the last hour, he'd moved over a hundred deck lounges to clear a path along the pool for the private 4th of July parade the Siena was holding for its guests later that morning.

"Excuse me," miss pink bikini called out.

"C-C-Can I help you, miss?" Skinny stuttered, nervous at addressing a guest for the first time.

"Can I get another towel please? This one has lotion all over it."

"Sure, I'll be right back," Skinny said and hurried off to the cabana supply room. When he returned with the towel she smiled enticingly and thanked him.

"You're welcome, miss," Skinny answered, backing away.

"Just a minute," she said, then glanced toward her parents who were several lounges away and lowered her voice. "What do you for fun around here? This place is so boring."

Skinny swallowed hard. "Is there something more I can do for you, miss?"

"Yeah, you can cut the 'miss' routine. How old are you anyway?"

"Eighteen," he lied. The Siena would not have hired him if they'd known he was sixteen. Thankfully for Skinny, few hotels bothered with background checks.

"I thought so. I am too. Is there anybody else our age around here? This place is like a dinosaur farm."

"I don't know if I should—"

"Delgado!" barked a voice from behind Skinny.

He turned and saw Landon the bell captain striding

toward him, his face knotted in a snarl. *Oh, shit*, Skinny thought. Things had gone sour with his boss from the moment they'd met. This was not going to help.

Landon's grimace changed to a fawning grin as he addressed the young woman. "Is this boy bothering you, miss?" he asked in a margarine voice.

"No. Not at all."

Landon then locked his eyes on Skinny. "You've got fifteen minutes to finish here, Delgado. Meet me at the entrance to the pool deck when you're done."

By the time Skinny wrapped up his work, the guests were gathering quickly around the pool for the parade. As Landon ordered, Skinny walked to the pool deck entrance.

From here he could see the parade line forming along the narrow side street off Collins Avenue. Leading the procession was a drum and bugle corps in floppy, wide-brimmed hats and red satin jackets, uniforms that seemed pimp-inspired to Skinny. Behind the musicians was Uncle Sam on stilts and bringing up the rear were a couple of cowgirls on horseback carrying flags.

As Skinny waited for Landon, he recalled the painful first meeting with his boss earlier that morning.

Landon had strutted up to him in the men's locker room, his nose in the air. "*Yo jefe. Tú haces que yo diga, comprende?*" he said in butchered Spanish.

"I speak English if that's easier for you," Skinny answered.

This seemed to anger Landon. "Oh, yeah? Well the meaning's the same, Delgado...I'm the boss and you do what I say."

The source of Landon's brashness was not hard to figure. Although the bell captain looked over thirty, he was several inches shorter than Skinny. After spending a couple of minutes around Landon, Skinny decided the words "angry little prick" fit his boss perfectly. To his credit, Landon was consistent. He was a bullying *pendejo* with the other porters as well.

Skinny's mother had heard about this job from a

neighbor who worked as a maid at the Siena. The neighbor had said the hotel was always hiring new porters. Now Skinny understood why.

The bugle corps broke into a drum cadence signaling the start of the parade as Landon appeared around the corner of the building.

Landon's grin worried Skinny. It had the look of revenge. "I got a special job for you, Delgado. I want you to follow the horses and clean up after them," he said, handing Skinny a broom and a dustpan on a stick.

As Landon turned and walked away, Skinny looked toward the horses and saw one of them expel a batch of hay dumplings onto the street. Holding the broom and dustpan, Skinny could see what would happen next: He would be cleaning up horseshit along the pool deck—right in front of the girl in the pink bikini.

"Not going to happen, you little prick," he muttered under his breath, tossing the implements into the bushes.

Ten minutes later Skinny was back in his street clothes aboard a bus headed south on Collins Avenue.

❖ ❖ ❖

After getting off the bus, Skinny walked for a block, climbed the steps of a weathered concrete pier and headed right, toward the side facing south. Leaning against the wall, he scanned the quarter-mile of sandy shore from the pier to the Government Cut jetties, looking for Loco.

The beach was packed with young bodies sprawled on a patchwork of towels covering the long stretch of yellow sand. Next to the beach was a graffiti-covered two-story parking lot where a few run-down food trucks plied their wares amid rows of clunkers. This undeveloped area at the end of Collins Avenue—an appendix of shoreline below the radar of most tourists—was a summertime mecca for local teens. The area was known as South Beach.

Normally, many of those lying on the beach would have

been surfing. But today, the water was nearly still, the waves just feeble ripples. Only a handful of surfers floated idly on their bright-colored boards, dotting the water like pins on a war map. Taking in the scene, Skinny felt uneasy. The crowd was strangely quiet, like everyone was waiting for something to happen.

Finally, Skinny spotted Loco along the edge of the water. His friend was skimboarding—tossing a two-foot disk onto the wash of a receding wave and then leaping onto the board, riding the film of water. When you caught the backwash just right, it was like gliding on ice. When you didn't, you could break an arm or a leg.

Skinny whistled with the distinctive double tweet used by everyone at Wynwood. Loco looked up and they exchanged waves. Taking off his street shoes and socks, Skinny rolled up his pants and started down the steps of the pier to the beach.

While stepping gingerly through the hot sand, Skinny was stopped by a pretty brunette in a granny dress and flip-flops.

"Have you turned on to Jesus, brother?" she asked smiling.

Skinny shifted from one foot to other, his soles frying in the hot sand. "Uh, no. I guess I haven't."

"Well, then you'll want to meet our pastor. He's going to be here later and—"

Suddenly, Loco appeared and tapped the girl on the shoulder. "Hey, you wanna fuck?"

While the girl gasped in shock, Loco grabbed Skinny's arm and pulled him away.

"Thanks for the rescue, man," Skinny said as they reached the cool sand at the edge of the water. "You were a little hard on her, though."

"She'll get over it. These Jesus freaks are worse than junkies—all doped up with religion and always looking to get somebody else hooked," Loco said with a dry laugh.

"Hey, what the hell are you doing here this early, man? Didn't you say you'd be working until four?"

Skinny chewed his lip for a moment. With time to cool off on the bus ride, he'd begun to regret what he'd done. "I quit," he said finally.

"Coño. The job must have been pretty bad," Loco said, putting an arm around Skinny's shoulder. "Let's go over to the jetties and sit down."

As they walked toward the granite boulders that lined the shipping channel into Biscayne Bay, Skinny told Loco about his run in with Landon and how he'd left the job without telling anyone. "What bothers me is thinking that I'm being just like my father," Skinny said, chin on his chest.

"Skinny, I've never bad-mouthed your father. But I'll tell you this, *mi hermano*... You tried to find work. This just wasn't the right job for you."

"Yeah, but where am I going to find the right job?"

Loco grinned. "I thought you'd never ask," he said, sitting down on one of the boulders. "Yesterday, I heard Chucho say that Armando is looking for somebody to stock groceries at his store. I think Chucho would put in a good word for you."

"Seriously?" Skinny said, thrilled at the thought of working so close to home. "I wouldn't have to catch any buses to get to work!"

"And you could even sleep in a little later, *dormilón*," Loco said smiling.

"Thanks, man!" Skinny said, then began jogging back toward the pier. "I'm going to Armando's right now."

"Hold up, Skinny," Loco called out. "It's the Fourth of July, man. Armando's is closed. You can start your new job with a day of vacation!"

Suddenly excited, Skinny ran back and pointed to a familiar chunk of granite shaped roughly like a face about thirty yards out on the jetties. "Hey! I'll race you to the Lincoln boulder."

"You're on!" Loco answered as they both began scrambling up the dark gray rocks.

Skinny quickly jumped into the lead. Although Loco was taller and more muscular, Skinny was agile and fearless, bounding from stone to stone without slowing down. When he reached the Lincoln boulder, Skinny thrust his hands in the air.

"The winner and new champion of the jetties, ladies and gentlemen, Victor 'Skinny' Delgado!"

Still a few boulders back, Loco stopped and slowly clapped his hands. "Nice going, *pendejo*," he said with a half grin. "Looks like carrying that lard all those years finally paid off."

"What's the matter, Loco? You jealous because I finally beat you?"

"Jealous? Ha! You may not be fat anymore, but you're still just as ugly."

They both laughed and sat down, stretching out the rocks.

"What's new at Curley?" Skinny asked, folding his hands under his head. Loco's mother had enrolled him at Archbishop Curley, the Wynwood-parish high school.

"Same old shit as Corpus Christi—a lot of rules and religion. Anything new at Jackson?"

"Yeah, I started Driver's Ed and I'm doing pretty good. Now all I need is a car."

"God, I hope you learn to drive better than my mom. She went to test drive a new Fairlane last week and rammed the car right into the wall of the showroom. When the salesman asks her what happened, she says, 'Thees leetle D is for Drive, no?' and he says, 'That's right, ma'am. But you needed to use that little R there to back out of here.'"

After he'd stopped laughing, Skinny said, "What about football? You going to try out?"

"I've had it with football, man. Too many coaches getting in your face," Loco said. "I like playing ball, but it's not worth all that shit. What about you? Are you trying out at Jackson?"

"I'd like to, but I can't. The old lady wants me to keep working after school starts."

"Skinny, if you take the job at Armando's, you can still try out for the varsity. Just go to the summer practices after work. If you make the team, maybe you can talk your mother into letting you play."

"Hey, that's not a bad idea—for a delinquent who thinks football sucks."

Loco laughed. "I'm just trying to help a friend who's a rah-rah dipshit."

Skinny slugged his arm, laughing along. "Yeah? So I should be a punk running numbers like you instead?"

"No way, man...You'd have to be a whole lot smarter."

A murmur of voices in the distance interrupted their banter. "What's going on over there?" Skinny asked, pointing to a knot of teens gathered near a food truck in the parking lot.

"Let's go find out," Loco answered, starting toward the group.

Once they got close, Skinny saw an older guy at the center of the crowd in a white shirt and black tie holding a brown leather Bible in the air. "The Lord Jesus is ready to wash away your sins!" the preacher said, the hair on his forehead matted with sweat. "You can sit beside Him in heaven, enjoying eternal peace—or you can spend the rest of all time burning in the fires of hell!"

Loco tapped Skinny's shoulder. "Let's split, man. I've heard enough."

As they were leaving, a guy in plaid surfer baggies ran up to the preacher. "Here you go, clown!" he yelled, squirting the man in the face with mustard from a squeeze bottle.

The preacher screamed in pain, covering his face as the mustard burned his eyes.

Loco's eyes narrowed. He began pushing through the

group until he reached the guy in plaid baggies. "Hey, asshole! What did you do that for?" Loco said, shoving him to the ground.

Angry shouts rose from the crowd, egging Loco on. "Kick his ass, man!" "Go on! Get him!"

The guy in the plaid baggies rolled to his feet and looked around, eyes suddenly wide with fear. The shouts for vengeance continued. "Hit him, man!" "Put his lights out."

After backing away a few steps, plaid baggies turned and ran toward the pier.

Loco was the first one after him. A moment later, the rest of the crowd followed. Skinny ran along with them, curious to see what would happen next. He wasn't worried about Loco. The redhead had never lost a fight.

As plaid baggies sprinted under the pier, Skinny noticed other teens along the beach rising to join the pack. By the time Skinny reached the shade under the pier, a stampede was underway. Almost everyone on the beach was on their feet and running behind Skinny, swept along by a magnetic mix of curiosity and boredom.

Plaid baggies looked over his shoulder in panic and turned away from the beach toward Collins Avenue—with most of South Beach on his tail.

As the young horde rushed into the hotel-lined street, people on the sidewalks backed away in terror.

Skinny felt a surge of excitement. The teens running alongside him were strangers but they now had a common purpose. Together, they were a force. Together, they had power. The realization made him tingle.

Then a memory surfaced—the riots in Havana after the fall of Batista. *Could that happen here?* he wondered.

Ahead of him, Skinny saw Loco slow down as the culprit ran into a hotel lobby. When Loco hesitated, Skinny finally caught up to him.

"Don't go in the hotel, man," he said, panting for breath. "They'll call the cops."

Hands on his knees and breathing heavily, Loco looked up at Skinny. "Maybe you're right."

Then, someone behind them shouted, "Don't let him get away! Go after him!" A swell of voices joined the call to keep up the chase. "Get him! Get him!"

Skinny looked behind him and gulped. Staring back was a sea of angry young faces filling the street. Somewhere during the chase, these hundreds of bored teenagers had become a mob.

Feeling like someone else was guiding him, Skinny jumped onto a bus bench and faced the crowd. "Hey, listen! Go back to the beach! That jerk will never do anything like that again," he yelled, waving them away.

Fewer voices rose this time. "No! No!" "C'mon, let's get him!"

"If you go in that hotel, they'll call the cops!" Skinny shouted. "Don't be stupid!"

Only a few die-hards remained now, still trying to stir the crowd. "Let's get him!" they called out.

Loco stepped up on the bench beside Skinny. "Hey, I started this thing—and it ends right here," he said, his voice calm and firm.

With a good deal of muttering, the crowd began to break up into knots of friends, no longer a creature with a single mind. Skinny exhaled slowly, the tension of the moment passing.

Stepping down from the bus bench, the pair began walking slowly back toward the beach.

"Thanks, man," Loco said patting Skinny on the back.

"What for?"

"You kept us out of trouble. That's a lot harder than getting into it."

Skinny looked toward the waves feeling odd, as if something around him had changed but he couldn't tell what it was. Then it hit him. For the first time, he felt like Loco's equal.

AUGUST

The Number 12 Dream Machine

The late afternoon sun glared painfully off the traffic inching past Jackson High. From a bus stop across the street, Skinny shielded his eyes and squinted down the long line of vehicles.

"Is the bus coming, Skinny?" Porkchop called out from a half-block away, hobbling toward the bus stop with Popeye alongside.

Looking down the stream of glinting chrome, Skinny spotted the baby-blue Number 12 several blocks away. "Take your time, Porkchop!" he yelled back, knowing the big defensive lineman was nursing a sore ankle.

After four weeks of pre-season football practices, Skinny was finally getting used to the mismatch between Porkchop's jumbo-jet build and his squeaky voice, a cross between Tweetie Bird and Nipsey Russell.

At first, Skinny had fought an urge to laugh whenever Porkchop spoke. But there was nothing funny about him on the football field. At a couple of cheeseburgers over 260, Porkchop moved with terrifying quickness and was a crushing tackler. His real name was Willie Anderson. The reason for his nickname was not hard to guess.

As he waited for his teammates, Skinny looked longingly into the ice cream shop on the corner. Coach Bellamy had told Skinny milk shakes would help him put on weight. When Skinny had asked his mother for an extra fifteen cents each day to buy one, her answer had not surprised him. "Oh? Your coach thinks you need milkshakes? Well, ask *him* to buy them."

Sighing, Skinny turned his attention back to Porkchop and Popeye who had now reached the bus stop.

Even though he'd just showered, Porkchop's ebony forehead was already trickling with sweat. "Man, it's too hot to be doing this shit every day. We're gonna be wore out before the first game."

Popeye slapped Porkchop on the rump and grinned. "There's a whole lot of you to wear out, Porkchop. The coach is trying to work off some of that candy ass on you, man."

Earl "Popeye" Price was the team's starting left linebacker and had earned his nickname from a pair of bulging forearms and a permanent squint in his left eye from a childhood illness.

"Shut up, fool!" Porkchop shot back. "Don't be talking that shit to me. Hell, you can't play nothing but left linebacker 'cause you can't see out that fucked-up eyeball," Porkchop said closing one eye and groping in the air like a blind man.

Skinny smiled. Since making the junior varsity football team at Jackson last year, he'd gotten used to the hard banter of his teammates.

"What's your narrow Cuban ass smiling about?" Porkchop asked, making sure Skinny wasn't left out of their hardnosed bonding. "I'll sit on you and squish you like a cucaracha."

"You gotta' catch me first, butter butt," Skinny replied, curling his fingers in an invitation.

"Even a fly gotta light some time, Skinny. You ever come down in the pits where the real men play and I'll roll up Popeye here like a newspaper and swat you dead, boy."

"Y'all shut up now. Here comes the bus," Popeye called out.

The battered Number 12 pulled to the curb, its brakes braying like a mule, and the three teammates quietly boarded the bus. Coach Bellamy had warned that any Jackson player who misbehaved in public would be dropped from the team.

Porkchop and Popeye walked toward the back in the near-empty bus and sat down. Skinny slid into the row in front and turned to face them.

Porkchop grimaced and rubbed the back of his thigh. "Man, now my hammy's oinking."

Popeye shook his head. "You skipped your salt pills again, didn't you? That's why you keep getting cramps."

"Man, those pills don't do nothing but make you thirsty."

"Then don't complain about cramps."

"C'mon, Popeye. We get one handful of ice for two hours of practice. Time we been out there a while, I'm praying for rain 'cause I'm ready to get down like a dog and lap me up a puddle."

"The coaches are just trying to make us tough," Popeye said. "Suck it up, man."

"Is your ankle gonna be ready for Edison, Porkchop?" Skinny asked. Jackson's opener against Edison High was only two weeks away. For Skinny, the game meant even more than the long-standing rivalry between the schools. He knew several of the Edison players from Wynwood.

Porkchop shrugged. "Hard to say, man. I've been icing it at home."

"Your momma gonna make you quit playing, Skinny?" Popeye asked. It was a problem they'd talked about on the bus ride home before.

"It doesn't look good," Skinny said. "My mother wants

me to ask the boss to switch my hours. Once school starts, I'm supposed to work from four to midnight. Unless I can talk her out of it, there's no way I'll make practices and games."

"That's too bad, man. We could use you for the Edison game," Popeye said.

At 140 pounds, the coaches did not consider Skinny sturdy enough to be a starter at flanker. But Skinny's elusiveness and speed had proved valuable in returning punts and kickoffs in pre-season practices. He'd taken back several kicks for touchdowns during their intra-squad scrimmages.

"Yeah, Edison's supposed to be tough this year," Skinny agreed and turned to look out the window, trying to imagine school without football.

For the first time in his life, Skinny did not dread the thought of starting classes again. There was a special feeling about Jackson that inspired hope. It was South Florida's first integrated high school, formed by the merger of the once all-white Jackson with Booker T. Washington, a shuttered Jim Crow relic.

Jackson's groundbreaking spirit seemed to bring out the best in most students, including Skinny. He was proud of his school—and playing football was wrapped tightly into that pride.

Football was a sport that forged bonds quickly. The brutal, grueling practices exposed a player's true fiber. You soon learned who was tough and who was a whiner, who was a team player and who was a prima donna. You might not know the name of a teammate's sister or even where he lived. But after four weeks of scrimmages, you knew the heart and essence of the guy lining up next to you. He was someone you could trust.

Skinny was devoted to Jackson's head coach as well. The day he'd asked to try out for the varsity, Skinny had admitted he might seem small but felt he could still help the team. "I only care how big your heart is, son," Coach Bellamy had told him.

There were guys at Wynwood who started fights and risked petty crimes trying to prove they were tough—to others and to themselves. For Skinny, putting on the pads and taking the field was proof enough.

Looking out the window, Skinny saw the Citgo station on 13th Avenue. Porkchop and Popeye would be getting off on 12th and transferring to the bus that would take them north to Liberty City—Miami's largest black neighborhood.

As the bus neared his stop, Porkchop tapped Skinny on the shoulder. "Hey, I've got an idea, man. Why don't you tell your momma you might get a scholarship if you keep playing ball?"

"Scholarship?" Skinny scoffed. "I don't even know if I'll make the varsity."

"Skinny, I've seen how Coach yells at you. He only does that to the good players. You beef up and next year, you'll be a starter, man. After that, who knows?"

"You really think I could get a scholarship?"

"My cousin Ernie's the same size as you and he went to Bethune-Cookman on a full ride last year," Porkchop said. "I'm gonna play for one too."

Popeye nodded. "Keep running back kicks like you've been doing and you might have a shot, Skinny."

The Liberty City-bound pair stood and Popeye tugged on the cord running above the window.

Skinny's eyes widened as the chime sounded. "My mother will *have* to let me play if it gets me into college!" he said excitedly. "And I can still work after school when the season's over."

"There you go, bro," Porkchop said, holding out his palm.

Beaming, Skinny slapped Porkchop's hand. "Later," he called out as his teammates stepped off the bus.

Once the Number 12 pulled away, Skinny began

counting down the streets to his stop. He could not wait to get home and tell his mother.

❖ ❖ ❖

Skinny walked to the corner of Third Avenue and anxiously looked down the street. There was still no sign of his mother. Heading back to his house for the third time, Skinny decided some music would help pass the time until he could share his plans for a scholarship.

Abuela glared at him as he walked into the living room carrying the Beatles' *Rubber Soul* album. "Are you going to play that *comemierda* music again?" she said, hands on her hips.

Ignoring her, Skinny slid the record out its sleeve and placed it on the recessed turntable of the blonde wood three-in-one. Over the last two years, Skinny had started a modest music collection, most of it Beatles and Motown.

"It's not bad enough that you play that garbage," *Abuela* said, sour-faced. "But only a *comemierda* would waste good money buying records when the same wretched music is free on the radio."

Irritated, Skinny lowered the needle onto the black vinyl LP and turned the volume all the way up. The opening riffs of *Drive My Car* roared through the house.

Covering her ears, *Abuela* walked to the wall outlet and pulled the plug. John Lennon's voice dissolved into a low growl before fading out.

"I have a right to play my music!" Skinny screamed.

"Show some respect, Victor! If not for me, then for your mother!" *Abuela* yelled back. "When she comes home from work, the last thing Alicia will want to hear is some long-haired effeminates howling like a troop of baboons!" *Abuela* shouted, thrusting her finger at him like a fencer. "Your mother works day and night to put food on the table for this family. Is it too much to ask for some peace and quiet when she comes home?"

"*Esta bien, Abuela*," Skinny said through gritted teeth, putting the record back in its sleeve. *Abuela* had played her trump card. He wanted his mother in a good mood tonight.

Heady with her victory, *Abuela* launched into a lecture. "To think that my daughter, who was the toast of Havana society, would be reduced to cleaning toilet bowls for those stingy Jews at the hotel. *Dios santisimo*, it's more than I can bear sometimes."

Skinny could not let his grandmother's narrowness pass. "It's not right to talk like that about Jews, *Abuela*," he said. "Don't you think people could say bad things about Cubans?"

"Oh? And what kind of bad things could anyone say about Cubans?" *Abuela* asked, spreading her palms. "Cuba has the most beautiful and virtuous women and the bravest, most industrious men. Look at Desi Arnaz. He came here with only a conga drum to his name and wound up owning half of Hollywood."

Skinny sighed, realizing his mistake. He did not want to get *Abuela* started on Cuba's merits. He'd heard her rant on that topic too many times. According to *Abuela*, all things Cuban were the best: The most beautiful flag. The most stirring national anthem. The loveliest beaches. The best weather. The list was endless.

Skinny also knew *Abuela's* attitude toward other ethnic groups. She was like a baseball manager who could sum up a rival batter in a single sentence: "Can't hit an inside fastball." *Abuela* had repeated her biases so many times, Skinny knew them by heart.

Puerto Ricans: "They wish to God they were Cubans."

Chinos (which to *Abuela* meant any Asian): "Good at running restaurants and laundries."

Italians: "Came to America to start the Mafia."

Jews: "Will sue you for any reason."

All other *Americanos*: "Complacent and lucky."

Afro-Americans: "*Americanos* without money."

Not wanting to poke at a hornet's nest, Skinny backpedaled. "I'm sorry, *Abuela*. You're right," he said. "*Mamá* deserves some peace and quiet when she gets home."

To avoid another battle, Skinny retreated to the kitchen. Maybe he could scrounge a snack before dinner. While opening the refrigerator, he heard the screech of the screen door and ran into the living room.

Alicia entered the house wearing her gray maid's jumper and a broad smile. "I have wonderful news," she said excitedly   .

"Tell us, *m'hija*. Tell us," *Abuela* said, pressing her palms to her chest.

"Well, to begin with, I won't have to wear this again," Alicia said, thumbing the collar of her jumper.

"Why not?"

"I've been promoted to Shift Supervisor, *Mamá*...and my pay is going to be fifteen dollars more a week!"

"*Dios santisimo!*" *Abuela* yelled and hugged Alicia, both women bouncing in celebration as tears of joy filled their eyes.

After they calmed down, Alicia tenderly touched Skinny's face. "Our prayers have been answered, *m'hijo*. Things are going to be better for our family."

"I have some good news too, *Mamá!*" Skinny said eagerly.

"What is it, *m'hijo?*" Alicia asked, drying her eyes.

"I'll be able to get a college scholarship if I keep playing football!"

Alicia's face turned cold. "I thought we agreed you'd start working after school once classes started?"

"Don't you want me to go to college?"

"Yes, but college is still two years away, Victor. Your family is counting on you *now*. You're outgrowing clothes faster than you wear them out. And you eat like a termite—although you're not gaining any weight."

"Think about how much more money I can make to help our family if I go to college, *Mamá*."

"*M'hijo*, it's going to be six years before you finish college and start making any money. What are we going to do until then? How are we going to keep this family fed? Who's going to buy the nice clothes you need to attend a university?"

"The football season only lasts ten weeks, *Mamá*. When the games are over, I'll got to work every day after school—I promise. Please, *mámi*, let me do this. Let me play football. It's my only chance to go to college."

Alicia stared at her son, apparently unconvinced. Then Skinny found a surprising ally.

"The boy deserves this chance, Alicia," *Abuela* said softly. "At least he's willing to work—unlike someone else in this house."

Alicia sighed wearily. "All right, Victor. My raise will get us by for now," she said. "You can play your football this year. As to next year...we'll see."

"Thank you, *Mamá*! Thank you!" Skinny said, grabbing his mother's hands and kissing them. He then bolted from the room and changed into his shorts and sneakers.

There was still time before dinner to get in some laps around the block.

SEPTEMBER

A New Season

Skinny stared into the night sky, mesmerized.
The football tumbling toward him out of the blackness above looked otherworldly in the glare of the stadium lights.

Skinny had never fielded a kick this high before. Under the unfamiliar lighting, the ball seemed to be floating in the same place. Not sure whether to move forward or back, Skinny stared at the ball, feet frozen.

From some distant place, Skinny could hear a faint buzz. It was the roar of the crowd at the Orange Bowl, on their feet and cheering for the first kickoff of the season. The buzz was soon drowned out by another sound—the pounding of his heart.

Finally, as the ball began to grow in size, he managed to gauge its flight. It was going to fall short.

Skinny charged forward frantically, trying to reach the ball before it hit the ground. By the time he closed on the ball, Skinny was at a dead run. Forming a basket with his arms, Skinny looked the ball all the way in. The ball slapped into his belly with a dull *thwap* and he cradled it against his ribs. A rush of pleasure washed over Skinny.

As he tucked the ball under his arm and turned his eyes upfield, his elation vanished. Instead of seeing a wall of white-shirted blockers ready to clear a path, a swarm of red jerseys was closing in.

The high, floating kick had given Edison's coverage team time to run through his blockers.

Skinny was operating on adrenaline and instinct now. Like every good kick returner, ingrained in Skinny's nervous system was a simple equation: It took just two good cuts to break a run—the first to escape containment and the second to evade pursuit.

As the wall of Edison tacklers drew closer, time slowed down for Skinny. The moment had come to make the first cut.

Skinny knew that the speed he had built up chasing down the kickoff was now his best weapon. He scanned the Edison players ahead and charged directly at the one farthest to his right.

Seeing his quarry coming directly at him, the Edison player slowed down, opened his arms and braced himself to make the tackle. It was exactly what Skinny wanted.

Skinny charged toward his opponent who was now almost flat-footed, certain the ball carrier was his. Then, an instant before the collision, Skinny planted his left foot and spun to his right. The Edison player lunged, but only managed to swat Skinny across the hips. Had Skinny not been going full speed, the Edison player's blow would have taken him down. But driven by his momentum, Skinny staggered for a couple of steps, regained his balance, and continued down the field.

That was cut number one. He had broken the containment.

Without hesitating, Skinny veered to the right. Vision was everything now.

As Skinny neared the sideline, he glanced left and saw

two Edison players taking angles to cut him off farther down the field. Gauging the first tackler's approach, Skinny's internal computer gave him the solution: He could simply outrun him.

Skinny lengthened his strides, his eyes straight ahead. Looking at his pursuers now would only slow him down.

The Edison player was getting close. Skinny could hear the rhythm of his footsteps in the grass, each stride getting louder. Then the footsteps stopped—followed by a crunching thud.

Without having to look, Skinny knew his pursuer had missed him in a futile dive.

There was now only one Edison player left to beat. From a distant part of his mind, Skinny recognized the number nine on his red jersey. It was his Wynwood buddy, Peanut O'Connor.

Peanut was clearly well coached, taking an angle that would intercept Skinny somewhere inside the twenty yard line. Watching Peanut draw closer, Skinny realized there was no way he could outrace him to the end zone.

The time for his second crucial cut had come—but first, he'd have to draw Peanut closer.

Skinny headed toward the flag at the corner of the end zone. Seeing Skinny's move, Peanut sped up to cut him off, closing fast from the left. Skinny let him get closer.

At three yards away, Peanut extended his arms, reaching for Skinny's shoulders. That was the moment Skinny had been waiting for.

As Peanut's fingertips brushed against his shoulder pads, Skinny ducked and hit the brakes. Unable to react fast enough, Peanut hurtled past him, arms flailing wildly.

Cut number two had been successful.

After nine more strides, Skinny coasted into the end zone.

Like the lifting of a fog, the distant buzz in Skinny's ears became the roar of the crowd.

❖ ❖ ❖

Rubbing her eyes and yawning, Alicia walked into the kitchen where *Abuela* was making breakfast for Marta and Rafael.

"It's Saturday morning, *m'hija*. Go back to bed," *Abuela* told her daughter, stirring the grits on the stove.

Alicia patted her mother on the shoulder. "Thank you, *Mamá*. But I want to see my children more than I want to sleep," she said before kissing each of the little ones on the cheek.

Abuela sighed. "Yes, they're growing up fast. It seems like only yesterday when—" The slam of the front porch door cut her off.

In a thunderstorm of footsteps, Skinny rushed into the kitchen. "*Mámi, Abuela*, look! I'm in the newspaper!" Skinny yelled, waving a copy of the *Miami Herald*.

"It must be a report on insolent juveniles," *Abuela* muttered without looking up from the stove.

Hearing the commotion, Juan came out of the bedroom, in his boxer briefs as usual. "What's going on?" he asked, bleary-eyed.

"I'm in the newspaper, *Pápi!*" Skinny said to his father. "Just like you used to be in Cuba!"

"Oh?" Juan said, arching an eyebrow. "Have you just written a stunning new dissertation that will turn the legal world on its ear?"

Skinny's shoulders sagged. "No, *Pápi*," he sighed. "It's just about playing football."

"I want to see it, *m'hijo*," Alicia said, walking closer.

Skinny's eyes brightened. "Here, it is," he said, pointing to the article. Alongside the story was a photo of a football player evading a tackler. "That's me in the picture," he said. "Number nineteen."

Alicia cradled her son's face in her hands. "That's splendid, Victor," she said smiling. "Tell us what the newspaper says about you."

Skinny translated as he read from the *Herald*. "The

Jackson Generals opened their season on a high note as Victor Delgado, a 140-pound, 5' 9" mighty mite, took back the opening kickoff 82 yards for a touchdown," Skinny said, holding his chin high as he finished.

"That's all it says?" Juan asked.

"Well, the rest of the article is about the game, *Pápi*, not just about me," Skinny explained. "We beat the other team 21 to 6."

"I am continually astonished by the foolishness of this country," Juan said, lips curling into a sneer. "The games of children are reported in the newspaper as if they're momentous events."

Alicia reached for the newspaper and gently ran her fingers over the article as if she were reading Braille. "This 'touchdown' you made...It's a very unusual thing, no?"

"Yes, *Mamá*, It means I ran the whole field without being caught."

"That certainly sounds like a valuable skill," *Abuela* said. "...if you're planning a career as a thief."

Alicia frowned. "Please, *Mamá*," she said. "Victor has done something important and we should recognize that."

"This is just the beginning, *mámi*," Skinny explained. "If I keep getting noticed like this, I'll start getting offers for a football scholarship next year."

"Remember, Victor," Alicia said, raising her palm. "We have to see what our situation is next year. I'm glad to see this football is making you happy—and if it brings a college scholarship, so much the better. But your family may need you to work."

Skinny hung his head, saying nothing.

"Besides, Victor. Why choose such a bestial sport?" Juan added. "This football lacks the beauty and elegance of baseball, which is a true test of athletic skill. Yes, of course, many people attend these football games—but only because they're played once a week. If only one baseball game were held in the major leagues each week the ballparks would—"

The phone rang and Skinny exhaled in relief as Juan stopped his lecture.

Alicia walked into the living room and picked up the phone. "*Oigo?*" she said into the receiver. After listening for few seconds, she held out the phone to Skinny and shrugged. "It's a man speaking English."

"Hello," Skinny said into the receiver.

"Hi, Skinny. This is Bill Bockman."

Skinny's jaw dropped. After a pause, he mumbled, "Uh, hi, Mr. Bockman."

"Hey, I could use some help in the yard. Are you interested in some work today?"

Skinny hesitated, still stunned. Janice's father had never called him before.

"I'll pay you five dollars," Mr. Bockman added with laugh. "I don't expect you to do this for free. We're not down the street anymore."

"Sure, I'll do it," Skinny said nodding.

"Good! Go get a pencil and let me give you our new address."

After writing it down, Skinny said, "I've got it," then added, "Oh, there's just one thing... My regular job starts at four so I'll have to leave at three."

"That's not a problem. Can you be here in an hour?"

"Yes, sir. I'll see you then," he said before hanging up the phone.

"Who was it?" Alicia asked.

"Someone who wants to hire me for some yard work," Skinny said, telling his mother only part of the truth—although he was not sure why.

❖ ❖ ❖

Skinny followed the house numbers along the palm-lined street until he reached the address Janice's father had given him.

The Bockman's new house looked like an oversized

wedding cake. Every surface of the white two-story home was covered with some type of fancy decoration.

As Skinny reached the arched opening on the front porch, he was startled by a voice from the hibiscus bush. "Well, if it isn't the football hero of 33rd Street."

A moment later, Bill Bockman stepped out of the bushes, his palm outstretched.

"Hi, Mr. Bockman," Skinny said, awkwardly shaking his hand.

Janice's father looked Skinny up and down and smiled. "You've stretched out a bit since the last time I saw you."

"Yeah, guess I have," Skinny said, studying the tops of his sneakers.

"I saw the sports section today, young man," Mr. Bockman said, stroking his beard. "An eighty-two yard return, huh? I guess at your size, you can't afford to get tackled. They might just break you in half!" he said, laughing at his own joke.

Skinny smiled, still staring downward, unused to the attention from Janice's father.

"Seriously, son...we're proud of you."

"Thanks."

Janice's dad stood there for a moment, trying to find something more to say. "Well, if you're ready, I'll show you where to get started," he said finally, leading Skinny to the side of the house.

Handing him a pair of leather work gloves and a bucket, Mr. Bockman explained Skinny's job, then went back to pruning the bushes out front. Skinny was to weed the knee-high flower beds all around the house—a job that, thankfully, did not look all that hard.

Once he started the weeding, Skinny tried to focus on the work and keep Janice out of his mind. But the chance she might be around was too powerful to ignore. With each plant he uprooted, more of his old feelings for Janice came surging back.

As the weeding took him to the back of the house, he finally saw her.

She was sitting on the diving board of a kidney-shaped pool, dangling her slim, tanned legs over the water and caressing its surface with her toes. Her delicate build of adolescence had blossomed into a curvier figure that was impossible to miss in the one-piece speedo clinging tightly to her skin.

As Skinny ripped a large bull thistle out of the dirt, the sound caught Janice's attention. She looked up and smiled.

"Hi, Skinny," she called out, waving him over.

He waved back but kept working.

"Come here," she said, brushing back on a strand of hair.

"I better get this done."

"Don't worry. You won't get in trouble. I've got some pull with the boss."

Skinny took off his gloves and walked to the edge of the pool. "You don't seem surprised about... well, how I look now."

"We girls have our ways of keeping up with these things," she said with a sly grin. "Did you bring your bathing suit?"

"No. I've gotta work this afternoon," Skinny answered and sat down next to her on the diving board.

"So how are things in the old neighborhood?"

"About the same," Skinny said vaguely. He was eager to share the news about the game but didn't know how to begin without making it sound like he was bragging.

Janice splashed the water playfully with her foot. "Have you seen Loco lately?"

"Not since football practice started," he said. "I heard Chucho got arrested, though."

"Do you think that Loco's going to get in trouble too?" she asked. Like most people from the neighborhood, she knew about Loco's connection with Chucho.

"I don't know."

"You and Loco were really good friends. It's strange not seeing you together."

"Loco is still my best friend, Janice. It's just that...you know, he goes to Curly and I go to Jackson. When I'm not in school or football practice, I'm working at Armando's."

"Yeah, you seem kinda busy these days."

"Hey, did you see the paper today?" Skinny asked, anxious to bring up the subject of the football game.

"Was there something important in it?"

Skinny lowered his head and stared at the water. "No. Not really."

"I'm just kidding, Skinny," Janice said, laughing softly. "I saw the article. My dad was impressed. He always wanted to play football. In fact, he started dropping hints about inviting you to the family dinner at the Order of Liberty lodge next week. I think he wants to show you off to his buddies."

"Really?"

"Yeah, he thinks I don't know what he's up to."

"What do you mean?"

"Dad figures that if he comes right out and says he'd like you to go with me, I'll invite someone else."

Skinny's heart began to race. In all the time they'd known each other, he and Janice had never gone out on a real date.

"So what are you going to do?" he asked, trying to hide his excitement.

Janice smiled and lightly touched his forearm. "I'm going to invite you, silly."

As Janice's finger slowly trailed along his skin, the excitement he'd felt crossing the end zone the night before suddenly seemed pale.

❖ ❖ ❖

"Yeow!" Skinny yelled as *Abuela's* needle nipped his skin.

"Stop squirming, *niño*," *Abuela* mumbled, holding a length of thread between her lips. "You're worse than a monkey with ants on his tail," she said, trying to take in a pair of pants several sizes too big for her grandson.

Skinny glanced nervously at the clock. "Hurry up, *Abuela*! They're going to be here any minute."

Abuela continued stitching calmly. "We had a saying in Cuba, Victor...'Dress me slowly because I don't have much time.' Being in a hurry is a state of mind, *niño*. It's not how fast you get something done."

Skinny looked down at his only pair of dress shoes. They were freshly-buffed, but he was disappointed they were the same black loafers he wore to school every day. "I don't understand why *Pápi* has more than twenty pairs of shoes and I only have these loafers and my sneakers."

Abuela's answer surprised him. "Because next year Juan's foot will still be the same size," she said without looking up. "There we are...You're ready."

Rushing past his grandmother, Skinny slipped on the powder blue blazer hanging on the door and dashed into the bathroom to look in the mirror. The gray mohair slacks *Abuela* had altered went perfectly with the sports coat. As *Abuela* had predicted, Juan's navy tie and silver clasp completed the outfit.

Skinny exhaled slowly, relieved to be finally ready.

His panic had started two hours earlier.

Returning from work, Skinny had casually told *Abuela* he wouldn't be home for dinner. "I'm going out with Janice," he said smugly.

"Oh? And where are you going with your *Americana?*"

When Skinny told his grandmother about the Order of Liberty dinner, *Abuela* nodded knowingly and then sighed. "That sounds very fancy, Victor. So, tell me. What do you plan to wear?"

Skinny's eyes widened. "*Dios santisimo!* I hadn't thought about clothes!"

"I didn't think so," his grandmother said, shaking her head.

Then *Abuela* took over.

She began by enlisting the neighbors. One provided the sports coat, another the trousers that had to be taken in. The tie and clasp had come from Juan's closet. In all, the boy's outfit was a communal effort—and *Abuela* had pulled off a miracle getting it ready on time.

With his outfit complete, Skinny was now preening in the mirror. While parting his sandy hair into a meticulous Princeton for the third time, he heard two short toots from a car horn.

Skinny bolted out of the bathroom and was nearly out the door when *Abuela* called out to him.

"Wait! There's one more thing you'll need, Victor," *Abuela* said holding out a white rose corsage. "Your girlfriend should be treated like a lady—even if she is an *Americana*."

Skinny's eyebrows rose in astonishment. "It looks great! Where did you get this?"

Abuela shrugged. "It was easy. Edita Jimenez from down the street gave me the flower from her garden. The lace is from the hem of a slip."

"Thank you, *Abuela*," Skinny said, kissing his grandmother's forehead.

Abuela flicked her wrists, shooing him away. "Go on. Get going, *niño*. They're waiting for you."

After watching her grandson rush out of the porch, *Abuela* turned away and walked back into the living room, wiping a tear from her cheek.

❖ ❖ ❖

Sprinting toward the Ford Fairlane, Skinny barely recognized the Bockman sisters. They were wearing eye shadow and mascara, making them look like grownups. Janice's hair was pulled up into a stylish twist that showed off sparkly, long earrings. Behind the wheel, Laura sported a towering beehive that brushed the car's ceiling.

"Hop in, Skinny," Janice said, opening the door and sliding next to Laura on the bench seat.

"This is for you," Skinny said timidly, holding out the corsage as he got in the car.

"Thank you, Skinny!" Janice said, eyes gleaming in delight. "Look, Laura. Isn't it cute?" she said, showing the corsage to her sister.

"Nice going, Skinny," Laura said as she put the Fairlane in gear and pulled away. "You scored some serious points."

Skinny looked at the floor uncertainly. Laura had always scared him. She was smart, pretty and spoke her mind, qualities that would terrify any male.

"Tie it on for me," Janice said, handing the corsage back to Skinny and holding out her wrist.

His hands trembling, Skinny tied the lace into a granny knot. "That's not too tight, is it?" he said, thrilled to feel the warm smoothness of her skin.

"No, it's perfect," Janice said, admiring the flowers.

"The corsage is darling, Janice," Laura said. "But it clashes with the shoes."

"Don't start on the shoes again, Laura!"

"I told her not to wear those shoes, Skinny," Laura said, turning the sedan north on 7th Avenue. "But my little sister thinks she knows better about everything."

"I got two compliments on these shoes the last time I wore them." Janice protested.

"It must have been someone who was half-blind and stuttered," Laura said tartly. "What do think about them, Skinny?"

Skinny looked at Janice's feet. Her shoes were black and had thin straps with tiny buckles. *What's the big deal?* he wondered. All the same, he was not going to take any chances. "They look nice," he said.

Laura shook her head. "I should've known better than to ask for fashion advice from the love-smitten."

Love-smitten? Am I that obvious? Skinny wondered as they drove north out of Wynwood toward Miami Shores.

Entering the Fraternal Order of Liberty hall, Skinny immediately felt out of place. Most of the other young men in the large, wood-paneled hall were wearing matching gray blazers with a fancy coat of arms on the breast pocket.

One of the blazer-wearing guys waved to Laura from a table nearby. Laura beamed him a lighthouse smile and waved back. "See you later, alligator!" she said before leaving the pair alone.

"That's her boyfriend, Mark," Janice explained, looking around the room. Janice then grimaced and quickly turned her eyes toward the floor. "Oh, crap. Here comes dad," she whispered.

"Hi sweetheart," Bill Bockman said, walking up to Janice. "Can I borrow Skinny for a while? I'd like some of the fellows to meet him."

"We just got here, Daddy," Janice complained.

"I won't keep him long, hon. I promise," her father answered, taking Skinny by the arm and leading him away. Entering a smaller side room, Skinny saw a group of older men in dark business suits. Most were smoking cigars and brandishing cocktails.

A tall, freckle-faced man approached them smiling, his hand outstretched. "You must be Skinny. Bill has been telling us about you. I'm Mike Somers."

Skinny shook the man's hand, feeling the coldness of the drink he'd been holding. "Nice to meet you, sir."

Mike looked at Janice's father. "Bill, when you said he was Cuban I was expecting somebody a little more...well... sun-tanned, if you know what I mean."

"I can tell you've never been to Cuba, Mike," said another man, joining the conversation. He was short and chunky, with strands of oiled black hair clinging to his forehead like wet seaweed. "I used to go to Havana all the time with a few guys from the office. They've got coloreds *and* whites down there—and some that's a little of both." The man then shook Skinny's hand. "By the way, I'm Pete DeLuca."

Mike nudged Pete in the ribs. "Yeah, I heard about your trips to Havana, Pete. They sure as hell weren't business!"

"That town was wide open," Pete said wistfully before

taking a long pull on his highball. "We sure had some good times down there. It was a shame to see Cuba go commie." Pete jabbed a finger into Skinny's chest and said, "Son, I hope the day comes when you can go down there and get your country back—even if those pinkos in Washington won't help you."

Bill Bockman patted Skinny's shoulder. "Well, my family and I have known this boy since he was just off the boat and could barely speak English. And, I want to tell you, we are proud to see him grow up to be just like a real American. Why, these days, you wouldn't even know he was a Cuban if you met him on the street. And now he's even playing football—and doing damned well at it!"

"Yeah, I saw the article about Jackson in the paper," Mike said. "Congratulations, son."

"What the hell, Mike? Since when do you read about high school sports?" Pete asked. "You and Mildred only have girls."

"I read the sports section every day, Pete. Hell, my bowels won't move in the morning without a cup of coffee and the *Herald*."

The men laughed for a moment, then Pete turned serious. "I guess with all the coloreds there at Jackson now, things must be getting pretty rough," he said to Skinny.

Skinny shrugged. "I haven't had any problems."

"This whole civil rights business," Pete said shaking his head, "it's just a communist front, you know. The reds are using the coloreds to stir up trouble with this integration thing," he said, downing the last of his drink. "I tell you, Miami is going to the dogs. I mean, all the Cubans are bad enough—sorry son," he said to Skinny, his voice slurred, "but what I'm saying is we need to snuff out that bastard Castro so your people can go back home."

Bill Bockman's face reddened. "Well, I better get you back to Janice or I'll never hear the end of it," he said to Skinny.

Once they were back in the main hall, Bill pulled Skinny

aside. "I just want you to know that the guys here in the Order don't care if someone is rich or poor—or where they come from. But when some of them get a little boozed up... well, you understand."

"Sure, I understand," Skinny said, confused by Mr. Bockman's apology. *Abuela* could be just as narrow without a drop of liquor. Maybe that's what happened when you got old. When it came to people who were different, you only saw what you expected.

Mr. Bockman smiled weakly. "I'm glad to hear that, son," he said, then shook Skinny's hand and returned to his friends.

Walking toward Janice, Skinny felt relieved. The conversation with these men had bothered him. But that feeling dissolved the moment he saw Janice smile at him.

"You're back just in time!" she said as Skinny neared the table. "The band's getting ready to start."

Skinny followed Janice's eyes to the corner of the ballroom where four pale guys in plaid jackets twiddled nervously with their instruments. When they finally struck up a day-old-soda version of *Everybody's Gone Surfin'*, Skinny cringed. The only thing more lame than the band in this place was the dancers. Watching their stiff jitterbugging, Skinny realized this was his chance to shine. He just needed the right song.

After a series of surf tunes, the band finally broke into a number with some soul, a passable rendition of *Midnight Hour*. Skinny took Janice's hand and led her toward the dance floor. He was going to kill her with his moves—and show up all these preppies in their fancy blazers. After partying for a year with the brothers and sisters at Jackson, he was ready.

Skinny started with the Shing-A-ling, pivoting smoothly side-to-side as Janice smiled in approval. Then he kicked it up a gear and broke into the Boogaloo. By the time the band reached the bridge, Skinny could see he had the crowd's attention. The time had come to really turn it on.

As he half-squatted to start the Philly Dog, the seat of his pants split.

Skinny bolted upright like he'd been goosed. In a panic, he pulled the down the tail of his jacket and backed away from the dance floor. *Goddamn you, Abuela*, he said under his breath, scuttling like a crab with his back against the wall until he reached the men's room.

Once inside a stall, Skinny wrung his hands in agony, wondering what to do. Looking down at his tie gave him an idea. He took off his pants and clamped the split seat together with his tie clasp. *This might work*, he thought, putting the pants back on. But there was no way he could sit down.

Janice looked bewildered when he returned to their table. "What happened?" she asked.

"Uh...Well, I think I pulled a muscle."

"A pulled muscle?" she said suspiciously

"Yeah, but it's fine now."

"Well, then you should sit down and take it easy."

"That's okay. It feels better if I stand...or maybe walk," Skinny said, sensing an opportunity. "You want to go for a walk?"

Janice smiled and rose from the table. "Sure, let's check this place out. It has some spooky old rooms I was always afraid to go in alone."

"Okay. Let's take a look," Skinny said, his pulse rising.

In the empty corridor outside the main hall, Janice took his arm as they walked.

"Those were some kind of moves," she said looking up at him, eyes fluttering. "I had no idea you could dance like that."

Skinny laughed softly. "If your family had stayed in Wynwood, you would have gone to Jackson and learned to dance like that too."

Janice looked away, her smile gone. "Dad said he ran out

of things to do with the old place."

Skinny nodded, realizing he'd touched a nerve. Maybe her father had convinced himself that was true. He seemed like a decent guy. In any case, he didn't want to ruin this moment with Janice. "So where are these spooky rooms anyway?" he asked.

Janice's face brightened, glad to change the subject. "This is one of them," she said as they approached the doorway into a darkened room. "Come on. I won't be scared if you go with me."

Following her into the room, Skinny stretched out his hand, trying to feel his way in the darkness. Janice took his hand and drew him toward her. The warmth of her breath on his neck made his own breathing quicken. Skinny hesitantly touched her face and she put her arms around his waist.

His heart racing, he kissed her, brushing gently against her lips. The kiss grew deeper and more sensuous as they pressed against each other, the caresses of her hands adding to his swelling passion. Skinny's arousal grew obvious and Janice did not back away.

The sound of footsteps in the hallway broke their embrace. "We better go," Janice whispered.

"Wait," Skinny said.

Feeling along the wall, he found the switch and turned on the lights. Skinny looked around a conference room with a long wooden table surrounded by ornate upright chairs. Revolutionary War paintings decorated the paneled walls.

He wanted to remember every detail of the place he'd first kissed Janice Bockman.

OCTOBER

The Visitors

M arta ran ahead of her family as they entered the Orange Bowl for the first time. Leaning over the lower deck railing, she scanned the field and yelled back to them over the din of the crowd. "There he is—number 19! He's standing right over there!" she said, pointing to a small figure among the cluster of players on the far sideline.

"Are you sure," *Abuela* asked, as she caught up to Marta.

"Skinny—I mean, Victor—told me Jackson's uniforms are green," Marta replied. "That's got to be him!"

"Yoo-hoo, Victor! We're over here, boy!" *Abuela* shouted, waving to her grandson.

"Don't be foolish, old woman," Juan said. "The boy can't hear you. We're in the middle of a crowd over fifty meters away." Juan then pointed to some empty seats to their right. "Let's sit over there. That spot should give us a commanding view of the game once the action begins."

"It looks to me like the game has already started," *Abuela* answered. "If you hadn't gotten us lost on the way here, we would have been on time."

"How would you know the game has started, old

woman?" Juan shot back. "Do you purport to understand how this American football is played?"

While Juan spoke, the crowd around them rose and roared as one of the players in maroon broke a long run and was tackled near them on the sideline.

"Listen to these people screaming, Juan. Do you think they're cheering the calisthenics before the game?" *Abuela* asked.

"Mother...Juan...let's not start an incident here," Alicia pleaded, noticing the stares from the people around them. No one else in the stands was speaking Spanish. Unknowingly, Juan had led them to the visitors' side of the Orange Bowl that tonight held the fans from Norland Senior High—a well-to-do suburban school.

Once they were in their seats, it did not take long for Juan and *Abuela* to resume their skirmish.

"The demeanor of Victor's team appears tense," Juan observed as he scanned the sideline. "I think they may be trailing the other team."

"I may be just a foolish old woman, Juan, but I think that's a scoreboard over there and Victor's school is named Jackson, no?" *Abuela* said pointing to the large electronic marquee over the end of the field. The score was Jackson 7, Norland 0.

Hoping to break up the fight, Alicia tugged on Juan's arm. "I don't understand this game. Do they get points for crossing those lines with the numbers on them?" she asked, pointing to the numerals along the sidelines.

"That's an interesting theory, *mi amor*," Juan said rubbing his chin. "Perhaps we should observe this in more detail."

"If that's the case, I don't think they want to go too far," *Abuela* noted. "Look at the numbers," she said pointing to the fifty yard line. "Once they get past the middle, the numbers start going down again. This game doesn't make any sense."

While the Delgados continued their debate over this mystifying sport, a man from the opposite aisle approached the family.

"Hi!" the man said with a smile a tad too wide. "I couldn't help noticing you folks speak Spanish. Is there a chance you're parents of a Jackson student?"

"My brother goes to Jackson," Marta answered for the family. "He's number 19. That's him right over there," she said pointing proudly across the field.

"I thought so," the man replied. "Listen, sweetie. Tell your parents they should move to the other side of the stadium. This side is for Norland High."

Marta translated the man's words for her family. After listening to Marta, Juan stood up, looked the taller man in the eye, and responded in a long stream of Spanish.

"My father says to tell you—very respectfully—that if you care to try and make him move, he will be happy to step outside and break your face." Marta said smiling.

Without another word, the man returned to his seat. After Juan sat back down, *Abuela* leaned against her son-in-law and nudged his ribs. "You don't look nearly as short when you're standing on those stones, Juan."

For the next two hours, the Delgado family watched the game, totally bewildered. *Abuela*—a fan of the real *futbol*—was most impressed by the punts and kickoffs while Juan had to admit the collisions were unquestionably manly.

The first time Alicia saw her son being tackled, she was horrified. After that, whenever Skinny had the ball, she looked away and made the sign of the cross. The halftime show was her favorite part, by far. Marta wolfed down several ballpark pretzels while Rafael mostly snuggled against his mother and snoozed.

During the remainder of the game, the man across the aisle stared straight ahead, never again turning his head toward the Delgados.

When the final gun sounded and the winning Jackson players walked to the center of the field to shake hands, they were surprised to hear a smattering of cheers from the dejected Norland side of the stadium.

"What's that all about?" Popeye asked, looking up into the opposing stands.

"Oh, my God—it's my family," Skinny said.

Embarrassed, Skinny quickly looked away. But as his family kept up their cheers, Skinny's features slowly melted into a smile.

DECEMBER

On a New Planet

The strobe light at the discotheque kicked in.

Carrying a brimming dixie cup of soda in each hand, Skinny stopped, suddenly disoriented as hundreds of teenagers dancing in the one-time warehouse became a flickering mass of frozen poses.

Around the dancers, the two-story walls were alive with amoebic shapes pulsing in lurid colors. Weird photos and silent film clips sporadically appeared on the ceiling. Thundering from large speakers all around the room, the bass line of *Spoonful* by Cream throbbed in Skinny's chest.

This orchestrated chaos was the main attraction of Miami's hottest teen disco: The Planet.

A *Herald* reviewer had called The Planet "an unholy syncretism of the San Francisco hippie scene with the over-the-top glitz of Miami Beach." That mattered little to Skinny. He was here to please Janice.

"The girls at school say the place is really cool!" she'd told him over the phone earlier in the week. "You want to meet there Saturday night?"

Eager to keep his new status as her steady, Skinny had agreed.

Now, he regretted the decision. From the moment he'd walked into the teens-only club in North Miami, Skinny had felt uneasy.

Although The Planet served no liquor, the place was like a zombie village. A lot of the young faces around him were glassy-eyed and clearly high. But that wasn't what really bothered him.

The teens flocking to The Planet were a smorgasbord of cliques from all over the Anglo sections of the city. Not really a part of any group, Skinny felt like an outsider. Still, he was fascinated by the social menagerie around him.

There were Surfers in abundance—the boys in Dewey Weber tees and baggies, the girls in bikini tops and cut-offs. A few had even painted a perfect white rectangle of Noxzema across their noses—just to make sure you knew they'd put in a long day at the beach.

Another common species was the Preppies. Sporting button-down shirts or pleated skirts, they mostly huddled against the walls, shooting sidelong glances and whispering as they took in the scene. Skinny imagined them as adults, living in Coral Gables and naming their children after some type of cheese: Colby, Brie, and Jack.

Finally, there were the Flower Children, both genders decked out in beads and bell bottoms, flaunting shoulder length hair that was always parted in the middle and invariably dead straight—in many cases, carefully ironed to get it that way.

After studying the fashion tribes around him, it dawned on Skinny they had one thing in common: all of them looked like their ancestors could have just stepped off the *Mayflower*. Although Skinny's features did not stand out at The Planet, he knew there was something inside that made him different—and he'd grown proud of that, although he was still not sure why.

Making his way through the crowd, Skinny spotted Janice at the small table she was holding for them while he went for sodas. As he got closer, he noticed a trio of Surfers around her.

"What's the matter, honey? Can't you speak?" a blond guy shouted at Janice over the music. She looked away, trying to ignore him.

Skinny put down the sodas and stepped between them. "She's spoken for," he said. Then, looking at the guy's face for the first time, was surprised to find he knew him. "Santiago?" he said in amazement. "I didn't recognize you with the blond hair, man. I haven't seen you since we played Little League at Wynwood."

Santiago's face hardened. "I don't know what you're talking about, man. My name is Sandy."

Skinny looked at the two Surfers with his childhood teammate and suddenly understood. Santiago was passing for an Anglo and had just been outed. "*Que pasa? Te da pena ser Cubano?*" he asked angrily—What's the matter? Are you ashamed of being Cuban?

"Cut the shit, spic!" Santiago said, clenching his fists. The other two surfers closed in on Skinny, glaring menacingly.

Skinny was scared. But there was no way he'd bail. Not in front of Janice. As Skinny and the trio squared off, a muscular guy with long red hair stepped up beside Skinny. "Is there a problem here?" he asked the Surfers with a cold stare.

It was Loco.

Knowing the redhead's reputation, Santiago backed down. "Just watch your mouth next time," he muttered to Skinny before leading his friends away.

Skinny turned toward Loco and smiled. "As usual, you showed up at the right time, man."

"You mean Santiago and his surfer buddies weren't inviting you to a Luau?"

Skinny and Janice laughed, relieved the tense moment had passed.

"To hell with that *pendejo*," Skinny said. "It's good to see you, man."

"Let's go out on the patio," Loco said, nodding toward

the back door. "It's easier to talk out there."

Holding Janice's hand as he walked behind Loco, Skinny noticed how much his friend had changed. Along with growing brawnier, Loco's thick auburn hair was now over his ears and parted in the middle, looking like a pair of rusty Brillo pads.

Out on the patio, the three of them stood for several seconds in an awkward silence. "I haven't seen you in a while, man. What have you been up to?" Loco finally said.

Skinny shrugged. "Football...work...you know..."

"I thought Catholic schools were really strict, Loco," Janice said. "I can't believe they let you have hair that long at Curly."

"They don't," Loco said grinning. "I got kicked out of Curly. I'm going to Edison now."

Skinny's eyes widened. "Edison? Are you shitting me?"

"I know how you jocks at Jackson feel about Edison, Skinny," Loco said smiling. "But I don't give a damn about football, man."

"Well, it's important to Skinny," Janice said. "He ran back three kicks for touchdowns this year. If he plays like that again next year, he might get a scholarship."

"That's great, man. I'm pulling for you," Loco said slapping his back. "So, how's your family? Is *Abuela* still cooking up those grits with a *huevo frito* on top?"

Skinny laughed. "*Abuela's* more forgetful nowadays—but she'll still scald your ears if you mess with her," he said. "How's your mom?"

Loco stroked his chin, his smile fading. "My mom's okay. Yeah, she's fine," he said. Then his face brightened. "Hey, are you guys doing anything for your head these days?"

"What do you mean?" Janice asked.

"Hang on a minute," Loco said and waved over a girl lurking in a dark corner of the patio. A slender brunette in low-cut bells and a black halter top walked toward them. To Skinny, she looked well into her twenties.

"We doing it?" the brunette asked Loco after reaching the group.

Loco nodded and she pulled three tightly-rolled joints from the pocket of her jeans. "They're on the house," Loco said proudly.

Janice gasped. "My God. Is that what I think it is?" she said, her eyes darting nervously.

"Listen, I think we better get going," Skinny said, taking Janice's hand and leading her back toward the door.

"I guess I'll see you around, man," Loco said to Skinny's back as he hurried away.

"I'm sorry, Janice," Skinny said as they walked back inside. "I didn't know Loco was dealing. That won't happen again."

FEBRUARY

The Chill of Morning

A small cloud of steam rose from Skinny's mouth as he yawned. He watched it drift away, bleary-eyed but mildly fascinated. Mornings cold enough to see your breath were rare in Miami.

Leaning forward on the wooden bench, he looked down the line of cars on 36th Street. The baby-blue MTA bus that would take him to school was nowhere in sight. "Shit," he muttered, tucking his hands under his armpits as his teeth began to chatter.

He yawned again, wishing he could crawl back into bed. After getting home from work at eleven, he'd been up until two studying for a History test.

As Skinny shivered and waited, a shiny red Mustang stopped along the curb. The driver tapped the horn and waved him inside. To Skinny's surprise, it was Hector Rivera.

Skinny hesitated. Here was Hector, who'd thrown his Roller Kings shirt in Skinny's his face—and gotten the better of him with Janice at Skateland, offering him a ride. Skinny knew all the jerk really wanted was to show off his new car. But the cold got the better of him. Skinny picked up his books and got into the Mustang.

"Nice day to take the bus, huh?" Hector said, smiling smugly. "Glad I don't have to do that anymore—not since I got this baby," he said, tapping the dashboard.

Skinny ignored him and looked out the window. He was not going to take the bait and give Hector a chance to brag. Then he realized something was wrong. "Hey, don't you go to Edison? What are you doing around here anyway?"

"Fuck Edison, man," Hector sneered. "I dropped out when I started working for Chucho."

"If you're working for Chucho now, what happened to Loco?"

"Haven't you heard? They put Loco in a foster home after his mother died."

Skinny flinched. "His mother died? How?"

"Car crash. She was drunk and went off some causeway ramp or something," Hector said, then slid a cassette into the eight-track player bolted to the dash. "Hey, man. Let me play you some Wilson Pickett on this baby. It'll blow your balls off."

The opening chords of *Mustang Sally* filled the car. Skinny stared straight ahead for a moment. Then he raised his foot and drove it into the tape player. The plastic cassette burst into shards.

"Hey! What the fuck?" Hector screamed, pulling the car to the curb. "That's a hundred-dollar eight-track!"

Skinny picked up his books, opened the door and got out. "Thanks for the ride, *pendejo*," he said, then slammed the door and landed a kick on the back fender before Hector drove away.

As he began walking the last five blocks to school, Skinny remembered how he'd walked away from Loco at The Planet. That wasn't right, and he knew it. He needed to see his friend again—now more than ever.

A Couple at the Beach

Perched on the concrete sea wall, Skinny scanned the shoreline. From the pier to the jetties, he saw only a handful of people along the quarter-mile stretch of South Beach. That wasn't surprising, though. South Beach was a surfing hangout and the waves today were puny.

Skinny looked behind him into the near-empty parking lot of the Miami Beach Kennel Club. Laura would be dropping off Janice soon. Between his long hours at Armando's and football two-a-days, he had not spent much time with Janice over the summer. He hoped today would make up for that.

But there was someone else he'd neglected—and making up for that would not be as easy.

After learning Loco's mother had died, Skinny had vowed to see his friend. But, the more he thought about it, the more his resolve had wilted. *What am I going to say? Will Loco even want to talk about it?* he wondered. *If he's in a foster home, how will I even find him?* For days, he dragged his feet, uncertain what to do. The days turned into weeks. Finally, the grim realization hit him. He'd waited too long. Loco would probably never forgive him.

Thinking about Loco hurt. And yet, there were so many other things going right. This time next year, he might be in college—with Janice as his girlfriend. Maybe Loco was not meant to be a part of the world where he was headed.

The sound of a car approaching broke his thoughts. His pulse rose as he spotted Laura's Fairlane.

Janice's sister looked worried as she pulled up near the sea wall. "Are you two going to be okay?" she said through the window. "This place looks like a ghost town."

"Stop being a mother hen, Laura," Janice said, getting out the car, beach bag in hand. "Go on, get out of here! Your dreamboat Brad is waiting for you," she said, smacking her lips in exaggerated kisses. As Janice leaned toward the car, Skinny got an eyeful of her curvy frame in a yellow bikini top and hip-hugging cut-offs.

Once Laura was gone, Janice took Skinny's hand. "Come on. I know a great spot to relax," she said, leading him from the parking lot to the beach.

Walking south toward Government Cut, they reached a bank of sand dunes covered in clumps of tall grass.

"This looks like a good place," Janice said, putting down her beach bag in a low spot behind the crest of the dunes. Sheltered by the tall grass, they had a view of the beach while standing up, but a cozy private nest lying down.

After they'd spread their towels in the sand, Janice unbuttoned her cut-offs and slowly slid them down her thighs, revealing the other half of a scanty yellow bikini. Watching the semi-striptease, Skinny felt his heartrate rise—along with a surge in his jeans. Lorenzo was back.

"Didn't you bring a swimsuit?" Janice asked, tossing her shorts on the beach bag.

Skinny swallowed hard. "Yeah, give me a minute," he said, then turned away from Janice and stepped out of his jeans. "Hey, is that a dolphin?" he said, looking over his shoulder. While Janice glanced toward the water, Skinny belly-flopped onto his towel.

"I didn't see anything," Janice said, facing him again.

"Huh? Maybe it was seaweed."

Janice's half smile made Skinny wonder if she'd caught on.

"You want to go for a swim?" she said.

"Not yet. I want to relax for a while."

"I guess Armando has been keeping you busy."

"Yeah, I put in forty-four hours at the store this week—along with football practices."

"I know something that might help," Janice said, sitting up. "Sometimes when dad's been working hard," she said, straddling his hips, "mom gives him a back rub."

Starting at his neck and slowly working her way down, Janice began kneading his spine. The stoking of her fingers, along with the rhythmic contact with her pelvis and thighs, put Lorenzo on the express elevator.

"When was the last time you were here?" Skinny asked, looking for a distraction that would get Lorenzo to a lower floor.

"At South Beach? I really can't remember. It's been a while."

"I remember when you and your family used to come here back in junior high," Skinny said. "Your dad used to park that old Dodge station wagon near the pier and go fishing," he said, the nostalgia finally getting Lorenzo to the basement. "You and Laura would surf and then your mom would break out the sandwiches for lunch."

Janice laughed softly. "That's right!" she said, then paused. "But I don't remember seeing you here."

"That's not a surprise. You hardly knew I existed back then."

"I did too!" she protested, playfully slapping his back.

"Oh, sure. And whenever we were together, you'd tell the other two thousand guys hanging around you, 'This is my fat little *friend*, Skinny.'"

"Take that back!" she said giggling, tugging on his swim suit and tickling his ribs. "You're saying I was a stuck up little bitch."

Caught up in her laughter, Skinny rolled over and grabbed her waist. "Oh, you want to fight, huh?" he said, pulling her down beside him.

Laughing, they roughhoused in the sand. After tussling for a while, they found their bodies pressed together in a tight embrace. Skinny stopped laughing and looked into her eyes.

"Do you know how long I've been in love with you?"

"No," she said, touching his cheek.

"The first time I wanted to tell you was at Shell's City— that day they wouldn't serve the black family. Do you remember?"

"Oh, my God, Skinny. We were just kids."

"That's how long I've known, Janice. I fell in love with you the first time I saw you—and I've loved you ever since."

Janice beamed, then closed her eyes and kissed him.

Skinny had waited for this moment almost as long as he could remember. Now, lying in the warm sand, feeling the smoothness of Janice's skin against him, he was filled with a glow of tenderness—and the heat of passion.

As their kiss deepened, he caressed Janice's waist. Then, very gently, he let his fingertips drift upward to the edge of her bikini. To his surprise, Janice pulled his hand to her breast.

Although he'd necked with Janice before, this was uncharted territory. As he began fumbling with her top, she helped him unfasten it. Then she calmly slipped off the bottom of her suit and helped Skinny shed his own.

What happened next was a poem without words.

When it was over, Janice looked at Skinny smiling, hair matted to her neck. "Let's get in the water," she whispered. "I need to cool off."

They both slipped back into their swimming suits and

rose from their private nest. After a few steps, they began racing for the ocean. Skinny got there first, diving into the surf. Janice followed and soon the two were thrashing in the waves.

The sight of Janice, wet hair framing her delicate features, was a vision Skinny wanted to savor forever. He opened his arms and she snuggled against him. Neither spoke as they clung to each other in the gentle surf.

After a while, Janice finally broke the silence. "Okay, I'm starting to get a little cold now."

"C'mon. Let's lay down on the jetties and dry off in the sun," Skinny said, nodding toward the line of dark gray boulders.

Coming out of the water, Skinny was pulsating with energy. "Hey, Janice. You see that boulder over there with the seaweed on it?" Skinny said, pointing to a stone about thirty yards away.

"You mean the Lincoln boulder?"

Skinny laughed. "I didn't think you girls knew about the dumb names us guys gave rocks."

"You'd be surprised what we girls know," she said with that half smile again.

"Well, I bet you I can get to the Lincoln boulder before you count to ten."

"Don't be stupid. You could hurt yourself."

"Naw!" Skinny scoffed. "Loco and I used to race there all the time," he said, grinning. "Go ahead. Start counting."

"No, Skinny. I'm not going to do it."

"All right, I'll do it myself, then," he said, scrambling onto the rocks. "One!" he yelled, leaping toward the first boulder. "Two!" he shouted, now in full stride across the tops of the rocks.

Continuing to count, Skinny felt a rush of adrenaline. The trick to navigating this uneven landscape was to keep moving. The moment one foot landed, you chose the landing spot for the other. It took agility and balance—but most of all, guts.

"Six!" he yelled, clearing the highest point so far. Then, seeing the boulders on the other side for the first time, Skinny knew he'd made a mistake.

The stones ahead of him were wet from the rising tide.

He tried desperately to stop. But that only made him stumble. His momentum threw him forward, slamming shoulder-first into the wet boulders.

"Oh my God! Skinny, are you okay?" Janice yelled.

"I'm fine," Skinny called out, trying to sound calm.

I've taken hits this hard playing football, he assured himself. Rising to his feet, he gingerly probed his right shoulder. It was swollen and numb.

Then he tried raising his arm. A searing jolt of pain drove him to his knees.

Then Skinny knew for sure. He'd never been hurt this badly before.

❖ ❖ ❖

Alicia bowed her head, dabbing at the tears forming in her eyes. "What in God's name were you thinking, Victor?" she said, her voice breaking.

"Look at how you've made your mother suffer," *Abuela* shouted. "What kind of a fool jumps around like a monkey over wet rocks? Did your brains just fall out of your head, boy?"

Juan glared at his mother-in-law. "Unlike your grandmother, I know you're not a fool, *m'hijo,*" he said icily. "But you leave me perplexed when you behave like such a colossal dimwit."

Sitting on the couch and still groggy from the painkillers, Skinny stared at the floor and said nothing. His right arm was in a sling and a figure-eight brace girdled his shoulders. On the couch next to him, Marta and Rafael were absorbed in a TV wrestling match, immune to the drama in their living room.

Skinny had come home expecting comfort and sympathy. Instead, the litany of blame had started the moment he explained how he'd shattered his collarbone. The excruciating pain as the emergency room doctor reset his clavicle hurt less than the scolding he was getting now. But that wasn't the worst part.

Six to eight weeks, the doctor had said. That's how long he would have to wear the brace. By then, football season would be nearly over. There would be no scholarship, no future. Everything he'd worked for, his dreams to help himself and his family, were now gone.

"Your pay from Armando's was finally letting us put away a little money," Alicia lamented. "Now we'll have to use it to pay for your hospital bill," she said, then sighed. "All the time you worked this summer was for nothing," she said, then turned her eyes toward the ceiling. "Oh, heavenly father, what did we do to deserve this?"

Like a voice from a Greek chorus, *Abuela* chimed in. "By the time you're able to lift a box of beans, somebody else will have your job at Armando's."

Skinny sat silently, his patience wearing thin. They were right. Running on the jetties had been a stupid thing to do. But bawling him out wasn't going to change anything. *Why can't they leave me alone?* he thought, his anger gaining ground over the guilt.

"So what were you trying to do, Victor? Impress your little girlfriend?" Juan asked smirking. "Did she swoon when she witnessed your manly prowess?"

"That's what comes from going out with an *Americana*," *Abuela* added.

Glancing toward the TV, Skinny saw a wrestling tag team mercilessly punishing their opponent. *That poor bastard against the ropes is me*, he thought, starting to fume.

Abuela leaned close to him. "Why can't you go out with a nice Cuban girl, anyway?" she asked. "You won't find a Cuban girl going to the beach with a boy without a chaperone," she said, wagging a gnarled finger in his face. "And these *Americanas* are dirty too. My God, Victor, they don't even bother to wash their private parts."

The last slur was finally too much.

"Shut up, you bigoted old hag!" Skinny screamed, rising his feet. "Just shut up!"

"Victor!" Juan said sternly. "Apologize to your grandmother immediately. That kind of disrespect will not be permitted in this house."

Skinny spun toward his father, the two suddenly face to face. "You're a fine one to talk, *papi*. Always screaming at everybody else but you never lift a finger to—"

Before Skinny could finish, Alicia stepped between them and slapped her son's face. "You will not speak to your father like that!" she said, trembling with anger.

Skinny was stunned. His mother had never struck him before. The blow turned everything inside him cold.

Without another word, he walked out.

Reaching his front-porch bedroom, he began slowly stuffing his belongings into a pillowcase, hampered by the sling and brace. Moments later, Alicia walked in.

"Don't be foolish, Victor. Where will you go?" Alicia said gently. "We're your family, *m'hijo*. We're all you have in the world."

Skinny said nothing as he finished packing. His clothes and records barely filled the pillowcase. Along with the three dollars and change in his pocket, this was everything he owned.

He stood and faced his mother. "You'll never see me in this miserable house again."

❖ ❖ ❖

Skinny dialed the payphone and waited restlessly for the line to ring.

"Hello?" said a voice in the earpiece.

"Janice, it's me, Skinny."

"Hi, Skinny. Are you okay? You still sound a little woozy."

"No, I'm fine. Can you talk?"

"Yeah, I think so. I'm on the kitchen phone and my family's in the living room watching Ed Sullivan."

"Listen, Janice. Something's come up. I've moved out of my parent's house. I'm going to quit school and split—maybe to California or something."

"Oh my God, Skinny, what happened?"

"There's just too much bullshit for me to put up with at home anymore. Look, I don't want to get into that right now. But there's something I need to ask you, Janice... will you come with me?"

The line was silent.

"Janice? Are you still there?" Skinny asked, his voice quivering.

"Yeah, Skinny. I'm still here."

"Well...What do you think? Will you come with me?"

"I can't, Skinny."

"Why not?"

"Skinny, that would be crazy. I mean, we haven't even finished high school. What would we do? How would we live?"

"We'd be together."

"I know, Skinny. But that's not enough."

"I love you, Janice."

"I love you too, Skinny. But is that a reason to do something crazy?"

"Janice...what we did today...well, it's hard for a guy to admit this, but that was the first time for me."

After a long pause, Janice answered. "Look, Skinny, I think you're just really upset right now. Why don't you go back home and we'll talk about this again tomorrow, okay?"

As he listened, a chill passed through Skinny.

"Janice...It was the first time for you, right?"

There was another long pause. "Does that really matter?" Janice asked softly.

Skinny stared dully at the phone. The seconds passed in silence. "No, Janice. Not anymore," he finally said.

He slowly put the phone back in its cradle, walked out of the phone booth and vomited into the gutter.

❖ ❖ ❖

Like someone walking in his sleep, Skinny started down the street, pillowcase slung over his good shoulder. He had no destination in mind, just an urge to be somewhere else—anywhere else. So he simply walked, staring down at his shadow under the streetlights, step following step until he lost track of time.

When Skinny looked up again, he was across the street from Wynwood.

For the first time since breaking his collarbone, he managed a weak smile. Just like returning a kick, his instincts were leading him out of trouble.

Walking into the park, he saw a group of longhairs near the bleachers. As he got closer, Skinny spotted Loco among them.

Would Loco be upset that he'd stayed away so long? It didn't matter anymore. He'd apologize to his friend, no matter what. He owed Loco that.

The guys by the bleachers turned toward him as he walked up.

"Skinny!" Loco yelled, a wide smile on his face. Then Loco's eyes widened as he noticed the sling on Skinny's arm. "What the hell happened?"

Skinny glanced at the guys surrounding Loco. "Can we talk—alone?"

"Sure, man," Loco answered, then turned to the group around him. "I'll get the material to you guys later, okay?"

The long hairs ambled away and the old friends sat down on the bleachers.

"*Que pasó?*" Loco asked after they were alone.

"Well, first off, I want to tell you that I've been an

asshole. I never should have—"

"Hold it, Skinny. You don't need to apologize for anything, man."

"No, let me finish. I acted like a prick, walking away from you like that at The Planet."

"No sweat, bro. I could see Janice was freaked out."

"That's not all," Skinny said, his eyes welling. "I should have come to see you when I heard about your mother. I'm really sorry, man."

Loco nodded. "Yeah, I missed you," he said softly. "They put me in a foster home in Hialeah after she died. But I split. You know me, man. I can take care of myself. And I know *you*, Skinny—maybe better than you know yourself. I figured you had your reasons for not coming around." Loco stopped and rubbed his chin. "Anyway, I'm glad to see you, man. With my mother gone, there's no one else I trust to always have my back," he said. "Now, tell me how you got busted up."

For the next hour, Skinny opened his heart to his friend. He told Loco everything that had happened—except for his moments on the beach with Janice. That was just between the two of them.

When Skinny was done, Loco said, "So what are you going to do?"

Skinny shook his head. "I don't know, man."

"Look, Skinny. If I have a roof, you have a roof. If I have a dollar, you have a dollar. You understand?"

Skinny closed his eyes tightly, trying to hold back tears, "*Gracias, mi hermano.*"

"You look like shit, man," Loco said, laughing softly. "Let's get over to my place so you can crash. It's probably going to be noisy as hell, but I don't think you're gonna care."

"What do you mean?"

"C'mon. I've got a car. I'll tell you on the way."

❖ ❖ ❖

"Where'd you get the car?" Skinny asked Loco from the passenger's seat of the blue Corvair.

"It's Beverly's—the girl I was with at The World. You remember?"

"Yeah, I remember. A brunette. Kinda skinny."

"That's Beverly. She works as a barmaid, but she's really cool," Loco said as he drove north from the park. "She's heavy into the head scene. The commune was her idea."

"Commune?"

"It's a cool scene, man," Loco said proudly. "Freaks from all over Miami are crashing there—a lot of them are chicks."

A few minutes later, Loco parked near a duplex on 40th Street. "The commune's around back," he said, getting out of the car. As they walked past a GTO parked across the street, Loco nodded to a pair of shadowy figures inside. He then led Skinny to a small windowless building behind the duplex that might have once been a one-car garage.

Nearing the door, Skinny could hear the muffled strains of *Manic Depression* by Jimi Hendrix. When Loco opened the door, the music assaulted him.

Entering the room, Skinny squinted into the darkness. Under the dim purple glow of an ultraviolet tube on the ceiling, Skinny could see at least a dozen bodies sprawled on an assortment of bare mattresses on the floor. Iridescent day-glo posters covered the walls. Rising above the bodies was the room's only furniture: an altar of cinder blocks enshrining a stereo turntable flanked by speakers blasting the Hendrix tune. The scent of cigarettes, reefer and sweat hung heavy in the air.

A few faces turned their way as Loco and Skinny stepped over the bodies, their teeth and eyeballs glowing an eerie pale violet in the UV light.

Loco gestured to an empty spot on one of the mattresses. "Here's a place where you can crash, man," he shouted over the music, patting Skinny's back. "Get some rest. I'll be back later."

With Loco gone, Skinny looked around for a friendly face. Everyone ignored him. It felt like being on a crowded bus full of strangers—except that most of the strangers were smoking dope or making out.

Exhausted, still foggy from the painkillers and drained of all feelings, Skinny curled up on the mattress. Before long, he was asleep amid the din, clutching the pillowcase that held everything he owned.

❖ ❖ ❖

Skinny opened his eyes, trying to get his bearings. The ultraviolet tube on the ceiling brought him back to reality—such as it was. It might be morning. Without any windows, he couldn't tell. The only sound was the soft hum of the still-spinning turntable.

Rolling over for a better look around, a sharp pain ripped through his shoulder. The anesthetics had worn off.

Now facing the other way, he saw Loco lying near him among the sprawl of bodies. Snuggled against his friend was Beverly, her arm draped across Loco's chest.

Sensing Skinny's movements, Beverly opened her eyes. She glared at Skinny for a moment. Then she shook Loco's shoulder, waking him up.

"How long is *he* going to be here?" she asked Loco, jutting her chin toward Skinny.

"As long as he wants," Loco mumbled, eyes barely open.

Scowling, Beverly rolled over, turning her back on them.

Loco yawned and looked at the watch on a wide leather band around his wrist. "Shit. I've got to get going. It's almost noon," he said, then rose and headed for the bathroom.

A few of the others began to stir. By the time Loco came back, someone had put an album on the turntable. The Doors' *Break on Through* welcomed Skinny to a new day. The only concession to morning was the volume. You could at least speak without screaming.

"I've got some business to do," Loco told Skinny. "I

should be back before dark."

A blond guy with shoulder-length hair called out to Loco from the other side of the small room. "God's children need some breakfast, man,"

Loco reached into his jeans and pulled out a few crumpled bills. "This is all the bread I've got, Joel," he said handing over the money. "I should have some more later," he said before heading out the door.

"Who wants to make a run to the Mayflower for donuts?" Joel called out.

A chubby brunette with bad skin said, "I'll go."

"Far out, Shelly," Joel replied, holding out the cash.

With Loco gone, Skinny could see that Joel was in charge.

The blond had the whole hippie look down pat. Along with his flowing hair, Joel wore a fringed leather vest over a tie-dyed tee, beads and bracelets, elephant bells, and Indian moccasins. Most of the others in the room were not as fully decked out in regulation flower child gear.

As Skinny watched Joel, they made eye contact. The blond stared back at Skinny like he'd just noticed dog shit on his moccasins.

Without Loco around, Skinny felt awkward and out-of-place, like someone who had stumbled into a party uninvited.

The party was just beginning.

❖ ❖ ❖

When he saw Beverly leave for work in a dress, Skinny knew it was nearly nighttime. Without a clock or windows, it was his only clue.

Since Loco had left, he'd dozed restlessly, his shoulder aching every time he moved. But that wasn't the worst of it.

He'd become the commune's resident leper. People kept their distance and avoided making eye-contact or speaking to him. Skinny wasn't surprised, though.

204 Raul Ramos y Sanchez

His Ivy League haircut and straight leg jeans stood out among the long hairs. The sling and bulky brace that made him look like a hunchback didn't help either. *Maybe they think a broken collarbone is contagious*, he mused.

He was also hungry. No one had offered him any of the donuts Shelly had brought back. He'd grabbed two glazed crullers out of the bag anyway. They were the only thing he'd eaten since lunch the day before.

The cold shoulder he'd been getting—and the gnawing in his belly—finally trumped the pain of moving and Skinny went out to look for Loco. Fortunately, the redhead was not far away.

Loco was near the same GTO they'd walked past last night, talking to the two guys inside. The driver was thin with a shiny, Elvis-style pompadour. Beside him was a stocky, square-headed guy with a burr. The three of them noticed Skinny and Loco waved him over. As he walked closer, Skinny noticed the sloppy paint job on the car.

"Hey, Loco. This boy don't look like the other hippies in your commune," the driver said in a Stars and Bars drawl. "You letting normal people in these days?"

Loco laughed. "Well, if by normal you mean hopelessly uncool 'sumbiches like you, I guess he's normal. This is Skinny. We go all the way back to our Little League days."

"Well, uncool or not, it's good to see a guy around here who don't look like my aunt Mildred," the driver said. "My friends call me Fabian and this here knucklehead is my brother Boo."

Skinny nodded a greeting. "You guys from Georgia?"

Fabian smiled. "Shit no, son! We ain't no red-clay-stomping crackers, We're from Paducah."

Skinny looked puzzled.

"That's in Kentucky," Boo added.

"So what happened to *you*, boy?" Boo said, pointing at Skinny's sling. "You get your arm broke in a wild orgy with them teeny-boppers in the commune?"

The brothers laughed, showing several gold teeth.

"It's a long story," Skinny said.

"Well, maybe you can tell us all about it sometime, Skinny. Right now, we've got to git," Fabian said, starting the GTO. "Y'all take care, now."

Watching the sedan rumble away, Skinny said, "They seem like nice guys. Those are the first friendly people I've met since I got here."

Loco laughed softly. "Yeah? Well, before you start getting chummy with Fabian and Boo, I'm going to let you in on something—for your own good," he said. "Everybody calls them the Romilar Brothers. They live out of that GTO and they holdup 7-11s and gas stations for a living."

"What?" Skinny said, mouth gaping.

"You can always tell when they've pulled another job 'cause they repaint the car," Loco said, then smiled. "That GTO's been more colors than a five-dollar crayon box—and the cheap 'sumbiches always use house paint and brushes."

"Why do they called them the Romilar Brothers?"

"Oh, I forgot that part, didn't I? They like to get high on Romilar cough syrup. It's cheaper than liquor—and it will really kick your ass."

"So why are *you* friendly with these guys?" Skinny asked.

"The brothers are like junkyard dogs, man. They protect the commune."

"If they're robbers, aren't you worried they'll rip *you* off?"

"The stashes we keep around are small potatoes to the brothers. The reason they hang around is for the girls."

Skinny shook his head. "Goddam, Loco. This is crazy."

"Look, Skinny. What I just told you stays between us, okay? Fabian and Boo act friendly and all. But they'll hurt anybody that gets them busted. So keep your mouth shut about this."

Skinny looked at the pavement. He had a lot to learn about this place. Do something stupid around here and a broken collarbone might be the least of your problems.

OCTOBER

Colonel Sanders Meets the Plastic Lackey

The chicken bones were piling up fast.

Sitting cross-legged on the floor, Skinny tossed another bone into the grease-stained paper bag in front of him. A picked-clean femur was all that remained of the second thigh Skinny had devoured in the last five minutes.

He sat in a circle with more than a dozen other commune members, all gorging on Kentucky Fried Chicken. Most of them had not eaten for days.

Skinny reached stiffly for one of the buckets of chicken in the center of the circle and fished out a drumstick. Three weeks after breaking his collarbone, he didn't need the sling anymore. But the shoulder brace remained and moving freely or lifting anything heavy without excruciating pain was impossible.

After taking a bite of the drumstick, Skinny turned toward Loco. "How much did you pay for all this chicken, man?" he asked, gesturing toward the three white cardboard containers glowing lavender under the UV lights.

"Nine bucks and some change," Loco answered, "Why do you wanna know?"

"Look, I know I've only been here a few weeks, and I don't work or anything—"

"How the hell are you supposed to work, Skinny?" Loco interrupted. "Your shoulder's still busted up."

Skinny nodded, aware that Loco had said that for everyone else to hear. "I know I can't work yet," he said. "But maybe I can help by figuring out how we can keep from going hungry so much."

The comment seemed to touch a nerve. Some hard looks turned Skinny's way—especially from Joel and Beverly.

"What are you talking about?" Loco asked, chomping on another wing

"Well, first of all, the problem isn't really money. You bring in cash all the time, Loco. And Billy and Slade have jobs. But we always blow the money right away and a few days later, everybody's going hungry. So instead of buying fried chicken and pizzas and burgers, why don't we stock up on cheaper food that'll last the whole week? Stuff like eggs and beans and grits."

Joel wiped his mouth on his wrist and sneered. "Man, that is so plastic."

"Sorry, man," Skinny said, rolling his eyes, "I didn't know being smart with money broke some kind of hippie law."

Joel stared down his short, narrow nose at Skinny and said, "God always takes care of his children, man. We don't need a bunch of tight-assed rules."

Skinny glared back at Joel. "So you'd rather blow all our money and then go hungry?"

"Look, man," Joel said, "if you don't like it, why don't you take your plastic attitude somewhere else, okay?"

Before Skinny could answer, Loco spoke up. "Hey, Joel. It's cool, man. It's cool," he said softly. Loco then pulled a baggie from his pocket. "Look...I scored some Colombian last night that's supposed to be outasite. You want to take a taste?"

"Far out!" Joel said, "Where's the pipe, Shelly?"

Skinny tossed the rest of his drumstick into the bag and retreated from the clot of bodies forming around the bag of weed. The redhead had managed to break up his fight with Joel, which was fine with Skinny. But he had no interest in the reefer.

Getting high made him feel worse, not better. The few times he'd toked up, Skinny had dwelled on all the things he wanted to forget—Janice, his family, his teammates and his lost chances for a scholarship.

But his life in the commune didn't offer much hope either. Although food was scarce, there never seemed to be a shortage of dope, albums, or cigarettes.

Joel's voice rose from the other side of the room. "That's some righteous shit, man!" he said, exhaling a large cloud of smoke. While Joel continued toking, Loco rose from the circle and motioned for Skinny to follow him outside.

As they stepped into the sunshine, Loco said, "Sorry about the hassle with Joel. I know he can be an asshole sometimes."

"I've got to tell you, man," Skinny said. "Things aren't fair around here. I mean, Billy Weeks works his ass off at the marina and gives away all his money. But he gets treated like dirt 'cause he talks like a cracker. And then you've got Joel who doesn't do shit to help anybody out but acts like he's the fucking pope of the hippies. That's not right, bro."

"Look, Skinny. Joel is popular with a lot of people—and they're people who buy what I sell. You understand?" Loco said calmly.

Skinny nodded. "Yeah, I guess so," he said, looking at the ground. "Hell, it's not like I'm bringing in any money either."

"I know you will when you can, bro," Loco said, then added. "There's something I've been meaning to tell you...I heard your father's been asking around for you at Wynwood."

Skinny stared at the ground, letting the news sink in.

He was happy to know his family missed him. Truth was, he missed them too. But there was no way he'd go back, no matter how hard things got. He'd sworn they'd never see him again.

Pápi can go fuck himself," he said.

❖   ❖   ❖

It was Saturday night and the commune was rocking. Sprawled on the bare mattresses were over two dozen young bodies in every shade of skin from vanilla to dark chocolate. Most were doing pot, hash, speed, downers, acid, or coke through an assortment of pipes, papers, pills, rolled bills and tiny spoons. The rest were either comatose or writhing in various stages of passion. Except for Skinny.

Seated with his back against the wall, he was reading a dog-eared paperback copy of *Valley of the Dolls* by the light of a Christmas tree bulb dangling from his neck.

A guy in pink glasses snorting a line of blow bumped against Skinny, knocking the bulb into his lap. "Sorry, man," he yelled over the music before hitting another line.

Skinny sighed and readjusted the light. His makeshift reading setup worked well enough on most nights in the dimly-lit commune. But this was a Saturday. "The hippie population doubles on weekends," Loco had told him shortly after Skinny had moved in. The wall-to-wall bodies in the small room were proof of Loco's point.

Starting the novel's fifth chapter, Skinny was startled by someone stroking his thigh. Looking up, he saw Shelly.

She leaned close, her breath warm on his ear. "You look lost in that book," she said over the music, still stroking his leg. "What's it about?"

Although this was the first time Shelly had paid him any attention, Skinny was not surprised. She was a runaway from juvi who had slept her way down the ladder of the commune's regulars. Now, she'd reached the lowest rung. Still, her caresses on his leg were hard to ignore.

"I found the book in a trash pile—which is where it belongs," he said nervously, then shrugged. "But it's all I've got to read."

"You ever interested in anything but reading?" she said, her hand rising higher on his thigh.

Skinny's breathing grew short as a civil war of urges broke out inside him. Lorenzo rose to attention, the conflict's first volunteer.

Shelly's come-on was hard to resist. After weeks of neglect, his nerve endings were screaming for attention. But would giving in to Shelly mean betraying Janice? And what kind of loyalty did he owe Janice anyway?

The civil war ended quickly.

"Shelly!" Joel called out, lying a few bodies away. "Want to try some Moroccan hash?" he said, holding up a pipe.

"Far out!" Shelly said, crawling over Skinny toward Joel.

After waiting for Lorenzo's return to parade rest, Skinny walked outside.

The moon was playing peek-a-boo with a band of silver clouds. Skinny sat by the door, staring at the sky, numb and empty.

After a long time, Skinny saw a familiar figure walking toward the door. Loco greeted him with nod. "What's up, man?" he asked. "You out catching a moon tan?"

"Something like that," Skinny said absently, rising to his feet.

"Far out. I've been waiting till we had some time alone to tell you ... I'm going to be away for a while—on business."

"How long before you're back?"

"Hard to say ... a few days ... maybe a week."

"Where are you going?"

"You don't want to know."

"What's the matter, man. Don't you trust me?"

"I trust you, Skinny. I'm just trying to keep you out of trouble. The less you know, the better."

"Then why did you bother telling me?" Skinny said

irritably.

"I need a favor," Loco said, pulling a folded envelope from his pocket. "If for some reason, something happens to me, I need you to give this to Chucho," he said, holding out the envelope.

Skinny shook his head. "I'm not going to help you do this, Loco. Not if there's a chance you could get hurt."

"Nothing's going to happen, man. This is just an insurance policy," Loco said. "I need you to do this, Skinny. There's nobody else I can trust."

Skinny sighed and put the envelope in his pocket. "Fine, I'll do it," he said. "But if you get killed, I swear I'm going to piss on your grave."

Loco laughed. "If this business trip goes bad, you might have to get in line."

❖ ❖ ❖

The argument with Joel began just before midnight—this one because Skinny did not agree the Grateful Dead were a better band than the Beatles. Furious that Skinny had once again openly questioned the commune's high priest of hipness, Joel huddled with Beverly in a corner.

Not long after, Beverly turned off the music and made an announcement. "Skinny is putting out bad vibes and bringing everybody down," she said stiffly. "Me and Joel think he should leave." Without Loco around, the others in the commune reluctantly agreed.

Skinny stared at his accusers for a moment, then slowly packed his pillow case and walked out, head held high.

Alone on the street, his resolve evaporated. *Why can't I fit in?* he asked himself. He had clashed with his family, with Janice, and now with everyone in the commune. *At least Loco believes in me,* he reminded himself, patting the envelope in his pocket. But that meant he had to stay close to the commune. There was no other way to keep up with any news of Loco.

Wandering dejectedly along the sidewalk, he spotted a sofa dumped in a trash pile by the curb. The couch was torn and threadbare but otherwise seemed clean. *What the hell,* he thought. *I'm not going to find a better place to crash tonight.*

Adjusting his shoulder brace, Skinny laid down and closed his eyes, trying to shut out the world. *I'll figure out what to do in the morning* he told himself, drifting into a fitful sleep.

A tap on the shoulder roused Skinny. Backlit by the glare of the streetlight, Skinny saw the boxy outline of Boo's head.

"You hungry?" the Romilar brother asked.

Skinny looked around, trying to get his bearings. "Huh?"

"Are you hungry?"

"Yeah," Skinny said finally. No one in the commune had eaten since yesterday. Their money for the week had already been blown.

"Good. Me and Fabian are hungry too," Boo said, his voice slurred. "C'mon, boy. Let's go get us something to eat."

Warily, Skinny picked up his pillowcase and followed Boo as he staggered toward the GTO parked a half-block away. The Romilar brothers were armed robbers—a group not known for their generosity. But the emptiness in his stomach voted down Skinny's qualms.

When they reached the GTO, Boo opened the driver's door and motioned for Skinny to get in. "You drive, son."

"My shoulder's still busted," Skinny said, patting his brace. "It might be safer if you drove."

"Trust me, boy," Fabian said woozily from the back seat. "We'll do a damn sight better with you driving."

Now Skinny understood why the brothers had asked him along. They were too stoned to drive. *Well, where else am I gonna find a meal right now?* he asked himself, sliding carefully into the car.

Starting the sedan and testing its power steering, Skinny

was relieved. At least he could drive without pain. "Where are we going?" he said after Boo got in the front seat beside him.

"Just drive. We'll tell you," Fabian answered.

Skinny pulled away from the curb. Under the car's headlights, the late-night streets looked still and gray. *Like a dead man*, he fretted.

"Gimme a hit, bro," Boo said reaching toward the back seat. Fabian passed his brother a smallish brown bottle. Boo took a long pull of Romilar, smacked his lips, and handed it back.

Fabian tapped Skinny on the shoulder. "Turn left up there on 2nd."

"2nd Avenue? We want to get there before daylight, don't we?" Boo said to his brother, then turned to Skinny. "Go on up to 7th."

"Don't listen to him, Skinny. Our momma rotted his brain with all the bourbon in her titty milk."

"Uh-huh. And what about you, Einstein? Didn't you have the same momma?"

"Momma raised me on formula. 'Bout the time you come along, she was too broke to buy it. So all you got was T–I–T."

"Well, if momma *did* have bourbon in her titty milk, it was 'cause she was never sober again after having a baby as ugly as you."

"Fuck you, Boo Fugate. Momma shoulda killed *you* in your sleep instead of her last boyfriend."

When Skinny turned on 2nd, Boo rolled his eyes but didn't complain. After a couple of more turns, they approached a darkened gas station.

"Pull in here," Fabian ordered.

"This place is closed," Skinny said, stopping the GTO by a gas pump. "How are we supposed to eat here?"

"Hush up," Boo said before stumbling out of the car holding a piece of wire and a grocery bag. "I'll be back in a minute," he said over his shoulder.

A soda vending machine stood against the station's outside wall and Boo went to work on it with the wire. Skinny couldn't see what Boo was doing but a few seconds later the machine came to life. With a loud clatter, it began spewing coins, one-by-one. Skinny cringed as each coin rattled through the machine's metallic guts. *Clink, clank, clunk! Clink, clank, clunk!*

Laughing, Boo tried to catch the stream of coins in the grocery bag, missing most of them. Despite the cool night breeze, Skinny began to sweat. *How could somebody not hear this?* he wondered.

To Skinny's relief, the noise stopped after a few seconds. "C'mon, man! Let's get out of here!" he called out to Boo.

After calmly picking up the coins on the ground, Boo got into the car. "This ain't enough, goddamit," he said, tossing the bag on the floor.

Skinny sped away from the gas station, trying not to squeal the tires and draw attention.

"You wanna knock over a store?" Boo asked his brother.

Skinny's heart, already thumping hard, began to rattle like a drum roll.

"Naw, we're too fucked up," Fabian answered. "Besides, we don't want to pop Skinny's cherry on a stick up."

Skinny exhaled, his sense of relief nearly orgasmic. "Well, at least we've got enough money to buy some burgers," he said, pointing to the bag of coins on the floor.

"We still need more," Fabian said. After another slug of Romilar, he began directing Skinny to a new destination.

A few minutes later, they reached a shabby two-story motel near the bay. "We hit this one a couple of times before. It's usually loaded," Fabian said as Skinny stopped at the edge of dimly-lit parking lot full of clunkers. "There it is, next to the stairs" he said, pointing to a vending machine against a ground floor wall lined with doors.

"Stay here where they can't see the plates and keep the

motor running," Boo told Skinny before walking unsteadily toward the motel. After a few steps, Skinny could barely make out Boo in the darkness. Moments later, the *clink, clank, clunk* began.

I'm going to regret this, Skinny thought. Getting into a car in the middle of the night with two stoned felons was incredibly stupid. As he stared into the gloom, visions of being handcuffed and put into a squad car crept into Skinny's mind.

A sudden burst of light made him wince. Someone had switched on the motel's flood lights, turning the area into daylight.

As Skinny's eyes adjusted, he spotted Boo desperately stumbling toward the car like two drunks in a sack race. Behind Boo, a man in boxer briefs stood in a doorway. "Call the police, Muriel!" the man yelled.

Trembling and ready to drive away, Skinny felt the cold, hard barrel of a gun against his neck. "Now, Skinny. Don't you even think about leaving 'till Boo's in the car," Fabian said calmly.

Suddenly, Skinny's fear of going to jail took a back seat to staying alive.

With Boo finally inside, Skinny floored the GTO and fled out of the parking lot, tires squealing. There was no point in stealth now.

"No, no, no! Slow down, boy!" Fabian yelled. "Turn right on Biscayne," he ordered. Still shaking, Skinny steered the GTO onto one of the few busy streets at this time of night. "Now just blend in with the traffic, nice and easy." Skinny realized Fabian was right. There was safety in numbers.

Cruising for a while among the other cars, Skinny calmed down enough for his hunger to return. "There's a Royal Castle coming up and the burgers there are cheap. How about we go there?" he asked, trying not to sound like he was pleading.

Fabian's answer surprised Skinny. "We heard you got

kicked out of the commune."

"How did you know? That just happened."

"Hey, we're fucked up a lot," Boo said, then gulped down another shot of Romilar just to prove his point. "But we keep an eye on what's going on."

"That's how we stay out of jail," Fabian added, tapping a finger to his head. "Anyway, Loco asked us to look out for you. He figured that little prick Joel would try to kick you out of the commune once he was gone."

Skinny turned to face Fabian. "You know where Loco is?"

"Never mind about that. And watch where you're driving," Fabian said. "The reason we need more money is to get you back in the commune. See, if you walk in there tomorrow morning with a couple of bags of donuts, they'll take you back," he said, then added, "although I still don't know why you and Loco want to live with all those weirdoes—except maybe for the pussy."

Skinny swallowed hard, his eyes welling. Loco had come through for him again. At least his childhood friend—and now two armed robbers—still had his back. "You guys are all right," he said, voice breaking with emotion.

"Now don't get all mushy on us," Fabian said, hitting the cough syrup again.

"Yeah, we still got to knock over at least one more pop machine," Boo added.

Skinny was calmer this time as Boo hit the jackpot with a vending machine outside a laundromat. Hefting the bag of coins they'd collected, Boo decided they now had enough.

A short while later, Skinny pulled the GTO into the all-night Mayflower Coffee Shop at 36th and Miami Avenue. With Skinny in tow, the brothers staggered inside and slumped into a corner booth. As Skinny sat down, Boo emptied the bag of coins on the countertop and began counting them. He lost track and had to start again several times.

An aging waitress arrived and looked at the coins with a wry smile. "Did you boys rob a juke box?"

Skinny stiffened, certain they'd been busted.

Fabian stared foggily at the waitress for a long moment. Then he smiled. "Why yes, ma'am. We did," he said before both brothers burst into laughter.

The waitress joined in the laughter as she took their order—three burgers and fries along with two dozen donuts to go.

The next morning, Skinny was welcomed back to the commune.

❖ ❖ ❖

The haul from the trash piles had been poor today. All Skinny had managed to salvage so far from the random heaps of refuse dumped along the curb in the neighborhood was a soggy month-old issue of *Life*. Without a television or radio in the commune, printed material from trash piles had become Skinny's only source of entertainment—and his lifeline to news from the outside world.

Then, in a mound of dead palm fronds held down by a bald tire and a broken baby crib, he spotted a prize: some pages from the *Miami Herald*.

Flipping through the two-day-old newspaper, Skinny saw the sports section. On page two was an article about Jackson. His school had won against Hialeah, the fourth win of the season against two losses.

Skinny rubbed his eyes with the back of his hand, trying to hold back the tears. Over eight weeks had passed since he'd broken his collarbone. The doctor had told him that's how long he'd take to heal. If he'd stayed at home and gone to school, he might be starting the next game.

Pulling off his shirt, Skinny unfastened his brace and threw into the trash pile. He then tossed the newspaper back into the trash as well. *That life's behind me know*, he told himself before walking away.

Later that day, Loco returned.

Skinny was reading his new magazine in the shade of the mango tree next to the commune when he saw the redhead approaching.

"Hey, do you know where I can find my friend, Quasimodo?" Loco called out, noticing the missing brace.

Skinny ran to Loco and bear-hugged him. "You fucking lunatic. I'm glad to see you."

"You worry too much, Skinny. I told you I'd be back."

"Here," Skinny said, pulling the envelope from his pocket and handing it to Loco. "Take back whatever this is, man—and don't do something this crazy again."

Loco tucked the envelope away. "You're not going to ask me what's inside?"

"Would you tell me?"

Loco smiled. "You can be a real *burro* sometimes, Skinny. But after a while, you catch on."

Skinny stepped back and looked at his friend. "You look tanned, man. You sure this wasn't a vacation instead of work?"

"I spent some time on the water, but believe me, it was all work. Anyway, the trip was worth it, man. Look," he said slipping a thick wad of bills out of his pocket. "We're gonna live better now. You'll see."

Many Unhappy Returns

Someone had fixed the large cracks in the apartment's windows with duct tape. The badly-worn linoleum tiles were curled and peeling away. The walls, long ago painted landlord-white, were now grimy and gouged. A bare bulb stared down like a prison guard from the ceiling.

Most people would have called the vacant, one-room apartment a rat hole. To Skinny, it was heaven.

Sitting in a sunbeam on a piece of cardboard and reading *The Diary of Anne Frank*, Skinny was relishing the light—and the silence.

Shortly after Loco's return two weeks ago, the commune had moved into an apartment across the hall. The commune's new home in this two-story building was a step up from the converted garage on 40th Street. The load of cash Loco brought back had paid for the move.

At first, Skinny was thrilled. The new place had windows and more space. But Joel had quickly ended Skinny's hopes of living someplace less gloomy. Their conversation that day was still fresh in Skinny's mind.

"These white walls gotta go," Joel decreed as the group

looked over the apartment for the first time. "I know where we can get some black paint cheap. We'll find some cardboard, paint it black, and cover the windows, too."

Skinny sighed heavily. "I suppose you're going to hang the black light and put up the concert posters again,"

"What's your problem, man?" Joel said irritably.

"I don't see why we have to conform to this whole hippie decorating thing. It's depressing."

Joel's face reddened. "We are *not* conforming!" he said. "We do it this way because we *like* it!"

Skinny stared at Joel for a moment, then said, "Yeah, I'm sure the housewives in Coral Gables say the same thing about their Early American furniture."

In the end, Joel won out. The windows were covered, the walls were painted black and the UV light and posters went up. The new apartment became a roomier version of the cavern they'd just left. Ever since, the vacant apartment across the hall had become Skinny's haven from the noise and the gloom.

He'd thought about leaving the commune and had come close several times. But the guilt of neglecting Loco after his mother's death held Skinny like a yoke. He could not abandon his friend again.

Finally able to work, Skinny had found a job cleaning the excrement of exotic animals at a pet shop wholesaler. He'd spent most of his first paycheck stocking the shelves of the kitchenette with staples. The look on Joel's face had been just as satisfying as no longer going hungry.

The sound of footsteps in the hall brought Skinny back to the present.

A swarthy guy with tightly-cropped hair stood in the doorway. He was painfully thin, his shoulder bones jutting sharply below a dirty gray sweatshirt. "Who the fuck are you?" he said.

Skinny thought he recognized the face under the scraggly beard. "Felix?" he asked, rising to his feet.

The guy stared back warily. Then his eyes widened. "Skinny?"

"Yeah, it's me."

Does he still hate me? Skinny wondered. One thing was sure. Felix wasn't the big, scary bully he'd been in the fourth grade. Skinny now stood eye to eye with Felix and seemed beefy in comparison—although Skinny had lost nearly fifteen pounds since moving into the commune.

To Skinny's surprise, Felix grinned. "What are you doing here, man?"

"I live across the hall."

"Oh, so you're one of the flower children, huh?"

Skinny realized that after two months without a haircut, he was starting to look like one. "I moved in with Loco a while back," Skinny said, trying to distance himself from the rest of the commune. "What are you up to?"

"Me and my homeboys just rented this place, man."

❖ ❖ ❖

Since moving in across the hall last week, Felix and the two guys who shared his apartment—Berto and Sonny—had been hanging around the commune. There was no mistaking the newcomers among the commune's flower children, however.

Felix and his cohorts kept their hair military-short. But the differences went deeper. Unlike the slow, slouching hippies, their new neighbors' movements were quick and purposeful—their eyes hard and darting. Both groups had one interest in common, though ... drugs.

Tonight, Felix and his boys were sitting in a circle around a hookah along with Loco and a few others from the commune. In the water pipe was some Lebanese hash Loco had scored earlier that day.

The hookah gurgled loudly as Loco sucked down a monster hit through the hose from the tall water pipe. The chunks of hashish in the clay bowl glowed bright red and then dimmed as Loco finally filled his lungs.

"*Oye*, Loco. Let me know when you're get tired of messing around with this pussy shit," Felix said, nodding toward the water pipe. "I can hook you up with something *for real*, man."

Loco finally exhaled. "What the fuck are you talking about, Felix?" Loco said, his eyes bloodshot. "That's some kick-ass hash, man."

"Shit," Felix scoffed. "You don't know what a real high is, man."

"You got something better?"

Watching from outside the circle, Skinny did not like where this was going. He knew Loco well. The redhead had a macho streak when it came to drugs. No amount was ever too much—or so Loco wanted everyone to believe. The redhead was already high. This was not a good time to prove how fearless he could be.

"Here, try a taste of this, man," Felix said pulling a small packet of tin foil from his pocket.

"What is it?" Loco asked.

"What's the matter, Loco?" Felix said, raising an eyebrow. "You scared of a *real* high?"

"Scared? Are you shitting me? Bring it on, bro," Loco said. He then reached for a small, brass pipe leaning against the wall. "Let's fire it up."

Skinny leaned toward Loco and tugged on his shoulder. "*Oye*, Loco. You don't even know what that shit is, man."

Loco shoved Skinny's hand away. "Stay out of this, man," he said. Loco then took the foil packet from Felix's hand and carefully placed the powder in the bowl of the small pipe.

Felix handed Loco a lighter. "Do it up, man."

Loco struck a flame, brought it to the powder and inhaled deeply. For several seconds he drew in the fumes, closing his eyes in the effort. Then he held in the smoke, letting it steep into his lungs before exhaling slowly.

When Loco's eyes finally opened, he seemed to be staring at a horizon very far away. He swayed from side to side, threw back his head and let himself fall onto the mattress.

"Far fucking out," Loco muttered staring at the ceiling, a look of stupefied bliss on his face.

"What did you give him. Felix?" Skinny said angrily.

"Whatever it is," Shelly said reaching for the small brass pipe, "I want some, too."

1967

NOVEMBER

The Horse Leaves its Tracks

Everything in the commune seemed normal as Skinny arrived from work. The regulars were sprawled in their usual places and, as always, they ignored him.

Eager to shed the smell of monkey dung still clinging to him, Skinny stepped over the bodies on the mattresses, grabbed a change of clothes from his pillowcase, and headed to the bathroom for a shower.

The bathroom door was locked, nothing unusual. So he waited.

Moments later, Skinny heard the toilet flush and Joel walked out, zipping up his fly. He threw a hard look Skinny's way before leaving.

What Skinny saw next, he would never forget.

Loco was slumped inside the clawfoot tub, barely conscious. A thin rubber hose was coiled above his elbow. On the mildewed floor tiles near the tub lay a dagger-like hypodermic.

Skinny ran inside. "Loco! Loco!" he said, shaking him gently. "Hey, man. Are you okay?"

"Skinny? Is that you?" Loco said, his eyes fluttering and

unfocused.

"Yeah, it's me."

"Skinny, this is *the* fucking trip, man. It's like acid, pot, and pussy all rolled into one."

After helping Loco out of the bathtub, Skinny led him to a spot on one of the mattresses. Sitting down beside Loco, Skinny stared at his unconscious friend.

Loco's fall into mainlining had been brutally quick. But looking back, Skinny had to admit he was not surprised. Loco would not back down from anyone or anything.

After smoking Felix's heroin for the first time from the hookah three weeks ago, Loco had gone back for more the next day. Before long, all Loco's attention was on scoring horse.

Felix was not giving it away anymore but Loco didn't care. In a very short time, the money from Loco's trip went up in smoke. Loco then stepped up the number of deals in pot, hash, and acid to make more cash for the smack.

That Loco would switch from a pipe to a needle seemed only a matter of time. He pushed everything to the edge—and that came with a price.

Still, that didn't lessen Skinny's pain.

Hours later, Loco finally woke up.

"So you're mainlining now, Loco," Skinny said, bringing his friend some water. "What comes after this, man?"

"Skinny, this feels so good, I really don't give a shit."

1967
DECEMBER

Guns among the flowers

When *Sunshine of Your Love* stopped in the middle of a Ginger Baker drum riff, Skinny bolted upright. Every head in the commune snapped toward the turntable, startled by the sudden silence. Something had to be wrong. The music never stopped on a Saturday night.

After lifting the needle from the Cream album, Beverly faced the group packed into the black-walled apartment. "Loco and Felix..." she said breathlessly, "they tried to hold up a 7-11 ... Felix shot the clerk."

Joel waved Beverly over and handed her a joint. "Toke up, baby," he said. "You need to calm down."

As anxious conversations broke out across the room, Skinny made his way to Beverly. "How did you hear about this?" he asked, hoping she might be wrong.

"Felix's roommate Berto told me," Beverly said, her hands trembling.

"Where's Loco now?"

"I don't know," she said, tears starting to flow. "Berto wouldn't say."

"Maybe Berto's right," Skinny answered. "The fewer

people who know where Loco is, the better."

"Why don't you get lost, man?" Joel said. "She doesn't need your stupid advice."

"I'm just trying to help. I've known Loco longer than any of you."

Joel's eyes narrowed. "Well, since he became a junkie, Loco's become a real drag, man."

Skinny stared at Joel for a moment, then punched him in the mouth.

Joel dropped to the floor, covering his face.

"You've had that coming for a long time, asshole," Skinny said, then walked out of the apartment.

Alone on the street, an urge to leave the commune hit Skinny again. The place had been a bad fit from the beginning. But he pushed the thought aside. He couldn't abandon Loco now. Who else here would try to steer his friend away from more trouble?

Once again, the danger signs had been easy to spot.

The first gun Loco ever owned had appeared shortly after he started mainlining. The redhead had said he needed the pistol to protect their stash—which had become more valuable now that he was holding smack.

"What about the Romilar brothers?" Skinny asked. "Isn't that why you want them around?"

"Fabian and Boo got busted," Loco told him. "Boo was so fucked up, he backed the GTO into a cop car."

After he got the gun, Loco began huddling quietly with Felix and his boys. The four would then disappear, returning hours later, usually loaded with cash. The reason behind those absences were now easy to guess. Tonight's holdup must have gone bad somehow.

During his time in the commune, Skinny had come to learn that convenience store stickups were not rare. The police would take descriptions and look for any suspects during regular patrols. But when a shooting was involved, the cops put on the heat. The police would follow any lead looking for Loco and Felix—and somebody around the commune would talk.

Checking his pockets, Skinny counted seventeen dollars and some change. If he asked for an advance on his pay Monday morning, he'd have enough to buy bus tickets somewhere out of town for him and Loco.

The only thing to do now was go back to the commune and wait to hear from his friend.

When he returned to the apartment, Beverly was waiting for him. "I hope you're happy," she said bitterly. "Joel just left the commune."

Skinny almost smiled. It was the only good news he'd had in a long time.

❖ ❖ ❖

Something poking his leg woke Skinny up. Looking around, he saw Beverly standing above him, prodding his calf with her sandal.

"Loco wants to see you. He's outside in my car," Beverly said, an edge in her voice. "He said for you to bring all your stuff."

Skinny jumped to his feet, packed his pillowcase, and raced past the slim brunette toward the door of the apartment.

He had not seen Loco since the news of the holdup three days ago. *Looks like Loco has the same plan in mind*, Skinny thought, lugging the pillowcase. *We'll get out of town before the cops can find him.*

Running out into the night, Skinny scanned the street for Beverly's car. The blue Corvair was parked under a mango tree, hidden from the glare of the street lights. Through the shadows, he could see someone in the driver's seat.

Skinny sprinted to the car.

"Loco! It's good to see you, man!" he said through the passenger's window.

"Get in the car, Skinny," Loco said dryly.

After Skinny was inside, Loco started the engine and started down the empty street.

"Great minds work alike, bro!" Skinny said excitedly. "I've been saving my money so we can—"

"Shut up and listen," Loco interrupted, staring straight ahead. His eyes were sunken and lined. "I thought I knew you, Skinny. I thought you were my friend. But I should have known better. From the time I took you in—"

"Loco, what the hell are you talking about?"

"I said shut up, godammit!" Loco yelled. Skinny then watched in shock as Loco reached under the seat and pulled out his gun. Loco did not point the black pistol at him. He simply held the gun in his lap, steering with his right hand. There was no mistaking what Loco meant by the gesture. Skinny kept quiet.

"I put up with your shit when you first came here, Skinny—always giving me lectures about smoking too much pot or dropping too much acid," Loco said bitterly. "Listen, asshole, I don't need a sermon about drugs from some *pendejo* who can't smoke half a joint without getting all teary-eyed for his *mami*. You're a lot like your grandmother, Skinny—always bitching and trying to run other people's lives.

"But I could have lived with that, Skinny," Loco said. "I could have lived with that. It was stealing the money that was the final fucking straw."

"Loco, I don't know what you're—"

"Godammit, Skinny! I said shut up!" Loco screamed and rubbed the gun angrily against his leg. Skinny was silent again.

"Don't try to deny it. I know you took the money, man. Don't try to make a fool out of me by lying."

Loco spit out the window and then continued.

"I took you in, Skinny. I fed you when you couldn't work. I kept you in the commune when everybody else wanted to kick you out. I even tried to fix you up with chicks—although you always managed to blow it. And then you fucking stab me in the back, man. You steal my money while I'm away hiding from the cops." Loco shook his head in disgust. "If we hadn't been friends when we were kids, Skinny, I'd blow you away right now," he said with an icy glare.

Loco pulled the car over to the curb. Skinny looked out the window and was startled by what he saw outside. They were in front of his family's yellow bungalow on 33rd Street.

Loco turned to face Skinny for the first time since he'd entered the car. "Before I leave, Skinny, I'm going to promise you one thing... If I ever see you again—around me or anybody from the commune—I'm going to waste you, man. I'm going to fucking waste you. Do you understand me?"

Skinny stared back at his friend, not wanting to believe what he was hearing.

"DO YOU UNDERSTAND ME?" Loco screamed, clenching the gun so tightly that it quivered in his hand.

Skinny nodded his head.

"Now get the fuck out." Loco said flatly.

Skinny stepped out of the car, pillowcase in hand, and watched his best friend pull away into the darkness.

FEBRUARY

A New Line in the Water

Juan cast the fiberglass rod with a fluid sweep. The hook and sinker flew in a graceful arc, landing more than thirty feet away with a gentle splash in the shimmering water. Watching his father, Skinny was surprised at the old man's skill with a fishing pole.

"I never knew you fished, *Pápi*," Skinny told his father.

"Before you were born, my father used to take Panchito and me fly fishing. Actually, your mother asked me give it up. She thought fishing was coarse. The only fishermen she'd ever known were the poor devils who made a living out of their little dinghies in Oriente."

"I didn't know that."

"That makes us even. I didn't know about this fishing spot of yours before today either," Juan said, gesturing to the waters below the Julia Tuttle Causeway.

"I've been coming here since I was eleven," Skinny said, remembering his times here with Loco.

Over the years, the spot had given up a lot of fish... snook, jack, and the occasional sea trout—Skinny's unforgettable first catch. The fish had always been welcome at his family's table. But the most precious prize he and Loco had ever come away with was the bond they'd formed sitting together on the sea wall while the cars buzzed overhead.

Suddenly, Skinny felt awkward being here with his father. Maybe *Abuela's* suggestion that they go fishing together wasn't such a good idea.

Sure, his father had tried to reach out to him since he'd come home two months ago. But their new relationship was still shaky. Skinny fidgeted with his reel, uncomfortable with the silence building between them.

"So tell me, Victor. How is work at the hotel?" Juan asked, clearly making conversation. Shortly after returning home, Alicia had found Skinny a job as a bus boy at the Everglades.

"Tiring...boring...humiliating...but the hours work out well with school. They're going to let me keep the four to midnight shift. That'll let me finish my GED classes and keep the same hours for college."

"That's good. Have you decided on a major yet?" Juan asked, adjusting the slack in his line.

"The scholarship program at Miami-Dade doesn't offer many choices. I'm going to major in Business."

"That's a sound decision, *m'hijo*."

After a few seconds, Skinny realized it was his turn to keep the conversation going. "What about you, *Papi*? Are you happy with your work?"

"Yes, I am. Being an editor doesn't put much food on the table yet, but it's a start. The circulation of *Zig-Zag* is growing."

"Wasn't there a *Zig-Zag* magazine in Cuba?"

"You have a good memory, *m'hijo*. It was one of the first publications Castro banned when he took over. Now, it's the first weekly in Miami published in Spanish," Juan said with pride.

"That's good, *Pápi*. Who knows? Maybe someday they'll have radio and TV stations in Spanish here too."

"I think we'll be back in Cuba long before that ever happens," Juan assured him. He then lit a cigarette and took a long drag. "I understand you're back together with your *novia*."

Skinny shook his head. "She's not my *novia* anymore. Janice and I are just seeing each other once in a while. That's all."

The two grew quiet. But this time it was different—more like the silence of friends.

After a few minutes, they heard voices in the distance. Skinny looked toward the sound and saw a father and son fishing not far away.

"No, Randy! No! Don't try to pull him in yet! Let him take some line, son!" the father shouted. The boy, probably around ten, had hooked a fish. The tip of his pole was curled toward the water and whipping back and forth as the fish struggled desperately to escape.

"Listen to me, boy!" the father yelled. "Don't pull on—" Before the father could finish the boy's pole went straight as the line snapped.

The tow-headed boy stood very still. Skinny could see that the kid was trying hard to hold back tears.

"How many times have I told you, son? Do *not* try to yank the fish in all at once! Boy, you can be useless sometimes!" the father yelled and then reached down, grabbed the handle of their tackle box and flung it into the bay.

The tackle box opened as it cartwheeled through the air leaving a trail of lures and sinkers in its flight before splashing into the water.

The boy dropped the fishing pole, covered his face and sobbed. Skinny turned away, unable to watch anymore.

"At least you let me make my own mistakes, *Pápi*," Skinny said to his father who had also been watching the pair.

"A hot house flower seldom survives in the jungle," Juan said. "Shortly after we came to this country, I realized you'd do best finding your own way, *m'hijo*. What could I teach you anyway? I was an academic who'd lived a soft life."

"You did what you could," Skinny said half-heartedly.

"You're being very generous with me, Victor. But I sense you don't mean it. Tell me the truth, *m'hijo*."

Skinny looked out over the water. The last few months had softened his feelings toward his father and his family. Now his father was giving him a chance to air the last of his bitterness.

"Well, *Pápi*," Skinny said cautiously, "I always wondered why you kept that money from the CIA and didn't share it with the family. Times were hard back then."

Juan laughed. "You still remember that? My God, I was feeling proud that day. I'd finally won big the night before," he said, then paused and looked away, his smile fading. "*M'hijo*, the only times I felt like my old self back then was when I won at cards. But that's behind me now. I haven't gambled since I started work." His face brightening again, Juan said, "Anyway, that night I finally had some real money to bring home—I made up the story about the CIA so I wouldn't embarrass you in front of your friend."

"What? You mean that money didn't really come from the CIA?"

Juan covered his mouth, trying to hide a smile. "I'm sorry, Victor. I probably should have told you the truth at some point. But I thought that crazy story I made up about the CIA was like The Three Kings or Santa Claus, a fantasy every child eventually figures out for himself."

Skinny was not convinced. "CIA or not, we kept right on eating grits and eggs."

"Do you think I kept that money?"

Skinny shrugged. "What else was I supposed to think?"

"Oh, *m'hijo*..." Juan said, lowering his eyes. "Your mother and I should have told you. We used the money to pay the rent, Victor. It would have been nice to splurge on better food. But paying ahead on the rent was the smart thing to do—even if it meant we had to keep eating those miserable grits," he added with a soft laugh.

A strange sensation passed through Skinny. He was looking at his father but he was seeing another person—a stranger, really. He was a short, bald, portly, rapidly-aging man with heavy glasses and a gentle grin. As he stared at the stranger, an odd idea dawned on him.

Maybe he and this man could become friends.

❖ ❖ ❖

"Our men's catch was good today," *Abuela* announced to the family as she carried four breaded snook fillets to the table. The delicately browned fish brought looks of approval from the faces around the metal table. Generously seasoned with garlic and cumin, the fillets were the crowning touch on a dinner of black beans and rice garnished with crisp *tostones* and sliced avocados sprinkled with lemon.

"Besides these snook, *Pápi* and I caught a couple of *gallegos* today—but we threw them back," Skinny said proudly.

Gallegos was the Cuban nickname for Crevalle Jack—a worthy fighter but a lousy meal. Cubans called the fish *gallegos* because their hatchet-faced profile and jutting underbite reminded them of Galician Spaniards. There was a time when even lowly *gallegos* were brought home to eat. But these days, things were getting better for the Delgados.

Alicia's English had improved—and that had led to another promotion. She was now head of housekeeping at the Everglades. The increase in her salary, along with Juan's new income from *Zig-Zag*, had led the family to an important decision.

The Delgados would be moving to a better house.

MARCH

One Last Look

The rental truck's horn tooted twice.

Bleep! Bleep!

Standing alone on the front porch of the empty yellow bungalow, Skinny understood the wordless signal from his family: *C'mon, we're waiting for you.* He turned to leave, but something held him in place.

For almost as long as he could remember, Skinny had longed for this moment—the day he could leave this wretched house. Now that the day had arrived, Skinny was surprised by his feelings.

The house they were moving into on Southwest 6th Street was better in every way—bigger, newer, and cleaner. So why didn't he want to leave? He looked around, trying to find the answer. He stared at the rusty screens, the worn floors and the chipped stucco walls, struggling to find whatever was holding him here.

A voice behind Skinny startled him.

"The old *bitongo* is anxious to go, Victor," *Abuela* said from outside the screen door. "He sent me to hurry you along. But go ahead and take your time,"

"Take my time? What do you mean, *Abuela*?"

"It can't be easy for you to leave this house."

"What are you saying, *viejita*? I've wanted to leave this place since the day we got here."

"Let me tell you something, Victor," *Abuela* said through the door. "When I was a young girl in Santiago, my family was poor. Back then, I used to dream about the day when I could leave our dark little house with a dirt floor and live in a big, beautiful home—a place with large windows, velvet curtains, and rich rugs. Your grandfather married me and made that dream come true. He was more than a rich man, Victor. Just like your mother, your grandfather had the soul of a saint. The years we had together were the best times of my life. But even during those times, a day rarely passed when I didn't recall something that happened in that dark little house...helping my mother fix a meal...a fight with my sister...a kind word from my father. Even today, I remember things that happened in that house like it was yesterday.

"So you can walk out right now...or you can stay and look as long as you like. It's all the same, Victor. You won't forget this house."

"I hope I never have to think about this miserable place again," Skinny said opening the screen door.

As the familiar screech rang out, Skinny stopped in the doorway. Without warning, a hot tear trailed down his cheek.

Abuela put her arm around her grandson's shoulders and led him toward the truck. "If it's God's will, you're going to live in better places during the rest of your life, Victor. But a person only has one childhood. You'll never forget the place where you changed from a child to a man. Whether you like it or not, this house will be with you always."

OCTOBER

Chucho's Last Favor

Victor was nearly finished shelving a cartload of books in the Fiction section when he noticed a middle-aged man walking toward him with a rhythmic, easy swagger.

His white guayabera, heavy gold bracelet and pointy two-tone shoes looked out of place at the junior college, a place where preppy or hippie styles reigned. The man looked familiar, but Skinny could not place him.

"*Tu eres Skinny, verdad?*" the man said as he drew near.

"Yeah, I'm Skinny," Victor replied in English. The sound of his old nickname seemed strange inside the library. Since he'd started classes at Miami-Dade two years earlier, he'd been using his given name with the professors and students.

"*El Loco te mando esto,*" the man said as he handed Victor a small, yellowed envelope. His business concluded, the man turned and walked away. Victor stared at his back, trying to remember where he'd seen him. As the man reached the library's glass doors, his name rose like a bubble in Victor's mind: Chucho.

Victor started to run after Chucho, then thought better of it. What was there to say? Then Chucho's words finally sank in: *El Loco sent you this.*

Victor stared at the wrinkled envelope in his hand, then walked into one of the study cubicles and looked around cautiously before opening it. He instantly recognized Loco's tidy, parochial-school cursive on the note inside.

Skinny,

Being in prison leaves you with a lot of time for regrets. God knows, I've done plenty of shit I'm sorry for. But there's one thing that I will never regret and that's having the cojones to drive you away.

It hurt when I did it, bro. But I'm not sorry. I know you never stole any money from me. I made that up to get you away from me and the rest of the junkies. After Felix and me knocked over that 7-11, I knew my life was pretty much over. When I saw that poor kid bleeding on the floor I realized we had fucked up royally. I didn't want to drag you down with me.

Things look bad here. I don't know how much longer I've got. I've gotten on the wrong side of some powerful people in the joint. It's better that you don't know who they are. You might be comemierda enough to try and avenge me or some stupid rah-rah shit like that. Forget it, Skinny. I fucked with the wrong people and that's my problem.

Chucho still owes me a favor or two. That's why I gave him this letter and asked him to deliver it to you if anything happens to me. I'm not afraid to die. I just don't want to go without telling you the truth.

Give my love to your family. I think about them often. You were the brother I never had.

Live well, Skinny. Make something of yourself. Do it for me, man. Saving you from me was the best thing I ever did with my shitty life.

Tu amigo siempre,

Loco

Victor carefully slipped the letter back into its envelope and tucked it away in his shirt pocket. After his shift at the library ended, Victor got in his car and instead of driving to his apartment in Hialeah, wound his way east along the nighttime streets to Wynwood Park.

Not much had changed at Wynwood.

A knot of teenagers hanging out around the bleachers suddenly stopped their banter, hushed by the strange man walking toward them in the dark—his stride slow but purposeful. Unsure if this was a lunatic or a cop, the kids retreated to the basketball courts. From the cracked asphalt, the teens watched the stranger climb into the bleachers and stop. What he did next left the youths baffled.

He seemed to be kneeling in prayer.

Epilogue

The Payment of a Debt

From the window of his penthouse suite on Fisher Island, Victor looked across the jetty-lined channel of Government Cut toward the shores of South Beach. He tried to picture the high-rise-studded coastline as it had been during the 1960s. The changes were so striking that he struggled to remember.

Back then, the trendy South Beach district had been a forgotten backwater, the threadbare domain of poor retirees and bored teenagers—one group waiting to die, the other waiting for something to happen.

Along the water's edge, the two groups had been separated by a concrete fishing pier, now long-gone. The old stayed north of the pier and the young gathered south. Like the pier, which had finally succumbed to the sea after a succession of hurricanes, many of Victor's memories had also washed away.

But a few recollections still remained clear.

The grassy dunes where he and Janice made love for the first time had vanished, paved over to create an asphalt pasture for a herd of sleek BMWs, Jaguars, and Porsches. Victor's memory of their embrace on those hot sands long ago brought a tingle of delight—and a twinge of sadness.

242 Raul Ramos y Sanchez

The passage out of innocence was always a one-way journey.

Victor sighed and turned his gaze toward the breaking waves. Although the once-untamed stretch of dunes was gone, the hard-packed yellow sands of the shoreline were still there, just as he remembered them.

Victor could recall the seemingly endless days he and Loco spent on those sands, riding their homemade skim boards along the edge of the surf, lunching for fifteen cents on a bagel and an iced tea with four spoons of sugar from the Walgreen's at the end of Collins Avenue. In his memory, that iced tea tasted better than Dom Perignon.

Still, Victor was a realist. His own sons had never known such frugal pleasures. And Victor was glad of that.

Enrique and Juan would listen politely about the hardships of his youth, if he didn't talk too long. Watching their eyes as he spoke, Victor was sure they thought he was exaggerating—especially now that Wynwood had been gentrified. All that his sons knew about his old neighborhood was the trendy bistros, clubs and art galleries that had sprung up in the area in this century.

Sitting in this condo perched atop the priciest real estate in Dade County, Victor found it hard to believe as well sometimes.

His life could have turned out differently. There were moments in those years when he'd come dangerously close to the undertow of drugs and crime. As his friend had done so often, Loco had saved him one last time. He'd tried to repay his friend in the only way he'd asked.

Sipping slowly on his single malt scotch, Victor let his mind wander back through the years.

After graduating from college in 1973, he landed a job as an intern at Haller, Adams & Schooler, Miami's largest PR firm. Blessed with a puppy's charm and the tenacity of a bulldog, Victor thrived. But the new turn in his life was not without sorrow.

The death of his grandmother in 1976, followed less

than a year later by the passing of his father, were blows
that struck hard—much harder than he had ever imagined.
The loss brought him closer to his mother and siblings and
they persevered.

When Victor married Isabel Lewis-Perez in 1978, Janice
Bockman was one of the bridesmaids. A friend of his family
to this day, Janice and her husband became Enrique's
godparents. As Victor's family grew, his life began to
blossom. The next two decades passed with the astonishing
swiftness that comes with contentment.

The loss of his mother in 1992 was another milestone
of pain. Before dying of breast cancer, she'd made Victor
promise to take her remains to Cuba. That pledge would
take fifteen years to fulfill when the Castro brothers finally
opened the island to their once-exiled countrymen.

In 1994, after 21 years in the public relations business,
Victor Delgado opened his own firm in South Beach.
Within two years the Delgado Agency was representing
celebrities from Miami's exploding salsa scene along with
several major-league baseball millionaires. The agency
flourished and nine years after launching his firm, Victor
Delgado quietly eclipsed the wealth his family had known
in Cuba.

His friends in political circles encouraged him to run
for office, noting his charisma, celebrity contacts, and
determination. Victor demurred. He was happy to stay
under the radar of the media he influenced so artfully for
his clients.

Victor was proud of how his siblings had fared. Marta
followed their father into law, eventually becoming a judge.
Rafael was a real estate tycoon in Chile.

To his clients, he was known as "Vic." To his employees,
he was "Mr. D." Very few knew the fit fifty-eight-year-old
was ever called Skinny.

But they were the people he cherished most in the world.

GLOSSARY

Abuela – grandmother
aqui está – here it is
bacalao – a particularly pungent form of salted cod
bitongo – spoiled, immature, self-centered
brujeria – (pronounced *brew-her-EE-ah*) the pejorative name for Lucumi, a Cuban syncretic religion merging African deities with Catholic saints.
brujo – (pronounced *BREW-ho*) a derogatory term for a Lucumi priest believed to practice the dark arts
café-con-leche – a typical Cuban breakfast drink, usually one part coffee to two parts milk, sweetened with sugar
cálmate – calm down
candela – an expression of accomplishment or audacity (literally: fire)
chica – a female term of friendship such as gal or chick (literally: female small one)
chico – a male term of friendship such as buddy, guy, or dude (literally: male small one)
chorizo – a reddish Spanish sausage
chulo – a pimp or ladies' man
chusma -- a person or thing that is coarse or vulgar
cojones – (pronounced *ko-HO-ness*) literally: testicles, used as an all-purpose oath
comemierda – literally: shit eater, typically used as fool or buffoon
comer dulces – to eat candy
cómico – funny
congrí – (pronounced *cone-GREE*) a Cuban dish of black beans and rice cooked in the same pot
confleis – a Cuban mangling of "corn flakes" used to define any kind of dry cereal
coño – (pronounced *CONE-yo*) literally: female genitalia, an all-purpose Cuban vulgarity used like "damn" to punctuate almost any expression
criollos – (pronounced *kri-O-yos*) Cuban-born people of pure Spanish ancestry
culo – ass, butt
Dios santisimo – Most holy God
dona – A mangling by Cubans and other Caribbean Spanish speakers of the English word "donuts"
dormilón – sleepy head
desesperate – a Spanglish mash-up of the Spanish word "desesperar" with its English equivalent "exasperate"
dulces – candy, sweets
El Encanto – a posh department store in pre-revolutionary Havana
El Señor – The Lord
embolia – a widespread belief in Cuba that bathing shortly after a meal causes a fatal embolism
entiendes – do you understand?
esbirro – thug, goon
esperate – wait, **esperame aqui** – wait here for me
está bien – multi-purpose term with varied meanings: okay, that's fine, I agree, all is good, yes
finca – a Cuban rural homestead or farm
gallo – (pronounced *GUY-o*) literary a rooster, used as a Spanglish play on words with the English word "guy." Often a companion word with grillo.
gracias a Dios – thanks to God
grillo – (pronounced *GREE-yo*) literally a cricket, used as a Spanglish play on words with the English word "girl." Often a companion word with gallo.
guajiro (male), **guajira** (female) – (pronounced *wa-HERO* or *wa-HEERA*) bumpkin, peasant, hayseed
guayabera – a square-tailed embroidered dress shirt popular with Cuban men, usually white

huevo frito – a fried egg
huevos – a euphemism for testicles
imbécil – although literally imbecile, among Cubans this word is less severe and closer
    to "dummy"
la zafra – the harvest, in Cuba usually meaning the sugar harvest
lechón – roast pork in Cuba (other parts of Latin America use this term for a suckling pig)
m'hija – (pronounced *ME-ha*) my daughter,
m'hijo – (pronounced *ME-ho*) my son
maricón – a derogatory term for gay men, often used to call someone a coward
mi amigo – my friend
mi amor – my love
mierda – shit (like its English counterpart, often used to connote a variety of meanings)
mi hermano (male), **mi hermana** (female) – (pronounced *ur-MAW-no* and *ur-MAW-naw*)
    literally my brother or my sister, often used as a bonding term between friends
mi papá es un habitante – my father is a bum
mira – look
mulata – female of mixed African and European ancestry, sometimes used to connote a
    sexual partner
mulato – male of mixed African and European ancestry
niña – girl
niño – boy
Nochebuena – Christmas eve, a day when Latin American families gather for a meal,
    similar to Thanksgiving in the U.S. – in some families the meal is followed by attending
    midnight Mass
no es nada – it's nothing
novio – boyfriend
oigo – how Cubans answer the telephone, literally "I hear"
oye – hey
papaya – Among Cubans, papaya is used as slang for female pudenda. Because of this,
    the fruit is called "fruta bomba" in polite Cuban conversation.
pápi – daddy
pinpollo – (pronounced *peen-PO-yo*) good looking guy, stud, hunk
por favor – although literally "please," in Cuba this all-purpose expression can be
    inflected to have a number of meanings depending on the context including: stop it, I
    doubt it, this is obvious, pay attention, etc.
por seguro – for sure
pendejo – (pronounced *pen-DAY-ho*) literally: pubic hair, an all-purpose Latin American
    insult with meanings including idiot, fool, jerk or creep
puta – like the English word "whore," puta can mean a woman of loose morals or a
    prostitute
que dices? – what are you saying?
que pasó? – what happened?
salud – health, often used as a toast
se llama – (pronounced *say YA-ma*) he (or she) is named...
silencio – silence
solterona – old maid, spinster
también – as well, also
tio – uncle, **tia** – aunt
vamos – let's go
vieja (female), **viejo** (male) – term of endearment for an elder. Diminutive: viejita or
    viejito
y que? – so what?

About the author

Raul Ramos y Sanchez

The Cuban-born author grew up in Miami's cultural kaleidoscope before becoming a long-time resident of the U.S. Midwest. The author and his work have been featured on television, radio, online, and in print media across the U.S. and abroad.

For more information, visit www.RaulRamos.com

Made in the USA
San Bernardino, CA
02 June 2016